MILE MARKER 33

MEREDETH CONNELLY MIND HUNT THRILLERS
BOOK 3

E.H. Vick

DARK TRIAD PUBLISHING

NEW YORK

Dark Triad Publishing
769 Broadway #1060
Manhattan, NY 10003

Publisher's Note: This is a work of fiction. Names, characters, places, and incidents are a product of the author's imagination. Locales and public names are sometimes used for atmospheric purposes. Any resemblance to actual people, living or dead, or to businesses, companies, events, institutions, or locales is completely coincidental.

Mile Marker 33/ E.H. Vick. -- 1st ED.
ISBN 978-1-951509-21-7

TABLE OF CONTENTS

CHAPTER 1 1

CHAPTER 2 13

CHAPTER 3 31

CHAPTER 4 41

CHAPTER 5 49

CHAPTER 6 55

CHAPTER 7 65

CHAPTER 8 83

CHAPTER 9 95

CHAPTER 10 101

CHAPTER 11 121

CHAPTER 12 131

CHAPTER 13 141

CHAPTER 14 151

CHAPTER 15 161

CHAPTER 16 185

CHAPTER 17 193

CHAPTER 18 205

CHAPTER 19 209

CHAPTER 20 215

CHAPTER 21 221

CHAPTER 22 247

CHAPTER 23 253

CHAPTER 24 261

CHAPTER 25...................................269

CHAPTER 26 275

CHAPTER 27 279

CHAPTER 28 285

CHAPTER 29 295

CHAPTER 30 321

CHAPTER 31................................. 333

CHAPTER 32 341

CHAPTER 33 347

CHAPTER 34 361

CHAPTER 35 365

CHAPTER 36 371

CHAPTER 37 379

AUTHOR'S NOTE 7/25/22 381

PATRON RECOGNITION 385

ABOUT THE AUTHOR 387

DEDICATION

For the real Sam Atallah, MD, with gratitude.

With special thanks to Vincent Soldano, who answered the craziest questions about driving a big rig like a psychopath without batting an eye, and to the members of BR549 for performing the song that partially inspired this story (*18 Wheels and a Crowbar*).

I hope you enjoy *Mile Marker 33* If so, please consider joining my online community—details can be found at the end of the last chapter.

CHAPTER 1

18 WHEELS AND A CROWBAR

North of Boise, ID

THE TRUCK DRIVER glanced at his insulated mug tucked into the cup holder, his eyes gritty and sore. His tongue tasted like flint, like a desert windstorm, and his stomach roiled—full of West Coast turnarounds and little else. A flutter of fear tickled his guts as he thought of the uppers. Drugs were not something his father approved of, but the man had never pulled twenty-one days and nights on the road like he just had.

He'd slept here and there—mostly during the daylight hours as he loved driving into the night's chiffon darkling embrace—but mostly, he'd taken methamphetamine when he could get it and relied on prescription Benzedrine when he couldn't. If you believed the fiction in his current logbook, he'd driven no more than twelve hours out of every twenty-four, but that didn't count his excursions since they were recorded in one of his *other* logbooks. He preferred wakefulness to sleep, even if that meant having a belly full of pills, even if it meant relying on a bottle of heat. Driving truck wasn't for weak old men, and he was neither weak nor old, so he saw no reason to act as if he were.

The modified Cummins engine in his rig thundered as he fed it go-go juice, and the compound-boosted turbos screamed a soprano sonata to the engine's raw bass. His tires hissed across the asphalt of Idaho State Route 55 as he sawed the front end back and forth across both lanes, hoping the motion would forestall the need for a caffeine and subsequent antacid infusion.

The moon kissed the hood of his Peterbilt 389, caressing the long, sleek nose of the tractor, dancing a second on the wide chrome grill and the heavy bull-bar bumper beyond it, then winking at him from the surface of the Payette River out his left window. The road followed the Payette north toward McCall and then joined US 95 for the long haul to Coeur d'Alene. In the moonlight, his truck looked quite black, the same as blood, though it was actually painted red—blood-red, to be sure, but red, nonetheless. He liked that. He liked it a lot.

With a sigh, he reached for the second of the two massive thermoses he carried in a box nestled behind his seat, hooking his finger through its handle and pulling it close. He had a travel mug in the cup holder in the console, and setting the thermos between his thighs, he flipped the travel mug's lid off. Next, he gingerly opened the thermos, knowing it was filled to the rim with black gold, then poured coffee slowly into the mug, his gaze darting between the road ahead and the mug.

His Pete had almost taken on the status of a loyal friend, of a living being, something he could always rely on—his father had taught him the value of preventive maintenance and repairs, and he'd taken that lesson to heart. It had served him well over his driving career, and he'd taken to carrying a lot of spare parts tucked away in the cab, in a hidden compartment in his wagon, anywhere else there was space, to be honest. He grinned and said, "You can't ever tell when you might need to replace a broken light, a bent bull bar." The sentence evoked memories of other nights, other hours spent penetrating the blackness, hunting for a prey, hunting for fun, hunting for—

"*JESUS CHRIST!*" he shouted as the molten orange Ford Fiesta ST lunged into the road from a parking lot on the left and accelerated hard, crossing all four lanes to drive in the outside northbound lane. The mug of coffee flew across the cab as he grabbed at the steering wheel, cranking it to the right, his foot coming off the go-pedal and hammering the brake, but both motions were wasted efforts, and he knew it.

There was no way he could avoid the stupid little car.

No way in hell.

The driver of the Fiesta seemed to know it, too, and he drifted to the left, dancing along the double yellow in the inside lane. He gave a jaunty little blip of his horn and waved.

The truck driver's blood came up in an instant, and anger seared him from within. *Another four-wheeler who thinks he's funny*, he thought. *Fine. Let's play.*

He downshifted and put his foot back on the accelerator, giving the truck the fuel necessary to bring all twenty-one hundred foot-pounds of torque screaming to life, fighting the trailer's desire to come alongside the tractor, to drag him down, to jackknife or worse. The modified engine roared, the compound turbochargers shrieked, and the Pete lunged ahead with a massive neck-snapping jerk.

He pointed his headlights at the little orange creep and let the beast under his hood eat. Without looking away from the Fiesta, he flicked on the custom lights he'd added to the roof of the Pete, and harsh, bright blue-white lights erased the darkness.

The thin man driving the Fiesta squinted against the rapacious glare and jerked his car away from the Peterbilt's path. The little Ford's tires screeched at the abuse.

But not as much as they were going to.

He knew exactly what he was doing. He didn't need to outpace the lighter car, all he needed to do was slide his nose closer to the rear end, and running deadheaded as he was, he could use most of the power to get there. He eased the Pete closer to the double yellows, a feral grin dominating his hate-filled expression. He flicked on the airbrakes and pumped his foot on the accelerator as he pulled next to the Fiesta, making and interrupting the high-pitched shriek each time he touched the pedal. He grinned as the driver fled to the outside southbound lane.

Cranking the big steering wheel first to the right, then even more to the left, he sent the truck careening toward the left side of the road, right foot planted, a low growl rumbling in his chest, and behind him, his trailer danced a jig, taking big swings toward both edges of the road. Though the driver tried to avoid him, the left edge of his bull bar clipped the Fiesta a few inches in front of the rear passenger-side tire with a satisfying crunch. He poured on the power and turned into the compact, shoving the back end of the Ford into a skittering slide to the shoulder of the road and river beyond it.

The pinheaded geek in the bright orange car panicked, jerking his wheel to the right and pounding on the accelerator, trying to get out of the 389's grill, but the only thing he accomplished against the mass and momentum of the big rig was to lose what little traction he had left on the front tires, and the Fiesta seemed to float in a lazy circle, heading across the nose of the Pete without so much as smudging the chrome bumper as the truck decelerated hard. The molten orange paint winked in his high-powered lights as the car spun across the double yellows.

He cranked the wheel to the right, lining up the nose with the middle of the Fiesta's body compartment, then slammed the go-go pedal to the mat. He smote the little car hard, lifting the passenger side tires a bit as he used his superior power and mass to shove the compact diagonally across the northbound lanes. The Ford slid from pavement to the gravel shoulder, and something caught on the driver's side—the lip of the wheel, a low-hanging suspension component, but it hardly mattered what—and the car went ass-over-teakettle across the gravel shoulder. Grinning, the Pete's pilot lifted his foot off the accelerator, watching the car tumble into the stubble and earth of a freshly mown hay field.

As the Fiesta came to rest on its driver's side, the passenger side tires still spinning, He pulled his rig onto the shoulder and set his brakes. He climbed down out of the cab, whistling a bright tune from his youth, and fetched his crowbar and a heavy one-handed sledgehammer from the toolbox. He trudged into the hay field, right arm cocked, crowbar resting against his collarbone, sledgehammer swinging in his left.

The driver's moans became audible as he approached the underside of the Fiesta, but he paid them no mind. The loudmouth pencil—pusher would be silent soon enough. His gaze searched for and found the black high-density polyethylene fuel tank right in front of the spindly rear axle of the vehicle. He ignored the fuel lines for the moment and gave the tank a thump with the bent end of the crowbar, then grinned wide. It sounded almost full.

"Hey, man!" yelled the occupant of the molten orange coffin. "Help me...I'm...I'm *pinned* in here."

"Right you are, chief," said the truck driver in his gravelly baritone. "Trapped, I'd say, if I were one to quibble about words."

"What the hell, man? Why'd you go all psycho?"

"You cut me off, geek. I don't like that."

"I was only having a little fun."

He swung his head ponderously from side to side. "I wasn't."

"Help me! I've got to get out!"

"I will." He paused for effect. "But not yet."

"What? Why not now?"

"Because I'm not ready yet."

"Then at least call for help!"

The trucker's answer was tilting his head back and laughing at the moon, and the driver grew silent. He listened to his echoing laughter, parsing what reached his ears for signs of EMS mobilization but heard nothing untoward.

"What..." The Fiesta driver's voice clicked as he swallowed.

"Sounds like you're going into shock, chief."

"What are you going to do to me?"

"What am I going to do to you? I'm going to help you, of course. I'm just making sure the car is safe for me to crawl in there and get you. What kind of man do you think I am?" The man trapped in the wreck said nothing, but the truck driver imagined his unvoiced reply: *The kind of man who runs innocent people off the road. The kind who flips cars into hay fields and refuses to help.* It was a fair assessment.

Grinning, he switched the sledge to his right hand and the crowbar to his left. He picked a spot and rested the pointed end of the bar against the HDPE gas tank. He drew back his right arm and gave the crowbar a solid, clanging strike.

"What the hell?" yelled the driver.

The trucker swung again, then again, putting more of his not-inconsiderable strength behind the blows and was gratified by the *thunk* of the crowbar penetrating the tank. Gasoline began to sluice around the tool steel.

"What're you *doing*? I smell gas! *Oh-my-God-get-me-out-of-here!*"

"Nah," grunted the driver of the big rig. "It's not safe for me with that gas leak you've got." He jerked the crowbar free of the gas tank and stepped back, away from the stream of gasoline jetting from the half-inch hole he'd made. He hooked the crowbar in his belt and fished in his jeans pocket with his left hand, digging for one of the free matchbooks he always grabbed when he stopped for fuel at one of the giant truck stops.

"Look! I'm sorry, okay? I'm sorry I cut you off! I'll never do it again, just get me *out*!"

"Where's the fun in that?" The trucker slipped the haft of the hammer through his belt on the side opposite the crowbar, looking for all the world like a gunslinger too stupid to make sure he carried actual guns into battle. He picked out a match, ripped it free, and struck it against the striker-strip on the back of the matchbook. The chemicals did their thing, and the match flared to life, adding the scent of burning phosphorous to the reeking gas fumes. His grin widened as he used the match to light the entire book, then flicked the fireball toward the closest rivulet of gasoline.

It went up with a *whoosh* and a blast of instant, eyebrow-singeing heat. He stumbled toward the molten orange Fiesta, a handful of steps, captivated by the dance of blue and orange flames. Eyes wide, lips distended in a maniacal grin, the freight hauler stood there until the flames had almost reached the car, then he turned and ran toward his Pete 389.

He'd just rounded the front end and was moving toward the toolbox when the *whoosh-thump* of the gas tank igniting shook the truck, and he changed his mind, yanking the door open, flinging the tools toward the passenger seat, slamming the door, slamming the truck into gear, and spinning the steering wheel hard to take his rig back onto the blacktop. He fed the angry beast under the Peterbilt's hood, checking his mirrors every few seconds to watch the molten orange fireball consume the molten orange car.

He forced himself to lift his foot, to slow down, to drive normally. Headlights peeked over the crown of the hill ahead, and he reached for his CB radio. "Come on, southbound. You on here?" He was parked, as he always was, on channel 19, the most popular band.

"Ten-four, northbound. You got yourself a black eye if you don't already know it. Left side."

"'Preciate it, good neighbor," he said, though it came out singsong: *pree-shade-it*. "I'll get that straightened out right quick. Listen here, some crazy seat cover in a four-wheeler just busted himself up good over my shoulder. Lost control, I guess."

"That fireball in the field?"

"I'd say yes."

"You gonna stop and talk to the bears?"

"Hell, no. I got deliveries to make. No time for dumb."

"Uh..."

"Let the locals deal with it. Where there's fields, there's farmers. Plus, he was right across from that wide spot in the road where you rent them kayaks."

"Ten-four."

The Pete powered up the hill, the semi's driver watching the southbound truck hit his brakes and slow as he approached the hay field. It didn't matter, that pencil-pushing loudmouth in the Fiesta was past talking to anyone. He wondered if it was worth the risk to pull over and change out the headlight the southbound truck had warned him of or if it would be safer to risk getting pulled over. He flicked his overhead lights on. At least that way he could claim he could still see despite the dead headlight.

CHAPTER 2

SHUTTER TROUBLE

Hanable's Valley, NY

WHEN SHE AWOKE, slow anger stole through her
like a sneakthief on a dark night. She'd fallen asleep.
Again. Her gaze flicked to the clock. The time she'd spent
struggling to remain awake prior to her last three-hour
nap had extended her record to exactly two hours and
thirty-seven minutes of wakefulness. She sucked a deep
breath into her lungs, then had to hold it, fighting not to
cough, not to jar the surgical wounds in her belly, and once
the urge had passed, she blew out a frustrated breath.

She was camped out in Kevin's La-Z-Boy, the one in
front of his giant television, and some idiot was blaring at
her about the Dow Jones. After an eternity of fumbling for
the remote, she managed to mute the television. She'd
been Kevin's "guest" for a few weeks by her reckoning,
which amounted to being a millstone around the man's
neck. Needy, bored, unable to care for herself, unable to
even shower without his assistance, her fight against

self-pity was constant. She couldn't even go for a walk—she was still too weak and having a pendulous bag swinging from her belly wasn't exactly conducive to a workout mood.

Right on cue, the hole in her guts loosed a stream of methane and digestive slop into the bag that hung from her flesh. Dr. Atallah, the surgeon who'd saved her life in Florida, had called it a temporary ileostomy—ten-dollar words for, "your colon is on vacation until further notice," and for, "say goodbye to social graces, and get ready to share every sound your digestive system makes with everyone in the room."

The hospital doctor had said she'd get it removed in two weeks—unless she misunderstood or was misremembering. Every physician she'd spoken to since had merely shaken his head and said something hopeful like, "It could be six months. Worst case a year." But they'd also backed up the surgeon's call, based on how low the knife wielded by Sonya—or was it Alex?—had ripped into her colon. There was evidently a good chance of being on a colostomy for life if they tried to connect everything back up and she blew out the stitches laughing—or coughing.

The urge was back, a tickle so deep in her throat it felt like it might live in the ostomy bag. She'd figured out that, for some reason, over-the-counter antacid helped—despite assurances that the cough was due to irritation and swelling in her throat and larynx due to being intubated during the five-and-a-half-hour surgery and then extubated in the recovery room. She reached for the end table Kevin had maneuvered next to the chair for her use, scrabbled around for the bottle of antacid, fought the damn cap open, then popped two of the chewable "berry-flavored" pieces of chalk into her already dry mouth. She grimaced as she chewed but felt the urge to hack her lungs out begin to abate almost immediately.

Her gaze crawled back to the clock on the soffit above the kitchen bar top, and she frowned. Kevin wouldn't be home for another few hours at least—and that was if he kept to his current pattern of checking out two hours early, but she knew he couldn't keep that up indefinitely. She could call him, and he'd be home before she could hang up—she knew that from experience—but she couldn't keep drowning the man in her inability to entertain herself for a few hours. The problem was that she couldn't do any of the things she liked to do. She couldn't workout, couldn't sit at the computer reading through forensic psychology papers dealing with the dark triad for hours on end, couldn't...uh...couldn't go in to work...

She shook her head and scoffed. "I need some goddamn hobbies," she muttered. During every moment of inactivity, Bobby was always on his phone—not talking but fiddling—and she picked hers up and looked at the apps that had come installed on it—social media stuff, mostly—then dropped the phone back to the table with a clatter. Meredeth let her head *thud* back against the overstuffed recliner and groaned. "What am I going to do?" Her eyes filled with stinging tears that she angrily wiped away with the back of her hand.

Dawn Connelly hadn't raised her to whine and gripe about what she couldn't change. She hadn't cottoned to melodrama and used to grow quite cross with Meredeth when she indulged. Even so, as fresh tears brimmed, Meredeth felt a little sniveling might be in order—as long as she got it over with before Kevin came waltzing in.

Her eyelids already felt heavy, but maybe that was the result of the tears. She had that exhausted feeling again despite the fact that all she'd done was open her eyes and move her right arm. *This is ridiculous*, she thought. "Stupid, even. When is this going to end?"

And, if she were honest, the fatigue and boredom were not the worst parts of her recovery so far... No, by far, the worst part was when she needed to change the adhesive wafer that secured the pouch's opening around her stoma. She couldn't do it alone, and that meant Kevin had to help. Each and every time, she was mortified as fecal matter squeezed out of the stoma in the middle of trying to get her skin clean and prepped. The odors were atrocious, though Kevin laughed it off with a reference to the drunk tank.

He had been so sweet, so kind and compassionate. But even so, he still had to look at her with shit on her belly, to see the end of her small intestines jutting from the pale skin of her belly like a whale breaking the surface of a calm bay, and he still had to carry the bags with her waste products in it out to the trash.

And to make matters worse, the Florida hospital had sent her on her way with products that were one size too small for her stoma, meaning she'd had frequent leaks, blowouts, and needed daily changes of the whole thing, instead of the advertised once every five days. It had left her skin raw and painful and would have made her wait even more unbearable if Darren hadn't sent in an ostomy nurse with thirty-five years' experience with the horrible torture devices.

The nurse had recommended a different brand of wafers and pouches—the ones she'd indicated were, in fact, roughly nine million percent more comfortable than the previous variety—as well as giving her and Kevin instructions about how to clean the area using adhesive removal wipes, and then using the skin prep wipes. The hospital had sent them home with only skin prep wipes and the barest amount of education she could imagine. The ostomy nurse had also given her a magic powder that helped her injured skin to heal—even while glued to a new wafer.

Even with the more comfortable gear, getting up and walking around still made her feel like she was being eviscerated, and there was no help for that. Time, the nurse had said, and allowing herself to heal.

Time, Meredeth thought with derision, *my archenemy in everything I do. Spend time up here with Kev, and there's never enough of it. Chase a serial killer, and it moves too fast. Sit around waiting for myself to heal, and it moves with such glacial slowness that insanity is surely in my—*

Her work phone jangled Bobby Van Zandt's ring tone, and she all but lunged at the thing and swiped accept. "Van Zandt! How are you?"

Bobby chuckled. "Someone's bored and lonely."

"You figure that out with your high-powered interview technique?"

"Which I learned from you, Mere, and I'm sure it really is high-powered, but nothing like that is required in this case. You grabbed it just as the second ring started."

"The phone was right beside me."

"Uh-huh. How are you doing? Is Kevin treating you right?"

Meredeth wiped away unexpected tears and drew a long breath through lips only just parted enough to allow it. "I'm..."

"If you say fine, I'm catching a flight."

"No, you're not," she said. "Having my business on display in front of Kevin is bad enough. To tell you the truth, Bobby, from a physical standpoint, and if we discount the constant, mind-numbing fatigue, I don't feel awful."

"And from an emotional standpoint?"

"I'm a mess," she said simply. "I don't do 'sit around and be waited on' very well. I don't want Kevin to have to go through this. I don't want this damn bag swinging from my guts. I don't want to sit around and do nothing all day."

"I figured that part might do you in."

For the second time, she swiped recalcitrant tears from her eyes. "Yeah, it would have if it weren't Kevin helping me, cheering me up, entertaining me."

"He's a good man, boss," said Bobby in a gentle voice. "This won't scare him away."

"I..." She found it impossible to talk past the sudden ache in her throat until she swallowed with a dry click. "I know, but that doesn't mean—"

"You didn't want to get stabbed, either. It is what it is."

"Yeah," she said with a sigh. "Let's talk about something else since there's not a thing either one of us can do about my situation."

"Okay."

"What does McCutchins have you doing?"

"I'm in Maryland with Dave Tilton."

"Uff. Sorry, Bobby, the Baltimore Brawler is a waste of your talent."

"Uh... You must be on pain meds."

"Not recently. I mean it, Bobby. I might get all the press, but I couldn't be half as effective without you."

"Well...thanks. I...uh... Anyway, McCutchins sent me to Maryland to help Big Dave wrap it up."

She couldn't help the lopsided grin that emerged on her face. "And you're not finding it much of a challenge?"

"Don't get me wrong, serial offenders are all dangerous, all challenging..."

"But?"

"But, yeah, it doesn't seem very hard."

"Tell me about the case."

"I don't know about that, Mere. You're supposed to be taking it easy."

"Bobby, if I take one more minute 'easy' I'm going to need a psychiatric hold somewhere."

His belly laugh rolled across the call like a cannon barrage. "So, business as usual, then?"

"Seriously, Bobby. I need something to think about except counting and recounting the days to the next appointment with the surgeon."

He hesitated for a few heartbeats, then said, "Yeah, I guess it can't hurt. You've probably already guessed the initial profile."

"Tell me what you've put together, then we can poke fun at Big Dave's version."

"Well, your instinct to cut deep hasn't left you." As soon as he said it, he clucked his teeth. "Sorry, Mere. I wasn't thinking."

"It's nothing, Bobby. I got stabbed, there's no sense tiptoeing around it."

"I just thought—"

"This won't get you out of spilling your profile. And yeah, my killer instinct is alive and well."

"Fine," he said with a chuckle. "Highly disorganized and impulsive black male, twenty to thirty years old, unemployed or employed in a dead-end job he feels is beneath him. It's likely he has trouble with authority and holding any job for longer than a few months. Given the brutality of the beatings, I'm putting him on the pro-football player side of the size spectrum. He leaves the bodies where they fall, and they've all been in West Baltimore. Statistics say he probably lives there, too, likely in the projects."

"Have you thought about gang affiliation as a driving force in the slayings? Maybe that's how he makes his money?"

"It could be. Some of the victims were members of the four big local gangs—in fact, one was a high-ranking enforcer for the East Coast Bloods. Other victims, however, had no affiliations we've been able to identify."

"Maybe customers of the unsub or his gang? Junkies too far behind on their payments?"

"I don't think so, Mere. The vics were in good physical condition prior to the beatings. It's almost like..."

"What?" she asked and leaned forward a little in her chair.

"It's like they are pro fighters. Lean muscle, strength, you know."

"Hmm."

"Tilton says we can rule out the enforcer angle, anyway. He said this guy's a wild card with respect to the gang hierarchy around here."

"How so?"

"He says there are four main gangs here these days—"

"And the unsub has killed from all four?"

"Bingo."

"That doesn't necessarily mean he's not in one of them. Maybe the beatings are punishments. That East Coast Blood, for instance, maybe he was skimming or using or breaking some other important rule."

"Yeah. I'll dig into it a little."

"The other thing to check is the local street fighting scene. There's usually a bunch of videos on the internet. A guy like this will be driven to seek that kind of attention."

"We'll check that, too. Anything else? Big Dave is giving me that saucy smile of his that says, 'Whenever you're done with your personal business, I'm ready to move.'"

"Not right yet. I'll text you if I think of something new." She switched the phone to the other hand and pressed her right hand against her belly as a spasm of uncomfortable sensation rippled through her. "Bobby?"

"Yeah, Mere?"

"Keep me in the loop, okay? Give me something to think about."

"You got it, boss."

"And don't get too comfortable with Big Dave. When I'm back to one hundred percent, you're coming right back to me."

"Wouldn't have it any other way, Meredeth."

"Good. I hate for you to be unhappy in your work."

Bobby chuckled. "That's a little more like the Meredeth Connelly I know."

"She isn't going anywhere."

"Good to hear. I'll call later?"

"You'd better."

"Hello to Kevin. And this time, I want you to really tell him."

"You two have given up your eldritch communications?"

"No need, now that he's got you under his thumb."

"Ah. Once I'm better, we're going to re-evaluate your deal with him. I can only worry about so many—"

"I've really got to go, Mere. Dave's moved on to loud sighs."

"Right, right. He probably wants food. Go, Bobby. I'll be okay, and we'll talk later."

"Right." He clicked off.

Meredeth took a deep breath and ran her fingers through her greasy hair. Showers were a big deal, requiring she virtually mummy-wrap her abdomen with press-and-seal film, three rolls of tape, and a little magic to keep her wounds and the ostomy junk dry. And her general lack of endurance meant she needed a shower chair and Kevin's help to finish bathing. It was so time-consuming; they'd settled on a shower every three to four days by unspoken agreement. She didn't enjoy days three and four, but she couldn't expect Kevin to work full-time, cook, clean, take care of her wounds and stoma, and all the other myriad duties, plus an hour's worth of prep and shower time every day. He'd never sleep.

Her eyelids tried to shutter her eyes, and her brain had that fuzzy feeling that meant she needed to sleep. *Again.* She lay her head back against the recliner's built-in pillow, heaved yet another sigh, and let her eyelids do what they wanted.

She was almost asleep when her phone gave its innocuous little buzz that meant she had an email on her Bureau address. *Maybe something from Bobby and Dave,* she thought. She reached for it and straightened up as she swiped away the lock screen. She tapped the email client and saw a new message.

It was from Meredeth Connelly, from her own Bureau email address, and she frowned at the screen. She'd had a cyberstalker for a while, but Ankou was the sender, and the emails had all stopped on his incarceration. He had no internet access, she knew, but that didn't mean some other prisoner who *did* have access wasn't willing to do his bidding.

Still, dealing with it would take fifteen minutes or so, and fifteen minutes of distraction was better than sleeping. She viewed the full email header and noticed that the from field and from email address had been spoofed, though the actual return address had not. With a lopsided grin, she took note of the address which was yourguardianangel in a domain named darkweb.ru. *That's smart*, she thought. *The Bureau has no leverage over a Russian domain*. No number of Federal warrants would get her the name registered with the account. That wasn't much of a loss, however. There was no verification of names attached to most email addresses, and it could very well be registered to Snow White. "Well, let's see what you have to say, Miss YourGuardianAngel," Meredeth murmured.

Frowning down at the screen, she read the subject line. "Be careful, Agent Connelly," it said. A spasm of annoyance flicked across her face, and she opened the email and read it.

> *Dear Agent Connelly,*
>
> *You don't know me, but I know you. I've heard stories about you all my life, both from my father and from my "uncle," though neither man is a blood relation. Both told me you are the enemy, but I don't believe them.*

Not anymore.

Look at me rattling on. Let me get to the point.

I've already told you I received an education on your life in the FBI and beyond. Partially, that's due to my uncle's obsession with you. We were instructed to call him "Uncle Kenny." I read in the press that you've recovered a slew of childhood memories, so I assume the significance of the name is not lost on you. Yes, my so-called uncle is your brother.

But that's beside the point of this message. You are in danger. Constant danger. Kenny is filled with rage and wants you punished, but he doesn't have the rocks in his head to make it last. Father does, and he's put a decades-spanning plan in motion with you as the end goal.

I'm sure he boasted about "his children." I am one of them, but not one he likes to acknowledge.

I'm in a fair amount of danger myself, and sending you this email only heightens that, so please don't spread it around like you did Father's.

What is the plan? It's too complicated to go into detail but suffice it to say that your next five to ten years are likely booked out. My so-called siblings (none of us are blood relatives, we're only a "family" because Father killed our own and made us live on his farm together while he "trained" us) will monopolize most of your investigations.

He's planned an order of events—though it may have changed since I fell out of favor. You met Alex, that psycho-bitch. You'll probably meet Mack or Lucy next. I pray it's not Lucy, given your current medical state. She's almost as bad as Alex.

Hell, they're all bad.

I'll help you where and when I can.

Yours,

M

Meredeth's brows had drawn toward the centerline of her forehead, and her frown had deepened into an ugly grimace. It was a long email for Doe, but she didn't know if she believed this "M" was a real person. Her thumb floated above the reply button, and she closed her eyes to think a moment.

For a moment, her old friend from countless crime scenes lurked around the edges of her awareness, giving her the occasional poke of soul-searing pain behind one of her eyes. She closed her eyes, drew a deep breath for the time it took her to count to four, held her breath for four counts, then exhaled it for another four. The headache retreated, but petulantly with a few more stabs of pain. The breathing pattern was a trick Bobby taught her—something from his days in the Corps.

Engaging might not be a good idea. Even if this was sent by a real person, Doe's control over his children seemed complete. Alex Delamort had killed on command, and though he'd had the perfect means of escape, he chose to stay, to try to gut her instead of playing it cool.

Her stomach gurgled and ejected a stream of waste into the ostomy bag. *Another punishment. Kenny must really hate me. Or John Doe does in his stead.*

She dithered, wondering if she should forward the email on to the tech team supporting the BAU, flip-flopping on the fact that they'd never been able to track down how Doe had hacked the high-security email server dedicated to Bureau emails to send her messages from her own account.

She shook her head and pressed reply. She sat staring daggers down at the phone for a few minutes, gathering her best interview techniques, her best negotiation tactics. Then, she wrote:

> *Greetings,*
>
> *This is going to get confusing if we both sign our emails "M," so I suggest we trade first names. Given what you've said, you probably already know mine—it's Meredeth—though your "father"*

may have called me Mercy. Kenny, too, for that
matter.

What is your name?

Hope to hear back soon,

Meredeth

She hesitated, her thumb hanging over the send button, then she steeled herself and tapped it. Meredeth sat staring down at the screen, hoping for a response sooner rather than later.

After a few minutes, she fell asleep, and her phone dropped into her lap.

CHAPTER 3

OVER HIS SHOULDER

David Branch's Farm, NY

MACK FOLLOWED ALEX into the barn, making a face at the cacophony coming from Randall's box. The boy never learned. His gaze drifted to Alex surreptitiously. She insisted on the fiction that she was a boy, hence wore boys' jeans, a loose T-shirt, and scuffed work boots. Her hair was shaved close to her scalp, but to Mack, she looked like a goddess walking.

"Randall, Randall, Randall," she mused. "What are we going to do with him? Nothing in Father's arsenal seems to work for him."

"More ECT?"

Alex shook her head. "Been there, done that. A thousand times. A thousand-thousand times."

"Hypnotics, then? Suggestion?"

Alex frowned at Randall's box. "He was the one Father brought after me. The second child Father saved, unless there were failures before me. He's never been out of the box. Not once in four years." She turned and lanced him with a severe gaze. "What should we do with him?"

"*We?*" asked Mack with a chuckle.

She took a half-step closer, and her right hand dipped to the fancy knife and sheath she had suspended through her belt. "That's what I said, isn't it? If you're going to follow me around like a damn puppy, I might as well train you."

"And is that okay with Father?"

"Sure, it is. He recognizes talent as easily as I do."

Mack felt his cheeks blaze with heat, and he knew he was turning cherry-red. "Well, thanks."

"Yeah, yeah. Answer the question, Mack."

He turned and surveyed the four columns of boxes stacked four high. Most were quiet; most of the occupants were going along to get along. "Randall is making things hard for everyone, right? He's a bad example?"

"A terrible example."

"And if he hasn't warmed up to the process after four years, it seems like the probability of him doing so in the future is low."

"I think you're right."

Again, Mack's cheeks blazed, but the sensation wasn't as intense as the first time. "Why is he still in the program?"

Alex shrugged. "You tell me."

"Because Father sees something in him?"

"Could be. Or he could be a test."

Mack snapped his gaze around to her face. "A test for who?"

"Me. *Us*."

Mack frowned. "But you already passed your test."

She narrowed her eyelids slightly. "How would you know?"

"Michelina—"

"That *bitch*! She knows better."

Lifting his shoulder the way he had back before... *Before*. "We're brothers and sisters. I was curious about you."

Alex cocked her hips and put one hand on the hilt of the knife again. "Look, Mack... I'm sure you're cute. I'm sure boys like you would be happy to—"

"Boys like me?" he asked with laughter in his voice.

"Yeah. Gay boys. I see the way you look at me."

"But I'm..." His brows bunched in confusion. "You're not really—"

"Go on," she said in a voice as cold as a medical examiner's table. "Tell me what I am and am not."

Mack stepped back and raised his hands in surrender. "*I'm* not gay," he said *sotto voce*.

"You must be, looking at me like that."

"No," he said. "I..." Mack felt as though he were walking on hair-thin ice covering a roaring river. "I think you might have taken my admiration the wrong way. You've made it so far, so fast. Even Father says you're to be admired."

She pulled her head back slowly, her gaze locked on his. "Well, I'm not gay, so you'd better make sure the only thing I see on your face is respect." She took a step to erase the space he'd made between them. "Got it?"

"Sure, Alex. Sure. Whatever you say." He dropped his hands to his sides. *What the hell*, he thought. *Michelina is just as cute.* It was a lie, but with enough practice, he'd come to believe it.

"Now, can we get back to work?"

"Yeah, of course."

"Then what should we do with him?"

"Randall? Kill him."

A slow grin spread across Alex's face, and she caressed the knife hanging from her waist. "Like you said, I've already passed that kind of test."

"Then..." Mack shook his head and shrugged.

"*You* haven't."

Ah, he thought. "Can I borrow your knife?"

"This one's mine. Find your own toy."

Mack arched his eyebrows as he looked away—the expression that had always gotten him in trouble with his mother. "Okaaay." He searched the worktable for something suitable, and there an array of implements lay on the table's top, but none of them called out to him. They were too...*up close*. Too personal, and he didn't even know the screaming kid.

Then he saw it and knew it was the right thing. He grinned to match Alex's expression and pointed at the control box. "Is he hooked up?"

Alex chuckled. "It only takes a second. Come on, I'll show you."

After they attached the electrical leads to Randall's training box, Mack walked to the ECT control box and stared down at the different switches and dials. "What do I do?"

"Are we killing him now?"

"Yeah, if this thing can do it."

With another one-sided grin, Alex nodded. "Oh, it can do it. It will be a grisly death for poor old Randall, and you know who will have to clean up that box?"

"Me?"

"The two of us."

Mack turned his attention back to the controls and found a knob labeled "Amperage." He spun it all the way to the right, then glanced at Alex.

"That's right," she said. "But you also want to crank the pulse width and frequency as far as they will go. It'll hurt more that way."

He did as she said, then glanced at her again. "Can I?" He reached a finger toward the button that would start the machine going.

"Once you press that button, there's no turning back. Are you ready for the consequences?"

"What consequences?"

She shrugged absently. "You might feel guilty or something."

"Did you? The first time?"

The one-sided smile surfaced again as she looked at him. "How do you know there's been more than one?"

"Oh, I don't. I just figured, what with you going out with Father all the time."

"Well, to answer the question, no, I didn't feel guilty. Or if I did, I don't remember it."

"Was it..."

"Was it good?" Alex nodded. "Better than diddling myself."

His blush was back with a vengeance.

"Relax, Mack. Everyone does it." She turned her attention back to the ECT machine. "This may bring up emotions, and Father may say you need more training in the box."

"Yeah, okay," he said.

"Then press it when you're—"

Mack mashed the button, and there was a sound akin to a massive short-circuit in one of the power transformers that hung from the poles around the farm. At first, Randall's angry screams twisted into something more like agony, and then, even those stopped. "Is that long enough?" he asked Alex in the relative silence.

"Nah, he's just seizing. You've got to keep that button pressed until he suffocates."

"*Cool*," said Mack.

"Yeah," she said and smiled at him—a real smile, one that reached her eyes. "Welcome to the *real* Family, Mack."

"Thanks, Alex. That means a lot."

"Keep your finger on the button. I'm going to get Father."

"Uh, okay."

"Relax. It's a *good* thing, and Father will be pleased."

Mack kept the button mashed until he could smell burning flesh, then went on holding the button down. His nostrils flared with the scent, and something inside him, something that felt like a reptile, like an alien, rolled over and took notice.

The door opened, and Alex slipped inside on silent cat-feet, and then Father's bulk blocked out the afternoon light. He rested his hand on Alex's shoulder and gave it a little squeeze. Then his gaze found Mack's, and the boy swallowed hard. There was no anger in Father's face.

There was no recognizable emotion on the man's face at all. He came closer and bent a little to peer at the settings, then sought Mack's gaze again. "You've done well, Mack. You've read about ECT?"

Mack shook his head. "No. I asked Alex, and she said—"

"*WHAT DID YOU SAY?*" Alex screeched. In a flash, she crossed from the door to the workbench, her polished steel knife flashing from its sheath like a bolt of lightning. "*WHAT DID YOU CALL ME?*"

"I..." Mack jerked his head from side to side as if he were the one with current flowing through his body.

"He made a mistake, Alex," Father said quietly, head tilted. His cold, assessing gaze was on her face, though she didn't seem to know it.

"Sorry, Alex," Mack said. "I misspoke, that's all."

"I don't think you did," rasped the girl pretending to be a boy.

"Mack, Alex is sensitive about his condition. You know that."

He swallowed hard and nodded.

"What *condition*?" Alex said in a cold voice. "Why are you implying I'm a *girl*? Girls are *worthless*! They are illogical, emotional barrens of the species!"

"Alex is a male, just as you are, Mack," said Father as though he hadn't heard her outburst.

Mack nodded again. "Yes. I understand. Sorry, Alex. I didn't mean anything by it."

Alex made no reply, except to narrow his eyes and glare at him from the delicate brows that made his face look so elfin. "I'm going to teach you to never make that mistake again. Get in your box!"

"Now, Alex, let's not be hasty. Mack is engaged at the moment, and if he lifts his finger, Randall may recover." He put a massive hand on Alex's tiny shoulder. "We don't want that, do we?"

"No," he all but snarled.

"Then ease off. Mack is sorry. He won't make the same mistake twice. He never does."

If anything, their father's words turned Alex's expression even uglier than before.

"Do you think it's been long enough?" Father asked Alex.

"What? Oh. I..." He shook himself and let his knife hand drop to his side as he straightened out of his crouch. "I think so?"

"You don't sound sure."

"I'm not. It's been about five minutes."

"How long does it take a person to suffocate?" asked Mack.

"Minutes," said Father in an offhand way. "More than on television but still single digits."

"Oh." After a quick glance at Alex's beet-red face, he looked down at his finger holding the button in. It had turned white, and though the pad of his finger hurt a little bit, the rest of the finger had gone numb. "Then if I hold it for ten minutes..."

"Yes," said Father. "Alex, sheathe your knife. Your brother isn't a suitable place to leave it."

Mack suppressed a shudder but squeezed his eyes shut as he heard the blade rasp on leather.

"Good," said Father in the same flat, uninflected voice he always used. "Anger can be a powerful ally, when *controlled*. It can be stored up, saved until it's appropriate to release—say when you are with someone who deserves cutting."

"Yes, Father," Alex said, and once again, his voice was calm, controlled.

"Very good." Father turned and placed a hand on Mack's shoulder. "And you. Your decision to continue the current for ten minutes is a sound one."

Mack looked up into the man's doll-like eyes and smiled. "Thanks."

"Did you intend to cause Randall immense pain?"

His stomach did a little flip flop. "I...uh... Randall's been..." He gave his head a sharp shake. "Randall has been a very poor example for the new kids. This seemed like a good teaching example."

"Very good. He's annoyed me for long enough. He deserves to die in agony." Father glanced at Randall's box. "That will be messy. You two will clean it up and make it ready for a new occupant. Have it ready by the time I return. It should be close to four in the morning." Father turned and strode through the door without another word, and outside, the Ford Bronco roared to life.

Mack could feel Alex glaring at him, could feel his raw rage again, and didn't like being the target of it. "I'm really sorry, Alex," he whispered without looking at him.

"Maybe," he said, "but in three more minutes, you will be for sure."

Mack shivered.

CHAPTER 4

READING THE MAIL

Hanable's Valley, NY

HER PHONE'S BUZZ woke Meredeth out of a light sleep, and she grabbed it, hoping it was a text from Kevin, or as a runner-up option, a text from Bobby about the Baltimore Brawler case. It wasn't, however.

It was an email. From her mysterious benefactor, "M."

Dear Agent Connelly,

I hope this email finds you recovering and in good spirits. For my part, I'm doing as well as I ever am, given my childhood.

I understand your desire to know my name, but for now, please allow me to hide behind the letter M. I need my privacy, and for some reason, I find it hard to trust anyone.

Yeah, childhood, again.

You're going to ask me how you can know I'm not my father. I will help you there. I'm going to tell you about Alex. And I mean I'm going to tell you everything, not Ankou's edited history.

You don't know what it's like to have someone destroy your personality and rebuild it any which way he wants. You don't understand the guilt of knowing your family died because of some psycho's desire to build his own "family."

The aim of this email is to help you understand. I know you have education in psychology, so I'm going forward with the belief that you understand the concept of psychic driving—at least the broad strokes.

That was Ankou's whole act: kidnap some kids, use psychic driving to first break them, then to rebuild them with what that psychopath calls ethics and morals. He did have a sense of right and wrong, but he doesn't have any respect for our societal norms or cultural standards. He thinks of society as a mewling child, and he aims to give it correction.

At least, that's what he says. Given his "grand plan," I have my doubts.

He kept us in wooden crates until we were broken, and he could start piecing us back together. I want to paint you a picture, here, so let me describe these coffins: two big sides forty-eight inches square mated by four rectangles that measured forty-eight inches by twelve. He fed us through a little flap in one of the sides. He had the boxes wired for sound, great big speakers mounted with their cones facing the top and bottom squares respectively. Oh, and he had one-inch circles of copper set into the bottom square. You know, for ECT.

Meredeth lifted her head and stared blankly at the television. The box sounded like something out of a torture chamber—and she supposed it was. She had studied psychic driving in grad school and knew enough to understand why the psychiatric community had disavowed it globally. She couldn't imagine using the barbaric method on *children*. Shaking her head, she returned her gaze to the email.

Let me anticipate your next question: Why am I writing to you?

By now, you know, of course, that Father's aim was to create an army of serial killers who were loyal to him and who would assist him in reaching his goals. You know, cogs in the grand plan. Alex was his first big success. I don't know if he killed perfecting the process, and if so, how many kids, before the girl who would become Alex, but I was taken soon after Father started rebuilding her after he'd torn her personality down to bedrock. The technique didn't work on the second kid—a boy he called Randall, who was electrocuted right next to me. I was number three. At one time, he considered me his first daughter—Alex was his first son, you see— but Ankou now considers me an apostate, a failure.

Alex is... Well, he's nuts. Father made him so. He wanted to know how far he could push Dr. Cameron's technique, if he could make a pre-teen girl capable of beating someone to death with a hammer. And he was successful. He wanted to know if he could rename her and have that name stick. When he achieved that, he wanted to know if he could make Alex think he was male. As you now know, he achieved both of those goals. I have no idea what Alex's original name was, so don't waste your time asking. Father turned Alex into a stone-cold killer and trained almost all his emotions out of him. The one he couldn't train away was the rage at being trapped in a woman's body. Alex wasn't transgender, but Father convinced him he was.

Did you know Alex tried to enroll in three different sex reassignment programs? Yep. Turned away after the psych evaluations each time.

Well, I think that's enough for now.

-M

When she reached the end, Meredeth returned to the top and re-read the entire message again. The implications were severe. John Doe could have actually done the impossible thing he claimed. He could have created a troop of serial killers and turned them loose on the unsuspecting world—just as he had crowed about in that original interview back in Buffalo right after his arrest.

Briefly, she wondered how many kids he'd broken irreparably perfecting the different techniques of psychic driving. It seemed likely that Delamort was an early success, probably having more to do with the woman's nature and mindset than his techniques given M's claim about the next kid and her own "failure." Her first exposure to Doe had been two decades before—in the spate of kidnappings across Western New York that populated those horror-boxes in his barn. M was a victim of that series, as was Alex and this Randall.

And that means I have a list of their real names! The idea sent tremors of excitement coursing through her. She'd had the case files unpacked and emailed to Bobby during the investigation into Doe's most recent series of murders, and he'd printed three copies out at Hanable's Valley PD...

With shaking hands, she grabbed her private cellphone and hit Kevin's icon. The phone rang three times before he picked up, which meant he was busy. "Kevin?"

"Well, hello there, FBI. Listen, I don't have time for a chat just now. I'm up to my alligators in assholes."

"Yeah, I figured by the delay in answering."

"Three rings? That's a delay?"

"You usually grab it on the first. But anyway, I'm not calling for a chat. I need something."

"Yeah, but you can't have *that* until your guts are back on your insides."

She cringed—flirting in her present state made her uncomfortable. "Uh, yeah, that's not it." Kevin made a funny little noise, and she thought it was likely a strangled sigh. "Remember the .40 Caliber Killer case?"

"Hard to forget it given what's gone on."

"Yeah. Remember when we reviewed the case files for the original kidnappings back in the late 90s?"

"Yes."

"Can you bring me one of the binders Bobby made?"

"Sure, I can, but, Meredeth, what's going on?"

"You know how Doe sent me those anonymous emails? I got another one from the mysterious M, and it struck me: I—"

"Wait a minute. *Another* one?"

"Yeah. I told you about the one from the other day."

"No, you didn't."

"But I..." She pursed her lips and made a face. "I *thought* I told you. Maybe I dreamed the conversation, or the pain pills scrambled my brains that day."

"Well, it doesn't matter now. Tell me about *both* of these emails. Maybe a buddy at BCI can—"

"The Bureau's Cybercrimes techies can't grab information from a Russian server—it could very well be viewed as an act of war—and I doubt a state trooper will be able to help get us information from a Russian provider. And we all know they will ignore any subpoenas from a US court." She sucked her teeth and grimaced. "Um, I mean to say that having your pal check them out would be great, Kevin. Thank you."

He chuckled. "Social graces still a work in progress, eh?"

"You know me."

"I do, and I respect you extra for trying given what's going on. Tell me."

"Right. The first email wasn't much. A warning, the author—who claims to be a woman I'm to call 'M'—called it. She told me a little of how Doe raised these kids to know me intimately, to follow my career. She...also mentioned my brother, Kenny. He was around enough to be called 'Uncle Kenny,' and the picture she painted of him is a grim one. She went over Doe's plan with a broad brush, claiming the details would be too complicated, too much."

"And this was when?"

"A few..." She grimaced and looked up and to the right. "I'm not sure my memory is accurate. Let me look at the date." She grabbed her FBI phone and backed out of the most recent email, then scanned up. "Ah, it was three days ago."

"The same day Bobby called about the Brawler?"

"Yeah. The email came in right after that conversation."

"I see," said Kevin. Meredeth could hear him jotting down notes. "And today's email?"

"I'd replied to the first one. You know, trying to draw her out. I said it would be confusing if we both signed our emails with an 'M' and asked for her first name. Today, she replied but wouldn't give me her name—and she explained that Doe renamed all the children as a part of the process to break down their existing personalities. The process is complicated, but it's based on the MKUltra experiments in Canada by the CIA. Dr. Cameron and all that."

"I must have slept through that lecture in my psych class."

"It's not discussed much. The psychiatric community effectively banned the process as unethical, and it is. Delamort is a perfect example of what can be done, how a mind can be twisted far from its origins." She glanced down at the long email. "Listen, this is a long email with a lot of detail about what Doe did to the kids. It would be easier to let you read it yourself."

"Forward both to me. I'll read them, and we can discuss it when I get home. I've really got to cut this short. The assholes are chewing on my alligators."

"Right," she said and couldn't help but smile. "When will you be able to get free?"

"Probably an hour or so. Will that do?"

"Of course, Kevin. Whenever you get finished up." She put some spring into her voice, but what she wanted to do was demand he drop everything and come talk to her. *Probably the meds*, she thought, but even as she did, she knew it for a lie. She needed to develop more patience.

And more social graces.

CHAPTER 5

CHARM CITY

Baltimore, MD

BIG DAVE TILTON lived up to his nickname. When he slouched, he reached the six-foot-six line on the door frames of convenience stores, and he must have weighed close to three hundred seventy-five pounds. But all that weight wasn't fat, as many a felon came to realize too late. Underneath an admittedly soft-looking exterior, Dave was as solid as stone. Add his Glock to that, and he was a formidable guy to mess with.

Despite all that, he was a genuinely nice man. A man who held doors open, who got things down from the top shelf for the "height-challenged" without being asked. Bobby liked him. He couldn't help it.

They sat in a West Baltimore police station watching videos of street fights in the area. Bobby lounged comfortably, ankles crossed, one arm draped over the back of his chair. Big Dave, on the other hand, sat hunched forward, his eyes intent on the computer screen. "He's going to get hit hard in a second," he said.

"Think so?" asked Cortez, the detective whose desk they sat at. "He's pretty quick."

"The big guy is, too. And he's been playing possum a bit. Trying to give the crowd a better fight."

Cortez shrugged. "Well, I guess we're going to find out."

Bobby thought Dave had the right of it, but adding his voice to the fray would only make the cop dig his heels in. He watched the two Black men circling each other in what seemed like a backyard—grass, a few chairs, and a chain link fence. A crowd of other men stood around cheering and heckling.

The leaner of the two took a couple of dance-like steps toward the brute he was fighting and swung for the fences. It was a haymaker to beat all haymakers, and it was obvious by his expression and the grunting effort that he thought it could be the blow that ended the fight.

It may have been—if it had connected. The bigger man dodged a half-step left, ducked under the sweeping blow, and hit the little guy with an upper cut that seemed capable of knocking his head clean off.

The leaner man stood straight up, eyes rolling around as if he were lost, swallowed blood flowing from his mouth, then his eyes closed, and he fell to the side like a tree cut at its base.

The bigger man danced around the circle, his fists shoved toward the sky in celebration of his victory.

"Well, shit," said Cortez.

Dave had a laugh like an avalanche—it started with a low rumble deep inside him, and when it finally burst its way out, it almost hurt to be near him—and the detective looked at him askance, his expression a mixture of scorn and distaste but also grudging respect. Big Dave seemed to get that look a lot. Almost everyone treated him like a big, dumb jock, though nothing was further from the truth.

"Good call, Big Dave," said Bobby. "How'd you know?"

Dave shot him a quick, eyebrow-arched look. "The big one was holding back. You could see his muscles twitch as his instincts called for a big right or something, but he never threw the punch."

Cortez hunched forward and stared at the screen, scrubbing the video slowly backward. "How'd you see that with this crap quality cellphone vid?"

Shrugging, Dave said, "I just watched him. He seemed more like the guy I imagine is committing these murders. He's got the strength, the endurance—and we know that unsub has the smarts to avoid getting caught on his first kill. Did the poster list the names of the fighters?"

Cortez gave up trying to see what Dave had seen and checked the description of the video, then shook his head. "Nada."

"Maybe your tech guys can pull the metadata off the video? We could track down the poster and interview him."

"Phone's probably stolen," grumbled Cortez even as he emailed the link to the techie. "Even if the video leads us to the guy who made the tape, he won't snitch unless we have something over his head, and even then..." He shook his head and shrugged. "It's a cultural thing."

"It's a place to start, though," said Dave.

Cortez only shrugged again.

"Dave's right," said Bobby. "A name gets us into the community, and if we—" his phone rang, and Bobby looked down at the screen while holding up one finger. The caller ID read, "McCutchins," and Bobby stood. "I've got to take this," he said to Cortez. "McCutchins," he murmured at Big Dave, who nodded.

"Work junk," Big Dave said. "Let's watch the next video while your tech guys crunch the first one."

"Yeah, okay," said Cortez as Bobby turned to leave them. "This time, say something when you see something. I want to see what you see."

Tilton chuckled. "Sure thing."

Bobby hit the accept button as he crossed the squad room and entered one of the interview rooms. "Hey, Jim."

"Van Zandt. How's the Brawler case coming?"

"Slow, but I've never seen a surer win. It'll just take time and good investigative work. Meredeth gave us a couple of ideas to check out, and we're already into one of them."

"Good, good." Jim cleared his throat. "How is she?"

Bobby's lips drew into a thin line. He didn't like playing middleman between McCutchins and Connelly, but they seemed to have some sort of old code that agents never spoke directly to one another about health issues. "She's doing about as good as can be expected."

"Going stir crazy, eh?"

"You got it. That's why I shared our Brawler profile with her."

"Smart move—she's a better profiler than Big Dave."

"True," said Bobby.

"But that's not the reason I called."

"No?"

"No," said McCutchins. "I got an email here from one of our crime analysts. She's found a few strange things in ViCAP and thinks they might be related. I'd like you to take a look."

"Okay. Can I share with Meredeth?"

"Sure, but don't let her mess around and do too much that it sets her back."

"No. I'll have help monitoring her."

"Ah. The boyfriend."

"Uh..."

"Relax, Van Zandt. I didn't snoop. It's a little obvious, though, don't you think? All of a sudden Meredeth Connelly has weekend plans? Then there's her sunny disposition of late. I've seen it all before but never with Connelly."

"You can take an agent out of profiling, but you can't take profiling out of an agent."

"That's it." McCutchins cleared his throat again as if the conversation had taken an uncomfortable turn. "Anyway, the first of the entries I'd like you to check out is a bit of road rage that ended in a car fire. Out in Idaho. I'll email the ViCAP ID numbers for the ones that tripped the red flag from the analyst. She'll keep me updated if she finds more, and I'll let you know."

"Sure thing, boss," said Bobby. "Big Dave can handle this part of the investigation. I'll sit there with my laptop and read up on the ViCAP entries. Should I email my findings?"

"Call. I don't want a paper trail on this yet."

CHAPTER 6

BUMPER STICKER

Yoagoh, NY

MACK SAT IN the back of the old Bronco, while Alex basked in Father's presence from the passenger seat. They were on a mission—Mack's first "procurement" mission. In other words, they were going to take another kid for the boxes back at the farm and kill everyone else.

His father's methods didn't seem all that elegant, but Mack supposed Father's cold efficiency—of which Alex had forewarned him—could be construed as elegance. He'd also told Mack to expect a kind of ninja prowess from the big man.

Mack wasn't little—far from it, actually—but their father made him feel so when they stood next to each other. His father's imposing presence elicited a desire to stand up straight, to throw his chest out, to *measure up*. It didn't matter that Mack was barely fourteen. In fact, his age might have made it worse.

He had to admit his present company had him a little intimidated. Sure, Alex was tiny physically, but he made up for it with ferociousness and a willingness to do *anything* to "win" as Alex called it. Whatever Father wanted of him somehow got rolled into "winning." He'd grown into the role of Father's second, and Mack could tell both of them liked that a lot.

The Bronco's oversized tires hissed along the damp asphalt—the salt trucks had been out an hour or so before, and despite the continued light snowfall, the roads were clear. They crossed into Yoagoh's town limits, and Father took his foot off the gas pedal, letting engine-braking slow them to the in-town speed limit. There weren't many people out and about at 2:43 in the morning, but headlights splashed across the Bronco's interior from behind, and Father's gaze zipped back and forth between the rearview mirror and his side mirror. Mack turned and hooked his arm over the seat back and looked out the rear window.

Whatever the car's make and model, it was big—boat big—and the driver had no sense of spacing. He was right up on them. As Mack watched, the car drew even closer until Mack couldn't see the lights or grill at all. "Asshole," he muttered.

"Eyes front," said Alex. "You don't want him getting a good look at your face, Mack."

With a grunt and burning cheeks, he turned to face the front. He felt an urge to count up the offenses of the man tailgating them, to *watch* and count, but he found he could tell how close the man was by the amount of light flooding the Bronco's cabin. "Are those his brights?"

Father said, "Yes."

"Doesn't that make it harder to drive?"

His eyes jigged to the rearview to look at Mack. "It does, Son, but you can deal with anything with the proper motivation."

Mack nodded as they slowed for Yoagoh's only stoplight—which was red, of course, to accommodate the complete lack of cross-traffic. As the vehicle rolled to a smooth stop, Mack rolled over the seat back to land on the box in the cargo area. The tailgate came open with a flip of his wrist, window and all, and Mack stood up, then jumped to the ground. He walked toward the car—a giant Cadillac Fleetwood from the early 1970s—and thumped his fist on the hood. An electric window whined down, and Mack stood straight, arms akimbo, hands drawn into fists resting on his waist.

"Get back in your damn car, kid. You don't impress me none."

"No?" Mack asked. He was proud that the nervousness he felt didn't make itself apparent in his voice. He strode around to the driver's side of the car.

"Get out of my way, kid, or you'll be sorry. I can promise you that. Let me around your slowpoke old man, and I'll be on my way."

"Oh?" Mack stopped next to the sideview mirror and peered into the car. The man inside was big—but not like Mack's father was big. The driver was almost hidden by rolls of puffy, soft fat. *He must weigh four hundred pounds*, Mack thought. *No wonder he needs a barge like this to get around.*

"Last chance, kid. If I have to get out of this car, I'm not getting back in until you've learned your lesson."

"Is that so? Better get to teaching me, then." Mack's voice was even, low volume, cold, as if the man were nothing, and he witnessed the effects of his words and timbre in the man's expression. First, there was a look of confusion that slowly crumpled into disbelief and then to anger.

"Kid..." The man shook his head. "Just get out of my way. I don't need no beef for beating on a minor."

Mack just looked at him, his face a slab of ice, incapable of emotion, of anger, of fear, of anxiety. "You talk a lot for a man too chickenshit to get out of his damn car. I get it. You're a fat hog. If I were as huge as you are, I wouldn't want to get out, either." He leaned closer and opened his eyes wide. "But you're going to have to, mister. One way or another."

The man's angry expression flickered for a moment—more disbelief, but this time, Mack thought it was tinged with fear—then settled into a rictus of fury. "Fat? Hog? Don't say I didn't try to warn you, kid. Don't say I didn't give you every chance."

Behind Mack, the two doors of the Bronco clunked open, and the Caddie driver's gaze flicked toward the truck. "Three on one, is it?"

"Nah," said Mack. "They want to watch me kick your ass is all."

"Sure, sure, kid. And when I'm beating you like a stepchild, your daddy's not going to wade in? Your sister isn't going to call the cops?"

"Brother," said Mack.

"Wuh-what?"

"That's my brother, not my sister."

"Since when do brothers have little baby titties?"

Mack took a menacing half-step and growled, "You want to get out on your own, or do you want to come out this window?"

The man heaved a sigh that shook his flabby man-boobs. "Yeah, kid. I guess I am. Get ready for the beating of your life. Your dad and little sister can't save you. I'm a black belt."

"Oh? In what?"

"Tae Kwon-Do. Still want to fight me?"

"Oh, *hell, yes!*" said Mack. "He's a *black belt in Tae Kwon-Do*, Alex."

His brother tittered and came closer. "Oh, goody," said Alex. "Father, shall we bet on the winner?"

"No contest."

"See, kid? Even your dad knows I'm going to beat you down."

Mack showed his teeth. "Talk, talk, talk. Get out and teach me a lesson, fat-ass." Some of his eagerness must have showed in his face or in his voice because the fat man's face drew into a prune-like example of confusion, and he pulled his chin back. "*Get out!*" Mack shouted as he grabbed the door handle and yanked the big door open.

The driver winced away as Mack stormed around the length of the open door and clamped his hands on his sausage-like upper arm. He jerked the big man but couldn't pull his bulk out from behind the steering wheel. He lifted his foot and planted it on the side of the car and tried anyway.

The driver's gaze swept across the three of them, then came back to Mack's face. "What the hell's the matter with you, kid?"

Mack leaned inside the car and shouted, "*I don't like bumper-stickers, you enormous pile of human waste! Get out of the car, or I'll pull you out in pieces.*"

The driver's brows drew together, and his fat, rubbery lips pouted, but he released the seat belt and shoved it to the side. Mack backed away to give him room. He swung his legs out and grabbed the door to pull himself to his feet. He glanced at Mack's father and said, "You seen all this. I gave him every chance."

Father nodded, his arms crossed, an expression that bordered on boredom on his face.

Shaking his head, the man turned to Mack. "Well, okay, then. Let's dance, kid." He dropped into a sloppy stance that Mack supposed was intended to look like a horse stance and shuffled forward like a crab.

Mack wanted to laugh at the ridiculous man. Part of their father's training regimen included Krav Maga—the self-defense and fighting system developed by the Israeli Defense Forces, and the fat man's training regimen consisted of lying about knowing martial arts and eating Twinkies.

As the driver moved toward him at a snail's pace, he kept repeating, "It's not too late, kid," and Mack kept rolling his eyes. Impatience nipped at the edges of his mind, but Father always said the measure of man is how calm he is in the moments before extreme violence. He tried to still his thoughts, to relax into the wait, but he was antsy and wanted to get over it. He glanced at his father's impassive face, and Father gave him a small nod of encouragement.

The fat bumper-sticker had stopped moving closer about four feet away. "Come on, kid, at least put up a fight."

Mack treated him to a half-grin. "You'll get your fight. I'm standing here waiting for it."

"Then put up your hands, boy!" the driver snapped. "Get yourself ready."

"I am ready," Mack said in a steely calm voice. To his surprise, he didn't need to pretend at calmness—he actually *was* calm.

The fat guy shook his head and muttered something about fighting children too dumb to put up their guard, then lunged toward Mack—a hippopotamus would have displayed more grace—swinging his right hand in a giant haymaker at Mack's head.

Mack stepped forward and to his right, then, with blinding speed, he made his hand into a blade and chopped the man in the throat, striking with the edge of his palm right in the fat guy's larynx as his father had taught him. He heard a wet pop, and the man went to his knees, both hands to his throat.

"Nicely done," said Father. "Clean up the mess, and we'll take the car back to the farm."

"Yes, Father," said Mack. He wasn't sure if he heard a note of disapproval in his father's voice. He glanced at Alex and found him giving the man a narrow-eyed glare. He bent to finish the fat man off.

"He's already dead, Mack. His brain just hasn't admitted yet. Don't waste any more time," said Father, his gaze zipping around the small four-corner "downtown" of Yoagoh. "We need to get out of here. Put him in the trunk and get that boat turned around."

"Yes, Father."

"And next time, consider your surroundings. This has been quite a risk. What if some insomniac is sitting in their dark living room watching the streetlight?"

Mack dropped his gaze to the asphalt. "Yes, sir. Sorry, Father."

"I understand you wanted to help me, but in the future, communicate your intentions first. We could have waited and run him off the road outside of town. He'd be just as dead."

Mack nodded again without looking up.

"And don't be glum. Enjoy this. You did very well. My comments aren't intended to berate but to teach."

Mack looked up at him and smiled. "Yes, Father. I understand." He hooked his forearm under the dying man's arm, then glanced at Alex. "Can you help? This guy weighs a ton."

"Sure," said Alex. He walked over and grabbed the man on the other side. "Come on, fat-ass. Time to get in the trunk."

CHAPTER 7

ON THE FLIP-FLOP

Hanable's Valley, NY

"HONEY, I'M HOME!" called Kevin as he came through the door. "I brought your case files, and I brought take-out from the diner. Don't worry, I remembered the hyper-unhealthy diet the surgeon put you on, although I can't see how people with permanent ostomies can survive with no vitamins, no fruits, and no vegetables. You have a choice between a cheeseburger and fries or fried chicken with deep-fried potato spears."

"Otherwise known as fries?"

"You got it, babe."

Meredeth pushed herself out of the recliner, a little groggy from the fatigue, and moved toward the kitchen. "Sounds great," she said in a voice blurred by exhaustion. "Did you get a chance to—"

"Yes, I read the emails while I waited for the food."

"Well?"

Kevin sucked his teeth, then drew a deep breath. "I'm not sure, to be honest. It doesn't sound like our buddy over in Wende. Not enough arrogance, not enough BS."

"Yeah, the tone is different from Doe's earlier emails. Of that, there's no question. But is M for real?"

"If it is a ruse by Doe, he's giving away a lot of information about his activities. The second boy was killed, right? There's no statute of limitations on that."

"True, but would this be admissible?"

"Maybe not, but it would get us back out there to search the entire farm. We could do that fancy ground-scanning stuff you Bureau people are so proud of."

"And what if he disposed of the bodies elsewhere?"

"With all that land? With that forest between the house and the road? My bet is all the dead kids are still on the farm."

Meredeth lifted one shoulder. "Let's eat. We can continue this argument with food in our mouths."

Kevin laughed and began setting out dishes. "Which meal do you want?"

"I can't believe my ileostomy requires a diet of French fries and meat."

"Sounds like a dream requirement to me."

"That's because you have a choice in the matter."

Kevin sobered. "True. Things will get back to normal soon, FBI."

She grimaced. "Not soon enough."

"I know it's hard, hon, but it's temporary. A few more weeks."

"I know, and I'm sorry to play the role of Debbie Downer. I don't usually indulge in self-pity."

"This is a unique situation, Meredeth. You can't eat as you please, you can't do much, you're tired all the time, and you're alone all day with nothing to occupy that high-octane mind of yours. I imagine the loneliness is staggering while I'm at work."

She drew a deep breath, too tired to rise to the bait, and slid the package of fried chicken and fries toward her place at the table and sat down. "The days are getting harder as I start to feel a little better."

"I've been thinking about that. I have quite a bit of time saved up. What if I took the week off, and we can hang out all day?"

"I already feel guilty about putting you through this, Kev," she said in a low voice, her gaze resting on her food. "I don't think wasting a week of your vacation-time to sit around your own house and watch me mope would do a thing to reduce that."

"FBI, don't be silly. Hanging out with you in any capacity could never be a waste of my time. I'm glad I can help."

She imagined Kevin meant those words to buoy her spirits, to make her feel better about the situation, but what they actually did was emphasize how much of a drain she'd become on him. She shook her head a little and picked up a French fry, more to do something than because she wanted to eat it—her appetite, which had been ravaging a moment before, was suddenly absent without leave. "I'm really sorry about all this, Kevin."

His lips made that thin white line—Kevin's default expression when he felt she was being stubborn. "First, none of this is your fault. Second—"

"It *is* my fault, Kevin. I let a serial killer fool me so thoroughly that I got stabbed from *behind*, and I never saw it coming."

He treated her to a severe expression. "Yeah, how dare you not anticipate that the *woman* you knew as the ADA for Pinellas County was actually the *man* who was abducting and killing blondes. How silly of you not to see that coming." His voice was filled with sarcasm.

She said nothing as he reached for the burger and arranged his food on his plate. She could see he was annoyed with her and that did nothing to help her state of mind.

"As I was saying, *none of this is your fault*. Second, I happen to enjoy having you around. It feels so...domestic, and I like that. Third, you are important to me, FBI. *Special*. That means I will do anything in my power to help you out, and you don't need to thank me, let alone feel guilty about it. Get it? Caring for you is not a burden—not in any way, shape, or form."

She swallowed a lump of raw emotion—relief, respect, love—that had lodged in her throat. "Thank you," she said. "You're wrong about that part."

"Always gotta have the last word, don't you?" His tone was still severe, but one glance at his face, at the laugh lines slowly forming, and she knew everything was all right.

"Well, *duh*," she said and laughed.

He took a bite of his burger and chewed a little but didn't swallow. "Now that I have the requisite food in my mouth, given—"

"Eww!" she said. "I can see inside your mouth when you talk."

"—the steps the sender took to hide from us, I think your only option is to try to draw them out." Wearing a grin, he chewed and swallowed. "Use your fancy-shmancy interrogation and negotiating training to get more information out of the sender."

"That's what I was thinking." She took a bite of chicken, chewed a few times, then ran out her tongue, laden with half-chewed fried chicken. "Now, we're even," she said after swallowing.

"Does that count as your obsession with having the last word?"

"Again, *duh*." She grinned at him, feeling better mentally than she had in a while. "Here's another last word for you: You are absolutely the best man I know, Kevin Saunders, and I'm lucky to have you in my life."

He showed her a saucy grin and said, "Well, *duh*." He took and swallowed another bite. "So? Do you think you can do what you do so well face to face in an email?"

After a curt shake of her head, she said, "I can write the words, obviously, but a lot of what I do involves reading body language, watching for micro expressions and behavioral tells. Obviously, I can't do that via email, but I may be able to analyze her word choices and get some of the same information."

"And you can use these first two emails as baseline data."

"Sure, though she's on guard, and the baseline won't be as reliable as say a couple of emails to her girlfriends."

"Okay, so we'll agree to cut you a break for getting some of it wrong. We *both* will."

"No idea what you're driving at, Saunders." She took a bite from her chicken breast to hide her smile.

"You'll note I wasn't asking you, FBI, I was *telling you*."

"Oh, I *like* it when you take charge." Instantly, she regretted the flirty nature of her tone and the words themselves, and an uncomfortable silence followed.

"As soon as you're ready, Mere," Kevin said softly.

"I know. I'm sorry for—"

"Listen, FBI, I have it on good authority—one Special Agent Robert Van Zandt—that you *never* apologize. Now, here you are performing random acts of contrition every time I turn around. Are you trying to make Bobby into a liar?"

She laughed and it felt *good*. "Okay, fine. I'm not sorry, and I'll do it again when you least expect it."

"Promises, promises." He got up and took the no-added-sugar ketchup out of the refrigerator and squirted some on her fries, then did his own as well. "Back to my point. This email interrogation is to be considered experimental, and you are not to expect perfection from yourself."

"Yeah, I got that part."

"Okay, then. Let's build that baseline."

Meredeth nodded. "The first thing to note, is that in the first email, M says she's worried about explanations being too long to commit to an email, yet she's very verbose. Do you agree?"

"Yes. What else?"

"She wants me to know she's studied my cases. My behavior, too, perhaps. She wants to appear knowledgeable, even 'revealing' that Kenny is still alive and served as an uncle figure to Doe's—what do we call them? Children seems to ignore everything he did to them, both before and after he took them."

"Victims?"

"I guess, though they are now active conspirators in his big plan for me."

"Some of them, anyway. And he brainwashed them."

"That's true. Back to M: she dropped the fact that the victims were raised with me cast as the enemy, the boogeyman. She also implied Kenny is unstable, likely psychotic, filled with rage, and that he hates me and wants to do me harm."

"All of which Doe already told you. She should have anticipated that."

"I think she did. She told me about Kenny to destabilize me emotionally. It's manipulation 101—get your target thinking emotionally rather than logically, and you're halfway to convincing them. She then dropped the bomb that she's one of Doe's children but emphasizes a certain distance from the others as well as pointing out that these emails put her in as much danger as they do me."

"And then she confirms Doe's story about the kidnappings, about building a perfect family."

"His grand plan, as well. But notice the level of detail in those last few paragraphs and compare them to the details in the paragraphs about me and Kenny."

"So, she's warning you about certain danger but doesn't or can't give you details. Then again, as she says, Doe probably changed the details after she broke with him."

"Or she has a Ankou-built psychological compulsion against giving up the details."

"She does drop a few names, though—Mack and Lucy."

"Which are meaningless. We can't track these people by generic first names."

"But maybe we can track the real names of the children Doe abducted twenty years ago."

"We can, but I doubt any of them are using those names. Hell, Doe did such a good job of obscuring his identity that we still don't know his real name."

"True enough. What can you glean from the second email?"

"She engages in idle chit-chat in the beginning paragraph, something she didn't do in the first email."

"That may be a sign she's warming up to you," said Kevin.

"It's possible, but I think it's more likely she now sees me as a person, rather than an idealized figure. Most of us are raised to be polite first, no matter what."

"Yeah. *Most* of us."

She grinned while shaking her head. "Hey, I said I'm working on it."

"You have a guilty conscience, FBI. What about the next paragraph? The one where she tells you why she won't give up her name."

"That's pretty straightforward. She says she won't tell me, then justifies it by claiming she has a hard time trusting anyone because of her childhood. In other words, I'm not going to give you what you want, and I'm going to make you feel sorry for me, so you'll drop it."

"And she tries to manipulate you further in the next paragraph when she dangles the carrot of giving you the unedited version of Alex Delamort's history."

"Yes, the person who stabbed me, but then she immediately goes back to the 'pity me' theme."

"Right, all while claiming it's to help you understand."

"And to confirm Doe's story about raising his victims to become as he is. She gives us details about his methods, which could be important in tracking down and stopping his other creations."

"His army of serial killers, you mean."

"Exactly. But you'll note she only really gives details about the two members of the 'family' who are already incarcerated—one who's already convicted and who will never step foot out of prison."

"Yes, and she does give a lot of detail around Delamort's training. More tugging on your heartstrings?"

"Probably, but it may not be conscious. Doe seems to have required his victims to kill someone on their own as a kind of graduation step. Since M wasn't killed back there on the farm near Yoagoh, we can assume she's committed at least one murder and was probably an accessory to others."

"Ah, I hadn't considered that. Then this not-so-subtle manipulation is to excuse her own crimes?"

"I think so but remember that I said she may not be conscious of the manipulation. She may be telling us this in the hopes that it will mitigate her responsibilities for her crimes—maybe to start building grounds for an affirmative defense."

"Not guilty by means of mental defect."

"Yep. The good old insanity defense. We could be called as witness for her defense."

Kevin grimaced.

"And remember this could all be unconscious activity."

"I'm not sure if that makes it better or worse."

"The real question is: what do we do now? Obviously, I need to write a reply."

"Yes, but this time using your fancy negotiation skills."

"Right. We need goals for this email and overarching goals for the entire sequence. All my communications with her need to be intentional, not happenstance."

"Extract enough information to derail Ankou's plan. How's that for a long-term goal?"

"It's a good idea, but it's not measurable. We either achieve it in total or we fail."

"True enough."

"Plus, how will we know when we have 'enough information?'"

"Then, how about we extract information that gives us leverage over him? And what about Delamort?"

"Yes, I suspect we will want leverage over both of them. Those are good."

"Next: Learn details on the other victims that will aid in their identification and capture."

"Perfect, as long as we include M."

"Find Kenny?"

Meredeth shrugged. "I'm not really sure I want to." She inclined her head. "I mean, I *do*, but I don't want to face the emotional wreckage."

"We only have the word of two serial killers that he's even still alive."

"True. Maybe the goal should be to extract information that confirms Kenny is alive. I can decide what to do about it after we know."

"Fair enough. What do you want to tackle in this first intentional email?"

"Hmm. I'd like leverage on Doe. I'd also like to hear more details about M, but I'm guessing she will deflect and tell me about Alex."

Kevin ate a few fries with a sober expression dominating his features. "Then do we beat her to the punch?"

"You mean ask her directly about Delamort and see if she provides the information?"

"And Doe. Don't ask her anything about herself."

"You're thinking is that she's compelled to deflect answers about individuals and only can get around it by answering unasked questions?"

"It's worth a shot."

Meredeth nodded. "It's a good idea." She wiped her hands on her napkin and picked up her phone. "Okay. Let's get a draft written, then we can sit on it and see what we think after dinner." She opened her email client and found

M's last message. "I'll say the sentence, and if you have no suggestions, I'll type it as is. Okay?"

"Sounds fine."

"Okay. I'll mirror her greeting style. Dear M. I hope this email finds you safe and well. I appreciate you helping me understand what life was like under Ankou's thumb. To be honest, I'm appalled by his actions, especially since you were all children."

"One suggestion," said Kevin.

"Yes?"

"We have your case files on these kids, right? Use her real name."

"Oh, we *can* because she said she was the third to arrive."

"Bingo. You've got the exact order in your notes."

She grinned and retrieved the three-ring binder Bobby had made for her during the .40 Caliber Killer case. When she returned to the table, she slid her plate toward the center and put the binder in its place, then opened it. "Okay..." She flipped to the police reports section. "Delamort's real name is Missy Smith. Randall, the boy M says was killed, was named Darrell Rogers. M's real name is Julie Fuchs."

"And the other sixteen? Who is Mack and who is Lucy?"

"We don't know the order they were taken. Maybe I should ask about that? Something like who was the next person to come to the farm after you?"

"Maybe? She probably won't answer."

"Maybe not, but we won't know that unless I ask her."

"Do it," said Kevin. He shook his head, a musing expression on his face. "Missy Smith? She hardly sounds dangerous."

"That was her name before Doe got his hooks in her. It's Alex now. He may not even remember the real name."

"This psychic driving is that powerful?"

Nodding, Meredeth slid the binder to the side and picked up her phone. "Definitely. How's this sound: 'Dear Julie, I hope this email finds you well and happy. In case you don't remember, the name your mother gave you was Julie Fuchs. I know that because you mentioned you were the third child brought to the farm after Ankou began his spree. I decided to call you by your birthname because you are not part of Doe's secret little family—at least that's how it seems to me.'"

"You left out that bit about appreciating her help."

Meredeth gave him a curt nod as she typed in the revised first paragraph. "Next paragraph: 'Hey, listen, I do realize you are putting yourself in danger by reaching out to me, and I appreciate your help in understanding what life under Ankou's thumb was like. That said, I don't want you to take unnecessary risks. Keep yourself safe—I'll be fine." She glanced across the table. "Good?" When Kevin nodded, she went on, "Third paragraph: Frankly, I'm appalled by what this man did to you and the others when you were children. Psychic driving, as you, no doubt, know firsthand, is a devastating technique—and that's for adults with a firm grasp on identity and personality. I can't imagine what it was like to go through that. You must be a very strong woman to have not only survived but come through it with enough of yourself intact to resist, to pull away. As you must know from studying my life, I know a little about what it takes to get away from a parental figure intent on doing you harm.'"

"That's great," said Kevin.

"On to the next, then: 'Would it be crazy if I asked you for a favor? It seems I'm destined to need Ankou's knowledge of his victims, and I have no leverage over him. He's already in prison, already sentenced to life and in protective custody since he's a serial killer, already has none of the privileges he'd like to have. Do you know anything that might give me leverage? Anything at all could help.'"

"Ask for where the bodies are buried."

She shook her head. "I think that's too direct."

"Well, you're the fancy interrogation expert."

She flashed a smile at him. "I appreciate the suggestions, though."

"Yeah, I know, Mere."

"Okay…this is me swinging for the fences: 'You're going to think I have my FBI hat on, and that I'm pumping you for information, but I'm actually very interested in how things were for all of you. It must have been strange, confined as you were, but I bet you could talk to each other through the walls of the boxes. Did you wonder who the others were? Did you exchange names? Real names, I mean. Also, I have a list of who Ankou kidnapped, so I know the order of the real names of the victims, but I don't have a mapping to the names you mentioned: Lucy and Mack. You don't happen to recall when those two came to the farm, do you?'"

"That will do it if anything will. What's next?"

"How about this: 'Did you know Alex was named Missy Smith prior to coming to the farm? And Randall? His name was Darrell Rogers. Does knowing their real names help? It would me, I think. I have to admit, I'm curious about Missy—Alex, as you know him. What was she—the original little girl—like before Ankou did all the twisting? Why do you think his methods worked so well on Alex, yet failed to move Randall at all and left you with enough independence to get away when you could?' Then, I'll sign it, 'Your friend, Meredeth.'"

"I think you could add something personal about learning your own birthname. Maybe tell her how it affected you."

"Not bad, Saunders. Not bad at all."

"For a small-town cop."

"Nay, fair sir. For anyone." She put her cursor at the end of the first paragraph. "Okay, I'm adding this: 'For me, learning my original name wasn't a positive experience, but I'm glad I know it. In my case, I was raised by a couple of great people, who gave me a new first name and formally adopted me, so I have their last name. That is who I am, Meredeth Connelly, not Mercy Reynolds. If your name makes you uncomfortable, please just tell me, and I'll revert to M.'" She glanced at Kevin. "Good?"

"Very," he said. "You're kind of good at this. You put that in the paragraph where you explained how you knew her real name?"

"Yeah, end of the first paragraph."

Kevin nodded. "I think it's good. The whole thing. Think it will work?"

"Maybe." Meredeth put her phone down and slid her chicken and fries closer. "I am worried, though. What if all this business about the names scares her off?"

"Then she's scared off, Mere. We can't second guess forever."

"No, you're right."

"In that case, let's finish dinner while discussing purely random topics and then you can send the email while I do the dishes."

"Or after *we* do the dishes."

"Oh, there aren't many. You need to rest."

"If I rest anymore, Kev, I'm going to end up under psychiatric care."

"You mean you aren't already?" He arched an eyebrow at her while wearing his cop face.

"Yes, Officer, that's what I mean." She giggled and found her appetite was back in full force. She took a monstrous bite of chicken and chewed it while grinning at Kevin.

CHAPTER 8

NOT RAMBO

West Baltimore, MD

BOBBY WAVED HIS hand and shook his head. "No way. I should be the one going in, Dave. I'm closer to the age of the crowds in the videos."

Dave's mouth split in a wide, toothy grin. He nudged Cortez, and both men chuckled.

"What?" asked Bobby.

"You might be the right age, hoss," said Big Dave, "but you're missing something big."

"Yeah? What's that?"

"You're White," said Cortez. "Hell, I couldn't even pull it off." He glanced at Big Dave. "Your partner, though, he'll fit right in."

"Really? It comes down to race? In this day and age?"

"Brother, you're in West Baltimore. And 'in this day and age,' *everything* is about race," said Cortez.

Bobby shook his head. "Then let me go in with you. I can be your White friend who wants to see the fighting firsthand."

"No, Bobby," said Dave, "that would be dangerous for both of us."

"Two clean guys with no facial hair? A White guy and a Black guy, and no one knows either one of them? You'd get pegged as cops in like twelve seconds." Cortez chuckled for a moment, then sobered. "I get it, Van Zandt. You're the junior partner, and you think it's your job to take the risks. It's just that in this case, your presence elevates the risks to certainties. These neighborhoods...it's not like the suburbs. Political correctness doesn't exist there. What does exist is heightened suspicion and a solid hatred of cops."

Bobby drew a deep breath in through his nose and shook his head. "Then what's my role?"

Big Dave lay an immense hand on his shoulder. "You sit in the van and make sure the recording is good. And, if something pops off, you're Johnny on the spot."

"You better believe it. I'll storm in there like a platoon of Marines."

"Just bring a few cops," said Dave with a smile. "Now, I'm going to get into some street clothes while you head down to the surveillance van and go on over to the abandoned storefront across from where the fights are going to happen."

"And don't worry," said Cortez. "I'll keep you company. You're going to want a vest, though. We've got one you can borrow."

"I think I'll change, too. That way if something does go down, I don't have to worry about ruining my suit."

"Meet you in the van, then. I'll get that vest."

"Thanks, Cortez."

The detective nodded and turned away, heading down the hall toward the armory, while Bobby grabbed his go-bag and headed for the locker room. When he headed out to the parking lot, the surveillance van was at the curb, and he climbed in. The exterior was painted a light blue, with a logo for a handyman company in yellow. All the paint was sun-faded, scratched, and rust was eating through the rear fenders around the tires.

The interior, however, looked like something out of a science fiction movie—lots of LED lights and a soft blue glow that was masked from the street by blackout curtains. Computers and recording equipment sat inside a custom-built enclosure that was more gamer's paradise than mobile surveillance set up. Even the chairs were comfortable.

"This hardly seems like surveillance," said Bobby.

"Hey, stakeouts don't have to be miserable," said Cortez with a grin.

The van's operator wore paint-stained white overalls and a painting cap turned backward. He started the van and headed for the location, driving sloppier and sloppier the closer he got to the abandoned store front. By the time he was headed south on Hammonds Ferry Road, he'd added a lot of erratic swerving and random braking to his repertoire.

"What's he doing?" Bobby asked.

"Acting drunk. No one questions a drunk guy pulling into an abandoned parking lot to sleep it off."

When the van arrived at the target location, it bumped over a few parking stops in the abandoned store's lot, then parked in the middle of the lane between two rows of parking.

"Are we clean?" asked Cortez.

"No one's watching me," said the driver as he released his belt and pushed his way through the curtains separating the front of the van from its cargo area. "We park this van down here in West Baltimore a lot. Everybody's seen it around."

"Good. Let's get the surveillance up."

Cortez and the driver got to work, and Bobby felt like a third wheel. He peeked past the blackout curtains. "Lots of foot traffic. Looks like a big crowd tonight."

Cortez grunted. "You see Big Dave?"

"He's hard to miss," said Bobby. "He's down at the street corner, in the convenience store's lot. It looks like he's talking to a couple of fight fans." Indeed, Big Dave was pantomiming the end of the fight they'd watched a few days back, the one where the big guy had played possum.

His audience looked on, nodding, but didn't seem at ease with Dave. "Maybe he's too big," muttered Bobby.

"Nah. People will warm up to him. We got one of our informants to claim him as a cousin from New York."

"Ah." Bobby pulled back from the window as the computer monitors showed views from cameras on the van's exterior.

Big Dave's voice crackled in the speakers, another animated blow-by-blow retelling of the fight. Then, "You know that man's name? The smart fighter?"

"Nah."

"Why you want his name?"

"I want to see him fight in person. Videos are great, but being there...mmm, that's the best."

Neither of the unknown speakers replied, and on screen, Big Dave was left standing alone. "Smooth, Tilton," he muttered. After ten or so suspicious looks, Dave waved his hand in dismissal and walked toward the lot where the fight would happen. "I don't think I'm blown, but I'm not going to get a thing from those guys."

"This is West Baltimore, baby," said Cortez into the microphone attached to the desktop.

"Heh," said Dave. He turned off the sidewalk and began striding down the semi-dark path that led to the rear of the old warehouse across the street.

"Are we going to lose video?"

"No, Van Zandt. Just wait." Cortez nudged the technician, and he flipped a switch. The grainy video was replaced with a crystal-clear infrared image. Big Dave was easy to spot—he looked like a giant standing amongst dwarves. "See there?" asked Cortez. "Live and in Technicolor!"

"Nice," said Bobby. "How do we identify suspects?"

"Big Dave's body cam." Again, Cortez nudged the tech, and he brought up another view—this one at the level of Big Dave's chest but grainy and frequently refocusing. "It's a button cam."

Bobby nodded.

"Hey, player," said Big Dave. "When's this shit kick off?"

The man standing in front of Dave turned and looked up at him, a little wide-eyed. "When it starts," he said in a gruff tone.

"Yeaaah, and when is that?" growled Dave.

"Why are you here if you don't know?"

"Jesus Christ, you boys are paranoid up in here. You see a badge or a uniform as you were checking me out?"

"Five-Oh is always trying to get up on us," said the man. "The undercards will start in a few minutes. The main fight is about an hour from now, depending on them undercards."

"Hey, man, I seen a fight on the internet. Big dude versus a lean brother. The big dude plays possum, then cleans the other guy's clock. You seen it?"

"Hasn't everybody?"

Dave shrugged, and his body cam view bounced. "I ain't from here, but I got a cousin lives a few blocks over. While I'm here visiting, I want to see that guy fight live. You know what he's called?"

"Man could get in trouble asking questions around here."

"Do I look like me and trouble is strangers?" rumbled Big Dave. "Why you think I'm visiting West Baltimore?"

"Nice touch," transmitted Cortez.

The man looked Dave up and down again. "You an East Coast Blood?"

"Who's asking questions now?"

"Yeah," said the man with a trace of a grin. "He goes by Hyena on the street. That's all you need to ask about."

"Cool," said Big Dave.

"He's the main fight," said the man. "He's probably going to watch the undercard fights, so he's probably already here somewhere."

"Thanks, brother," said Dave. He turned and walked to the back of the crowd.

"Give us infrared," said Bobby, and the tech made it so.

Dave moved around the edge of the crowd, stopping frequently to scan the crowd. After the third such stop, he said, "I see him. Moving in."

"Take it slow," said Cortez into the mic. "Don't push."

"Right," muttered Dave. He pushed his way toward the inner ring of the crowd—a loose circle in which the fights would happen. He stopped next to a man who, in infrared, had the contours of a silverback gorilla. "Hey, man," said Dave. "You Hyena?"

"Body cam!" said Cortez.

The man was light skinned, bald, and in his early thirties. He was built like a Titan, though he looked just shy of six feet tall. He looked up at Dave, eyelids narrowed, mouth a grim slash. "Who's asking?"

"They call me 'Big Dave.'"

"Yeah, no shit. Your mama survive your birth, big dog?"

"Big Dave. And yeah, I was smaller then."

"Got jokes, too? You fight?"

Dave shook his head. "Too old."

"Your size makes up for that little bit of speed you lost."

"Maybe," said Dave with another shrug that bounced the camera all over the place. "But I only hit people for money."

Hyena inclined his head toward Dave. "I can see that attitude. But you can make bank in West Baltimore if you fight. Big sasquatch motherfucker like you could clean up."

"I'm only here until the pigs settle down back up in NYC, but I'll think on it. I'm staying with my little cousin."

"You do that. Look for me at the next fight if you want in."

"Sure," said Dave. The fighter nodded and started to turn away, but Dave lay a thick hand on his shoulder. "Hey, man, I saw you fight on the internet."

"Yeah?" said Hyena with a narrowing of his eyes.

"Yeah. You fought a lean dude and played possum until you caught him slipping."

"Rassclot," he said. "He should've known better."

"You fight pretty good. You get some training somewhere?"

Hyena chuckled. "Damn straight. I trained in the West Baltimore streets."

"I hear that." Dave rumbled a chuckle. "You got good instincts." Hyena shrugged and made to turn away, and again, Dave lay a hand on his shoulder. This time, however, Hyena shrugged him off and whirled to face him, eyes blazing.

"I don't like no motherfuckers touching me," he grated.

Dave put up his hands. "Don't trip, don't trip."

"And where's all these questions coming from? Why you hassling me?"

"I'm a fan, Hyena! I'm not trying to wear you down."

"You a fan? You just want to run your trap at me? Well, I come here to *fight*, not talk." The people around them had backed away, leaving Big Dave and Hyena in an informal ring, and the crowd had grown silent. "You said you staying with your little cousin? Who's that?"

Dave gave the name of Cortez's informant.

Hyena hunched his shoulders and lowered his jaw. "That asshole's a rat," he hissed in a low voice. "You a cop."

He hadn't asked a question, but Dave said, "Nah. You see a uniform? A badge?"

Hyena looked up at him from under the bony ridge of his brow. "That's what all UCs say. You definitely a cop. Know what we do to cops around here?"

"Shit," muttered Cortez. He picked up his hand-held. "Get ready to move."

Bobby was already up, one hand on the side door of the van, the other holding his Glock. He peered over his shoulder at the screen. "Ask him. Ask him, Cortez!"

Cortez nodded and leaned forward to speak into the mic. "You want us to move?"

"No," said Dave. "Player, you got me all wrong."

Hyena circled to Dave's left, away from his right hand. He hadn't raised his own hands yet, but he'd clenched them into fists.

"Hold on, brother. Hold on." Dave held his hands out in placating gesture, and as he did so, Hyena attacked.

The fighter came in low, his head tucked toward his chest, knees bent, swinging his right fist in a brutal, tight arc targeting Dave's spleen. As Big Dave dropped his left arm to block, Hyena bent even lower and wrapped his arms around Dave's knee, hugging it tight to his chest.

"Come on!" Dave shouted as he lifted both arms high over his head, interlaced his fingers, and brought both hands down on Hyena's back with a sickening thud.

Bobby rocked the van with the force he put into opening the sliding door, then bolted across the street. Cortez followed, mumbling curses and wrenching his weapon out of his shoulder holster. "Move in! Move in!" he shouted into his hand-held.

Running flat out, Bobby streaked across the street, ignoring the honking horns and the screeching tires. He sprinted down the worn footpath along the side of the disused warehouse, skidding around the final corner and into the weedy lot where the fights were held. The back row of the crowd looked his way and bolted to all points of the compass. Bobby ignored those he could, shoved away those he couldn't and screamed, "FBI! Make way!" The knot of spectators around Big Dave and Hyena was a tight one, and they were so focused on the fight, they didn't even turn as Bobby shouted.

Behind him, he heard the battle rattle of the SWAT team moving in, along with a bunch of uniforms and the detective squad from Cortez's precinct. He ignored all of them, punching, pushing, kicking his way toward the center of the knot.

"Down on the ground!" the SWAT commander boomed through a megaphone. "Get down now!"

That woke up the onlookers to Dave's fight, and the thick knot loosened, allowing Bobby to push his way to the center. Big Dave lay on his back in full guard, his legs clamped around Hyena's middle, holding the fighter away with the superior length of his legs. He had a gash under his right eye. For his part, Hyena seemed intent on breaking through Dave's guard and going full beast in order to mount the FBI agent for a massive helping of ground and pound.

The cold muzzle of Bobby's Glock pressed into his ear brought him around, however, and he held up his hands in surrender.

CHAPTER 9

SANDBAGGING

Hanable's Valley, NY

"RELAX, FBI. IT'S only been a few hours," said Kevin. "Getting all hopped up won't change a thing, yet it *will* wear you out. You need to rest, to heal up, to get ready for that second surgery. You can't keep on this way."

Meredeth nodded and closed her eyes. "I'm not good at waiting around."

"Then let's go do something."

Shaking her head, she held up her hands. "Like what?"

"A drive in the country?"

Her eyes lit on his face. "Yeah, maybe over to Yoagoh."

"To the Branch farm?"

"Yeah. Maybe there's something there to—"

"Two different crime scene teams have sifted the dirt and dust over there, Mere. There's nothing there."

"Maybe so, but even a fruitless search will get my mind off the potential disaster of M getting spooked and never emailing me again."

Kevin looked at her for a few moments, then stood and walked toward the bedroom. He came back wearing a windbreaker with "LAW ENFORCEMENT" stenciled across the back. He had a second one in hand for Meredeth. "Put this on."

She got out of the recliner with a groan. "I need to...use the bathroom before we go."

Kevin nodded and lay the jacket across the back of the chair. "I'll be right here. Unless you need help?"

Meredeth smiled at him but shook her head. "I've figured out how to get it emptied on my own without painting the walls or my legs. It'll just take a moment."

"Ten-four, FBI."

She did her business, then slipped out of her baggy nightgown and into a too-large T-shirt and a pair of athletic shorts with an elastic waistband, but that waistband irritated both her stoma and the wide cut across her lower belly. She rolled the waistband down twice, then moved to the closet to borrow one of Kevin's ball caps. She pushed her greasy hair into a ponytail that jutted from the rear of the hat, then threw some ostomy supplies into her purse.

In the living room, she slipped into Kevin's spare windbreaker, and he looked her up and down. "Do I pass muster?" she asked.

"Of course. I was just thinking you might want a shower instead."

"I can survive one more day."

Kevin shrugged, then turned and led her out to his HVPD cruiser, holding her door for her while she grunted and groaned her way into the car. "You sure this is a good idea?" he asked.

"We won't know until we try. But don't worry about...anything. I brought supplies in case of emergency." She patted the purse on her lap, and Kevin issued a single, curt nod, then closed her door and went around to get in on his side.

Yoagoh was about an hour away, and truth be told, Meredeth worried she wouldn't be able to stand the pain and irritation the waistband of her shorts was causing her, but if she said anything, Kevin might insist they stay in. She needed a change of scenery, pain or no pain.

"It's not like you could have done anything different, you know," said Kevin.

"I could have slowed down. I could have taken baby steps. It was only the second email I sent her, and I was pretty aggressive."

"Not in my opinion. You pushed a little—but for information we need. Exchanging emails that give us nothing is a waste of time."

"Maybe so." She sighed and looked out into the dark night, watching the silhouettes of trees and power poles flit by. "If I've scared her off, I don't think I can bring her back around. She'll think I'm manipulating her."

"Like she's doing to you?"

"Yeah, well."

"Relax, Mere. Maybe she's making dinner and will reply after that. Maybe she's working late. Maybe she hasn't even seen your reply."

"Yeah, I know."

After a mile or two of silence, Kevin asked, "So, how are you doing?"

"I'm fine."

"Good, we've got that out of the way. Now tell me how you're *really* doing."

She lifted the shoulder closest to him and let it collapse against the seat back. "It's hard, Kev," she said in a soft voice.

"No doubt it is, but keep in mind it's temporary."

"Not temporary enough. I want this thing off me. I feel like it's pulling my guts out every time I stand up. And it's worse when I walk."

"It's hard on you. Convalescence, I mean."

She nodded. "It feels too much like spinning my tires, too much like *waiting* around for the shoe to drop."

"It'll be over soon. I promise."

"I know, Kevin. We will see the surgeon soon, and he'll tell us the date all this ends."

"That's right. Your appointment is at the end of the week?"

"Yes. Friday afternoon."

"There you go."

"I know. I'm so tired all the time, too, and the constant consumption of liquids is going to have me wearing a rut in your pretty wooden floors."

Kevin chuckled. "Don't worry about any of that, Mere. Just focus on healing, and the rest will follow. And you heard Dr. Atallah as well as I did. You've got to hydrate or run the risk of kidney failure."

"Yep," she said, forcing a positive note into her voice. "Now, where do you think we should focus? The house or the barn where he did all the torturing?"

"Our only hope of finding something new is to find a hidden spot, a *secret* spot. Do you have any ideas on that?"

"The basement?"

"The report I got from Schweighart was that they went over the basement with a fine-toothed comb. That was Doe's command center, after all."

"True, but it's not unheard of that a man like him might dig out a secret vault down there."

"This isn't a root cellar we're talking about, it's a real basement with concrete block walls."

Meredeth shrugged. "Maybe one of the outbuildings will be a better target. I don't remember reading anything about a CSI search on the outbuildings—except the barn, of course." She cocked her head to the side. "Did Butch say if they ever found the kid you three chased out by the barn?"

"I'd have heard if they did."

"That's too bad. *If* M responds, I'll have to ask her what she knows about the next generation of victims."

"Good idea." He gave her a long look. "We're about half-way to Yoagoh. Are you feeling good enough to continue on?"

Meredeth sighed. The truth was, the shorts were killing her, and her guts felt like a gurgling, leaky mess. "There's probably nothing out there, anyway."

"Then I should turn back?"

"Yes. I enjoyed getting out, though, and it did get me out of my head. That said, I really need to get these shorts off."

A grin twisted Kevin's lips as he slowed, then swung wide to the shoulder and turned around.

"Dirty old man," Meredeth muttered through her broad grin.

CHAPTER 10

HOW ABOUT YOU, HYENA?

West Baltimore, MD

"I GOT NOTHING to say to you, pig." Hyena, also known as Martin Webster, sat hunched in the corner, his head leaning on the wall beside him, his hands cuffed to the ring on the table.

"Technically, I'm a Fed—*Feeb* if you want it to be insulting," said Tilton. He had a bandage over the laceration Hyena had given him below his eye and had changed into his dark blue suit. "You're smart enough to know the difference."

Webster scoffed and rolled his eyes.

"If you want to talk to a police officer, I can step out."

"I don't wanna talk to none of y'all."

He'd said the same thing a few minutes before, but so far, he hadn't exercised his rights. Even so, Dave was being especially careful not to cross any line that might give Webster a technicality to exploit.

"You want me to leave?" asked Dave.

"*Shit*. Like you're going to do it if I say it. I don't care what you do, and that goes for your friends behind the glass. You ain't got nothing on me. I was defending myself from a sasquatch."

"Assaulting a Federal Law Enforcement Officer. We've got that in spades, brother. Video"—Big Dave ticked the points off on his fingers—"and audio, plus about forty sworn cops and one agent who can testify to the assault. You're going to jail, player...unless you've got something to trade."

Hyena hit him with a penetrating glare. "Like what?"

"Like the Baltimore Brawler. You've got to know him."

"Why? Cause I'm Black? I got news for you, *brother*, you're black as a coal mine, yourself. Sounds like you got to know the man, too."

Big Dave smiled. "Are you really trying to accuse me of racism? No, you've got to know him because of the fight game. A man of your skill, he'd watch you, maybe hang out with you."

"Nah," said Webster. "Nah. I don't hang out with psychos."

"Like Ricky Schneider?"

"Who's that?"

"You know who it is. He was beaten to death a month back. Right after that fight of yours that's all over the internet. The ME puts the time of death between two and five hours after your fight."

"What you trying to say?"

"Chances are, the Brawler attended that fight, got all worked up, then went out hunting."

"Nah," said Hyena, with a sour twist to his lips.

"For curiosity's sake, where were you after that fight?"

"Home. Took a shower, then ate a little and watched me some MMA."

"Alone?"

"Well, I ain't married, and I ain't got no roommates, so yeah."

"Did you order food or get takeout?"

"Nope. Leftovers."

"Then you have no evidence that can be verified that proves you were at home?"

"Just my word. You think *I'm* the Baltimore Brawler? You got screws loose, man. How hard did I hit you?"

"Not that hard, as a matter of fact," said Tilton.

"Hard enough to pop that cheek open."

Dave shrugged again. "Tell me about Ricky."

"Yeah, I knew Ricky. Everyone did."

"When was the last time you saw him?"

Webster scoffed. "You assholes always want to play games. You know he's the one who filmed that fight."

"Yes, we knew that. Did you talk to him at the fight?"

"Yeah."

"What about?"

Rolling his eyes, Webster turned his face away. "Am I arrested?"

"You are, Martin."

"*Don't call me that!*" Webster snapped. "That's my daddy's name."

"Okay, no problem. But whatever name you want me to call you, you are under arrest for assault on a LEO. I haven't decided whether that will be a federal charge, or if I'm going to let Cortez charge you."

Once again, Webster heaved a sigh. "Bet I'll be home before you, Fed."

"Maybe so, but you will eventually go to prison—*unless* you have information to trade."

"So, I either turn rat or I go upstate?"

"That's about the size of it," said Dave.

Webster closed his eyes and shook his head. "It's safer to go to prison. You'd know that if you grew up where I did."

"I grew up in Harlem in the Eighties, Webster. You think my life coming up was easier than yours?"

"Whatever, man," Hyena muttered.

"Yeah, whatever," said Dave with a hint of iron in his voice. "Help me understand Ricky's movements that night."

"What movements? He taped the fights on his cellphone. I don't know anything else about it."

"Detective Cortez tells me you're an East Coast Blood."

"Yeah? So?"

"And Ricky was, too, right?"

"Yeah, like about fifty million other dudes."

"Tell me something, Hyena. When we start processing all the data from tonight's fight, are we going to find that the Bloods run those fights?"

"You might. How would I know? I don't run them."

"Surely, you know who is paying you your prize money."

Hyena shrugged and leaned his head against the wall again.

"So, two Bloods, at least one of them high-ranking... Say, player, where do you fit in the hierarchy?"

"Man, I ain't going to tell you nothing about the Bloods. You think I'm crazy? Folks get killed over shit like that."

"Is that what happened to Ricky?"

Hyena scoffed. "Tell the truth, does anyone fall for shit like that?"

"You'd be surprised," said Dave with a grin. "Most criminals are pretty stupid, but you aren't, Hyena. You're *smart*. That's why you should get out in front of all this."

Webster shook his head, a grimace on his face. "I'm thirsty."

"Would you like something to drink? A soda? Water? Coffee?"

"Dr. Pepper, but only if it's a Zero drink. Otherwise, anything Zero or diet."

"You got it." Tilton got to his feet and looked down on Hyena. "In the meantime, think about what I've said. You're smart enough not to go down for something stupid when there's an easy solution."

"Yeah, yeah." Webster sighed and lay his head down on the table.

Big Dave nodded once, then turned and left the interview room. Instead of heading to the vending machine, he entered the observation room. "Well, what do you think?"

"Cagey," said Bobby. "What's he hiding?"

Cortez shook his head. "You two don't get West Baltimore. If you went out and pulled in a ninety-year-old grandmother, she'd tell you the same as Hyena did. It's a cultural thing."

"No, it isn't," said Big Dave. "It's the same all over, Cortez. Snitches get stitches. Blah, blah, blah. All that goes out the window when self-interest is involved."

"Then why isn't he giving you information?"

"This first part is about building trust and establishing a behavioral baseline," said Bobby. "This isn't going to be quick, by any means. Dave is working on getting him to answer questions without all the teeth pulling. Then he'll move on to trawling for important information."

"And I did try to speed up the process, but the second I brought up Ricky Schneider, he clammed up. He's not ready yet."

"Uh-huh," said Cortez, sounding unimpressed.

"Hey, Dave, do you mind if I call Meredeth and run this by her?"

"Not at all, Bobby. She's one hell of an interviewer."

Bobby nodded and pulled out his phone. "I'll get the drinks. Anyone else want something?"

"Coffee," said Dave. "Then I can blame the delay on having to make it."

"You got it. Detective Cortez?"

"Coke's fine."

Bobby turned and exited the observation room, dialing Meredeth's number as the door swung shut. It rang twice, then the call was accepted. "Hey, Mere. How are you doing tonight?"

"I'm worried and in a little pain from a drive we just attempted. We made it halfway before I asked Kevin to turn around."

"Wow, that's a big step for you, Connelly."

"What, taking a ride?"

"No, admitting you aren't Wonder Woman and heading back early."

"Yeah, yeah. If you're just calling to bust my chops—"

"Can't a guy have a little fun? Nah, skip that. I am calling in Bureau interests. We grabbed a guy who fits the profile tonight. He's a fighter we found in videos on the web, and he actually freaked out and attacked Big Dave."

"And he lived? Dave must be getting soft."

"When I got there, Dave had the guy in full guard and was holding him away from his head. The suspect is named Martin Webster, but on the street, he goes by Hyena. He's good enough to fight in pro MMA contests."

"Then why isn't he?"

Bobby frowned. "That's a good question. He has no serious record—some shoplifting as a juvie, one joyriding rap."

"Not the usual pedigree for a gang-banger."

"He's smart, Mere. And he has a strategic mindset. I bet others took the rap for his crimes."

"You mean he set them up?" she asked.

"Maybe, but I was thinking more along the lines of recruiting younger Bloods to go do while he was on overwatch."

"Or manipulated people without his level of smarts."

"Or that," agreed Bobby. "But listen: Big Dave's doing the interview, and it's moving like sludge in the arctic. The local detective is getting antsy, putting out the 'this is a waste of time' vibe."

"Does Dave know you're calling?"

"Of course," said Bobby. "He endorsed the idea. For some reason, he thinks you are a good interrogator. I think it's because he doesn't have to work with you."

"Nice. Kick a girl while she's down."

"That's the only time it's safe to kick you, Mere."

"Ha. Let me guess... Snitches get stitches."

"Got it in one. He thinks we're asking for his help in identifying the Baltimore Brawler. Dave made out like we think the unsub attended the fight and got all wound up by Hyena's fight."

"That's pretty smart. Get him talking, then get him to say something only the Brawler would know."

Bobby reached the vending machine and started the fight of getting the thing to accept his dollar bills. "That's the idea, but we're running into brick walls all the time." He bought a Coke for Cortez. They didn't have much selection for Zero drinks, just Coke Zero, so that's what he got for Hyena.

"Well, you did say this guy was smart."

He turned and walked across the break room toward the coffee urn, looking for cups as he went. "Yeah. He's probably guessed at the strategy."

"Then it's time to change things up."

"Yeah? I should tag Dave out?"

"I was thinking more good cop, bad cop. Have Dave keep on building the trust, and you be Johnny Privilege. Be demanding, be insensitive. In other words—"

"Don't even say it."

"—just be yourself." She chuckled. "Hey, what's good for the goose..."

"Right. How far do we take it?"

"All the way to a confession. Threaten to add charges, even ones he knows he didn't commit, and promise to make them stick. You're the bad cop, remember? You would absolutely plant evidence on this Hyena character. You would lie on the stand."

"Okay. What else?"

"Set up your phone so I can hear you guys and hook up your earpiece."

"Can do. What about Dave?"

"Tell him to play along, unless you can somehow conference him in and get his earpiece in."

"He's 'making coffee' right now, so he's in the observation room. We can do that."

"Good, that will make it easier."

Failing to find a tray, Bobby shrugged and put the cans of soda in his front pockets, then filled two disposable cups with the foul-smelling brew that served as coffee in the precinct house. "All right. I'm heading back."

"What's this guy like? I'll need you to communicate what you see. And be obnoxious with the negotiation tactics I taught you."

"Right." He jogged back to the observation room and handed Dave his coffee and the Coke Zero for Hyena. He explained what Meredeth wanted while he gave Cortez the regular Coke. "Hey, Mere? I'm going to include Art Cortez in the conference call. He's the local detective, and he can describe Hyena's reactions."

"Great idea. Do it."

They got everything set up and made introductions between Meredeth and Cortez, then Bobby and Dave re-entered the interview room. Dave went through the door smiling, Bobby with a crumpled up, angry expression. Dave put Hyena's drink on the table next to him, then sat across from him. Bobby dragged a chair away from the table, making as much noise as he could, then slumped into it.

"Hey, skel, wake up!" he said in a loud voice.

Hyena lifted his head, glanced at Dave, and rolled his eyes, then reached for his drink and popped the top. After he'd taken a long draught, he glanced at Bobby. "Uh-oh, I'm in trouble. The White people are involved."

"Funny," grouched Bobby. "You want to waste my time with nonsense? I'll waste your life with a big rap."

"Assault ain't no big rap," scoffed Hyena.

"Who said anything about that charge?" snapped Bobby. "You screw me, I'll screw you. You might find that charge elevated to attempted murder. I've got your gun out in the car."

"Man, I don't have no gun. Don't need one."

Bobby shrugged. "You do now."

"You can't do that!"

"Can't I?"

"*Good,*" said Meredeth in his ear. "*Now, Dave, give Bobby an out.*"

"Let's all just calm down a minute. We're all friends here, right?"

"Your boy don't seem to be on the same page."

"I'm not his 'boy,' and I'm only saying that I'll go tit-for-tat with you, puppy dog."

"Big man in the middle of all these cops. Sasquatch over here went toe-to-toe with me, you ain't done nothing but wave a pistol around like Rambo."

Bobby shrugged and looked pointedly at Dave. "You going to do this, Tilton? I don't want to be here all night."

"Right," said Dave, turning back to Hyena and rolling his eyes. "Let me do that."

"*He's looking at Dave, now,*" said Cortez. "*He looks a little suspicious, but I think he's taking a side.*"

"*Naturally. He's going to side with Dave, and that's what we want.*"

Dave took a sip of coffee. "We left off with you thinking about helping us out with respect to Ricky Schneider. In exchange, we'll talk to the local DA and tell her you are a cooperating witness with us. Your charges will disappear. You can walk right out of here as soon as we're done, most likely."

"*If* what you have to say is worth our time. If you don't..." Bobby let the thought trail away, then took a sip of the horribly bitter coffee.

Hyena pointed at Bobby with his chin. "He always a dick like this?"

Dave chuckled. "That he is."

"Big White man working with us darkies," said Hyena, shifting a decidedly hostile gaze to Bobby.

"*I think we got him,*" said Cortez. "*He's giving Bobby the stink eye.*"

"Listen," said Dave, "you can help me out here. One brother to another. Van Zandt isn't my real partner. His is out on medical, and mine's on vacay, so the bosses paired us up. All I want to do is close this thing with Schneider so I can get the hell away from him."

"*Nice job,*" said Meredeth. "*Now, Bobby.*"

"Yeah, hardcase, help *me* get away from *both of you*. Help me get the hell out of Baltimore," said Bobby with a sneer. "I'm so far above the level of this BS that I can barely breathe down here in the gutter."

"Gutter, huh?" asked Hyena. "This is my hometown, motherfucker."

"Sorry for you," said Bobby. "But you can move out. Or I can send you to prison for life."

"Let's not get off on a tangent," Dave said, shifting his gaze to Bobby, mirroring the suspect's hostility. "Can you just shut up for a while? Christ, it's like having my four-year-old grandbaby in the room."

Hyena laughed. "He does seem like a little kid, don't he?"

"You should see him eat," said Dave with a small smile.

"Yeah, yeah," muttered Bobby as he took out his phone and pretended to read social media.

"Yeah, you read your phone, little White man."

"*Hyena's looking pretty pleased with this. Smug,*" said Cortez.

"*Get into it, Dave. This might be our best chance,*" said Meredeth.

"If the bear wants to put his brain to sleep, let him," said Tilton. "Tell me about Ricky."

"You already know he was a Blood."

"Right," said Dave. "So are you."

"Maybe, maybe not."

"Oh, for Christ's sake," muttered Bobby.

"Fair enough," said Dave. "Just ignore him. That's what I try to do. How long did you know Ricky?"

"All my life," said Hyena. "We came up together, went to the same schools, played in the same weedy lots."

"Then you owe it to him to help us find the man who killed him."

"I ain't owe him nothing. That man's dead. He's beyond caring."

"Not religious, huh?"

Hyena shook his head in the negative. "Got no time for all that holier-than-thou bullshit."

"Me, neither," said Bobby without looking up from his phone.

Hyena looked at him and grimaced. "Then maybe I better start making time for church on Sundays."

Bobby shrugged.

"To his memory, then," said Dave. "Help me put his murder to bed. Give his family that closure."

"Closure?" scoffed Hyena. "Man, I thought you grew up in Harlem? There ain't no closure. That's a lie White people made up. Time's the only thing that helps when your sister gets shot and dies in the ambulance."

Dave spread his arms to grip the corners of the table. "Then give *me* closure, and let's get away from *him*."

"One day, Tilton, you're going to work for me, and you're going to find out I have a very long memory."

Hyena turned away from Van Zandt. "He ever *do* anything, or is he all talk?"

"Go, Bobby. Come in hard."

"Try me, punk. See if I'm all talk. I'll do what I have to in order to see you with thirty years to life. At the very minimum."

"What's that supposed to mean, Van Zandt?" demanded Dave.

"You *know* what it means, Tilton. We'll elevate his charges. I'll get up on the stand and swear before God to tell the truth, then lie my ass off."

"You'd do that?" Tilton shook his head sadly. "You're okay with breaking the law to get what you want?"

"Of course, he would," said Hyena. "That's the only way this little bitch can face someone like me. Lie, plant evidence, cheat. You're one of those amoral motherfuckers, ain't you?"

"Sure, why not?" said Bobby, leaving which question he was answering in ambiguity.

Rolling his eyes upward, Tilton gripped the table tighter. "Dear Jesus, give me strength." He lowered his gaze to find Hyena looking at him with open speculation. "Did you see anyone at the fight? Someone who got a little rowdy?"

Hyena lifted his shoulders. "There's always some, but the Bloods keep them in line. That fight, though, I do remember someone. He stayed back in the shadows and just stared at me."

"Maybe he was gay, too," said Bobby.

"Can you just *shut up*, Van Zandt?"

"*Okay. Time to get rolling,*" said Meredeth. "*Start pressing.*"

"What did he look like, Hyena?"

"He stayed back, like I said, but he was big. I think I seen him on the stroll, but he ain't a Blood. Maybe contract help."

"Would Ricky have known him?"

"Probably hired him."

"To do what?" asked Bobby.

"What you think, White boy? He was muscle, plain and simple."

"*This is probably true,*" said Meredeth, "*but I bet the man he's describing is in the landfill rolled up in a carpet.*"

"And you saw him at the fight? He was just staring at you, watching the fight instead of doing security?" Dave leaned back and took his hands off the table. "Ricky might have noticed. He might have fired this guy, and it enraged the man. Maybe the other killings are just camouflage."

"Yeah," said Hyena, sitting up in the chair for the first time. "I bet you're right. I bet that's it. Find that man, and you'll close all them cases they're talking about on the news."

"He use a hammer?" asked Bobby.

"A hammer?"

"Yeah. The ME said the blows were too hard to be inflicted by a human hand. He thinks it was a one-handed sledgehammer."

"Naw, man. Them fools got beat down, that's all."

"You think so?" asked Dave. "None of the victims had defensive wounds."

"Well, they wouldn't, right? I bet that guy who killed Ricky went all ninja on 'em and snuck up behind, punched them in the side of the neck, right under the ear, and bang! Out go the lights."

"The ME did say there was bruising on the left side of the victims' necks," said Bobby.

"Sure," said Hyena. "He punched them in the neck, then went on beating them until they kicked."

"Why would someone do that?" asked Dave. "Cowardice?"

"No, player! He got paid to send a message to the neighborhood. They wanted something ugly, something to get on the news."

"They?"

"Yeah," said Hyena. "Whoever hired him."

"Would the Bloods do something like that?" asked Bobby.

"Could be they might, if the circumstances was right."

"Say they wanted to get a message to the other gangs in West Baltimore..." murmured Dave.

"Could be the Bloods wanted to shout from the roof tops of the world."

"And the beatings? How are they affiliated with the gang?" asked Bobby.

Hyena cracked a half-smile. "They bloody, ain't they?"

"And that's enough? Wouldn't everyone beaten to death be bloody, no matter who dished out the punishment?"

"You ain't too bright, are you, white bread?" Hyena grinned at Dave. "You sure he's FBI?"

"Hey, I've got the badge to prove it," said Bobby. "Now, answer my question."

"Well, *yeah*. That's how beatings work. But...say the shot callers want to make a statement. They'd have the street crews spreading the word, wouldn't they?"

"Would they?" asked Tilton.

"*If* it was the Bloods that ordered the hits, and *if* they wanted anyone to know."

Big Dave nodded. "And is that what they wanted with Ricky?"

"Ain't nobody come right out and say it, but then again, they didn't really have to."

"This guy they hired... You sure you don't have a name?"

"Even a street name would help," said Bobby.

Hyena bounced his gaze back and forth between them, grinning.

Tilton leaned across the table and fixed Hyena with a solemn gaze. "You know your statement has to be factual for the DA to care about it, right? I've got a feeling you're holding something back."

"He's grinning at them like a...hyena," said Cortez.

"He wants them to figure it out. He wants the credit, but he wants you two to work for it. Just come out and ask him. And, Bobby? Remember negotiation tactics."

"Come on, Hyena," said Bobby. "Admit what you did."

Hyena turned his grinning face in Bobby's direction. "What do you think I did, agent asshole?"

Big Dave leaned back in the chair and looked at Bobby.

"I know you think I'm some rich White dude from the suburbs, and that I can't possibly understand your life. I get that much, and to tell the truth, I probably can't identify with the things you've had to do to survive. And I *am* from the suburbs, but I'm not rich. So, Hyena, listen: I *want* to understand. Would it be so crazy to explain why you agreed to murder all those people?"

Hyena froze, his smile becoming a rictus. "This ain't really the place, player."

"It's all we have."

Webster glanced at the mirrored glass separating them from the observation room. "This being recorded?"

"You know it is, Hyena. This isn't your first time in a police station," said Dave.

With a half-grin and a shrug, Hyena drew in a deep breath. "Yeah." He threw another glance at the mirror. "If a guy was to go against his principles and tell a tale or two, he'd probably want it on the news."

"*You've got him!*" crowed Meredeth. "*Good work.*"

CHAPTER 11

BILLY BIG RIGGER

Yoagoh, NY

ALEX DROVE THE Ford Bronco, one wrist draped over the twelve o'clock position of the steering wheel. He was a careful driver, never speeding, never taking big chances, and Mack admired him for that. For his own part, Mack had learned to drive out in the pastures and loved the roar of power the Bronco made when it lost traction in the mud. There was just something about the low grunting burble, about the feeling of power, that appealed to him.

It was the first time Father had allowed them off the farm alone. He had tasked them with picking up supplies he'd ordered at the big hardware store in Jonodot, and he'd trusted them to go alone. He'd even given them cash to pay the bill, and whatever he'd ordered must have been expensive as he'd handed over five crisp hundred-dollar bills. Mack patted the pocket that held the cash.

"You couldn't have lost the money in the roughly forty-five seconds since you last checked that pocket. Relax, Mack."

"Yeah," he said. "Isn't it strange Father sent us out unsupervised? And with all this money?"

"You've worked hard, Mack—almost as hard as I have. Father is a fair man, and hard work earns his trust." He looked at Mack askance. "You know what I mean by hard work?"

"Yes. Working Father's program, not necessarily sweating out in the fields."

"That's right. And the other night, what you did to that fat ass in the Caddie. That was impressive, and even more so because you used initiative. Father doesn't think he needs to worry about you any longer. You've *proved out*, as he likes to say."

"But we could just drive away."

"But we won't, and he knows that. Where could we go? Who better to guide fledgling killers than an absolute artist at the craft? A master of death?"

"What if we stopped killing people? Five hundred dollars is a good stake."

Alex laughed. "Who's this 'we' you keep talking about? I'm not going anywhere, Mack." He gave Mack another quick look. "And to be honest, neither are you. I know that. Father knows that. You're one of us."

Mack grinned and shrugged. "Just thinking out loud."

"I know."

The sound of an airhorn made them both jump, and Alex's gaze snapped to the rearview. "*Jesus*, he's close!"

Mack turned and looked out through the tailgate's window. A giant Peterbilt long-nosed truck was right up on them—close enough that he could see the driver's annoyance-filled face as the man reached up and blew the air horn again.

Mack turned and faced the rear, drawing his knees up under him as he did so. He pointed at the driver of the truck and shook his head.

The trucker's response was to blow the horn again.

"This jerk could use a lesson in manners."

"I...I'm going the speed limit. Why is he acting this way?"

With a chuckle, Mack said, "Some people are born needing an ass-whipping. Randall was one. That Caddie driver was another. I'm adding this guy to my list, too."

"Who are you, Santa Claus?" asked Alex, but his gaze was locked to his mirrors, and he didn't put much into the jibe.

"Yeah, sort of. But a Santa whose best present is you never see him. Look out!"

The bobtail Pete roared into the opposing lane, the shriek of its turbo loud to Mack's ears. It had a fancy paint job, and more bling than a jewelry store—chrome and lights and everything Mack could think of. The truck whipped by them, then crossed back over the double yellow lines too early, and Alex had to jerk the wheel hard to the right to avoid being struck. His face had gone bone-white, and he gripped the steering wheel like a drowning man holding onto a life ring.

The passenger side tires dropped off the shoulder into the scree of old rubber, salt, and gravel. Almost immediately, Mack heard the evil hiss that meant the tires were losing traction. "You're going to skid!" As soon as the words left his mouth, the big four-wheel drive vehicle spun in a loose circle, and Alex spun the wheel into the spin, jamming on the brakes at the same time. Luckily, the ground past the shoulder was flat and relatively free of big rocks and trees. They came to a halt staring in the direction they'd been traveling in and sat for a moment, watching the Peterbilt drive away.

"That jackass!" snapped Mack. "He almost *hit* us!"

Alex nodded.

"Let's go, Alex! Catch him!"

With a head shake, Alex opened his door and got out.

"What are you doing?" demanded Mack.

"You drive."

He didn't need to be asked twice. He unfastened his seat belt and jumped into the driver's seat, applying the brakes, and levering the gear selector out of park and into drive. As soon as he heard the passenger door slam shut, he accelerated away, the big tires spitting gravel in their wake.

It didn't take him long to catch up to the truck, but once he did, he was at a loss of what to do. "I can't run him off the road," he said. "He out masses us by a metric shit load."

"This was your idea..."

"I know, but what do I do now?"

"Follow him? He has to stop eventually. We owe that guy."

"Agreed." Mack stayed back, giving the trucker plenty of room, but at the same time, keeping the truck always in sight—which wasn't all that hard given the flashy paint, the chrome, and freaking size of the monster.

"What are you planning, Mack? Remember what Father said."

"Word for word. 'In the future, communicate your intentions first.' What I intend to do to Billy Big Rigger—"

"Billy Big Rigger?"

"Trucker slang for a guy who goes in for the chrome and extra lights. Like that guy up there. Anyway, what I intend to do to Billy up there is pull him out of that rig and then let inspiration take me where it will."

"That will make it hard for me to support your play. Any hints?"

"It will involve punishment, then...he needs killing."

Alex grinned. "See? You're one of us. There's no better place to be than Father's farm for us."

"Think Father will let me keep the truck?"

"It's possible. Haven't you two been fixing up that Cadillac, though?"

"Yes, to sell it. We forged a bill of sale from the fat guy to one of father's special identities."

"Then maybe he can do the same for the truck."

"I hope so," said Mack. "But not for sale."

"You like that thing?"

"Hell, yes. I like the noise, I like the paint, the chrome, all of it. Not to mention the fact that if we were driving that and he were driving this, he'd already be dead."

"So..." Mischief danced in Alex's eyes. "You're a Billy Big Rigger?"

Mack glanced at him and grinned. "I guess I am."

They followed the truck through Yoagoh and on the road toward Jonodot. Billy Big Rigger must have finally noticed them keeping up with him because he slowed, then slowed again and again, until they were going twenty miles an hour under the speed limit, but Mack resisted the provocation and slowed to match his speed. The air horn on the truck blew a couple of blasts, and Mack tapped the horn in response.

"What are you doing?" asked Alex.

"Picking a fight, I hope." He swerved into the opposing lane and goosed the Bronco as if he were going to pass. The trucker swerved to ride with one side of his vehicle in each lane, and Mack backed off, then swerved toward the shoulder on the other side. Billy swerved to block him again, and Mack pressed the horn for a long blast.

The truck slowed to twenty miles an hour in response, so Mack pulled in close, riding his bumper the way the man in the Caddie had ridden theirs. He turned on the Ford's headlights, set them on bright, then hit the switch for the off roading lights mounted to the Bronco's roof. All told the roof lights totaled fifty-five thousand lumens, and Mack knew getting hit by them was like getting struck by lightning.

The trucker swerved to get his mirrors at an oblique angle to the roof lights, but Mack swerved with him, this time not trying to pass. "I want to irritate him into pulling over so he can kick my ass."

"Blow the horn," suggested Alex. He opened the glove box and pulled out the handheld spotlight their father stored in the vehicle for hunting deer. He plugged it into the cigarette lighter and switched it on. Then, he rolled down the window and stuck his hand out, aiming the light on the truck's passenger side mirror.

"Good idea," said Mack.

"I know," said Alex with an air of arrogance. "I have them a lot."

The truck slowed to an idle, and Mack slowed with him, holding the horn down and revving the big block engine in the Bronco, blipping the throttle, then letting off, making the whole vehicle bounce—including the lights. Billy blew the air horns in a sustained blast, then slowed to a stop.

"Show time," said Alex. "How do you want to play it? Want me to get out, too?"

"Let me go to him first, okay? I don't want to spook him into jumping back in the truck and taking off again."

"Okay. When you want me to come, wave or something."

Mack nodded as he opened the door and got out. He plastered a wide smile on his mug and walked toward the trucker—who was roughly ginormous. He was tall, but what made him look so big was a barrel chest, wide shoulders, and an impressive set of arms. "Howdy, neighbor," he called.

The trucker narrowed his eyelids and frowned at Mack. "You're just a kid."

"Almost eighteen," he said with a shrug.

"Old enough to know better," growled the man.

"So are you. You ran us off the road back there."

"You was poking along like my grandma going to Sunday meeting."

"And so were you, just now."

"I didn't try to *blind* you."

Mack chuckled. "What's the matter? Can't take the same bullshit you dish out?"

"You wasn't even driving! It was your girlfriend."

"Uh, that's my *brother*, Billy Big Rigger."

The trucker's face tightened like a hand closing into a fist. "Watch what you say to me."

"Why? Are you going to beat me up?" Mack grinned like a fool.

For a moment, the trucker only looked at him. Then, "Are you crazy kid? Is that the story here?"

"Crazy? No. But I do hate rude drivers like you."

"Kid..." The trucker shook his head and frowned. "I could whip you with one arm. You need to apologize, then get back in that piece of shit Ford and go home."

"Nah," said Mack. "And don't talk about the Bronco that way. It has feelings, too."

"Shit for brains," said the trucker.

"Don't get mad, *good buddy*," he said with a leer.

The man's face soured even more. "You shouldn't use slang you don't understand."

"I know exactly what it means."

"Do you? You just called me a homo."

"If the shoe fits..."

"I see," said the man as he half-turned toward his truck, but then threw a punch with all his weight behind it. Like with the Cadillac driver, Mack side-stepped and aimed a chop at the man's larynx. "Good try," said the trucker as he dropped his head and took the strike on his forehead. He stepped forward to grapple, and behind Mack, Alex opened his door and jumped to the asphalt.

Mack met the trucker's advance, hooked one arm under the man's left arm, threw his hip into the man's gut and yanked, throwing the man to the road's surface. He took a running half step and kicked the big man in the belly as hard as he could. "Want in, Alex? Come on if you do!" He swung his leg back and kicked the trucker in the face as the man tried to push up to his hands and knees, and blood exploded across the macadam.

"*Jesus Christ!*" the trucker shouted.

Mack kicked him again for his effort, this time catching the back of the man's elbow, delighting in the sickening crunch of the joint dislocating and in the shrieking wail let loose by the trucker. He aimed another kick at his face and connected.

Then, Alex was there on the man's other side, aiming his own kicks, stomping on the man's hand, stomping on the small of his ankle, kicking him in the liver. With Alex to back him up, Mack took a more calculated approach, laying a heel kick across the man's kidney, then another to the base of the trucker's neck.

A little breathlessly, Alex said, "Who knew running errands could be so much fun?"

They kept on until the trucker stopped twitching, then shoved him into his truck's sleeper cabin. Mack climbed up in the truck.

"Do you even know how to drive this thing?"

"Piece of cake," said Mack with a smile. "I'll follow you to the hardware store."

CHAPTER 12

ON THE SIDE

Hanable's Valley, NY

MEREDETH DISCONNECTED FROM the conference call to West Baltimore, smiling from ear to ear. "They've got him, Kevin!" she said.

"I gathered. Is he confessing to all the murders or just one?"

"He's not confessing yet, but they've got him making demands that his statement be leaked to the press, and I'm sure he's *going* to spill the beans as soon as they get the details worked out. They'll probably have to do a plea deal—take the death penalty off the table, but he won't get to kill again."

"Are you sure about that? He kills with his fists, and I bet he'll do a lot of fighting in prison."

"True," she said with a shrug, "but everyone will know he did it, and more charges and adseg will be his reward. I don't think he'll kill many inmates."

"You've got your rose-colored glasses on tonight."

She smiled at him. "Thanks to you."

"Nah. I just drove."

"And brought dinner, helped me with the email to M, talked me down off the metaphorical ledge, and made me laugh. By my count, that's about a bajillion I owe you."

"You can make it up to me after the surgery is done and you've fully recovered. Which reminds me, I still have to get up to Buffalo and buy one of those canvas director's chairs."

She grinned but also blushed a little.

"But right now, I'm beat. I think I'll turn in. You coming with, or are you going to stay up until four in the morning again?"

"I'm coming. I might as well sleep in the bed instead of the recliner."

They got up and moved toward the bedroom, turning off the lights as they went. After getting ready for sleep, they climbed into Kevin's big king-sized bed. He turned to face her and smiled. "You're beautiful, lady, and you should know that."

Again, Meredeth blushed and grinned. "You are going to spoil me...turn me into one of those girls on social media who are always shouting for attention."

"I'll give you all the attention you want."

"I know, Kevin," she said. "And that's why I love you."

His eyebrows arched. "Got over the anxiety, I see."

She simply shrugged. "Well, you've seen me at my worst. I've got to say it now, so you don't go and start dating that goth chick at the diner."

"I'm old enough to be her father."

"So? She flirts with you every time we go there. She's got a daddy complex, maybe, or she loves the uniform."

"She's just being nice."

Meredeth shook her head and chuckled. "Men are oblivious. Look, when a woman smiles at you from across the room, it means she wants you to come over and talk to her. When she's always touching you, like goth-chick does, it means she's very interested in touching you some more."

"She pats me on the shoulder."

"And rubs it. She runs her hand down your arm when she's dropping off the check or a drink refill—even when it's *my* drink she's refilling. There's no question, Kev, you've got a not-so-secret admirer."

"Mere, I didn't encourage—"

"I know, Kevin. You can tell I know that because you're not shot in the guts."

Kevin laughed long and hard while Meredeth looked on grinning. When his guffaws died down to occasional chuckles, he asked, "Should I tell her I'm taken? How do I let her down easy?"

Meredeth shook her head. "You don't, Kevin. It would only embarrass her. She'll get the message when you don't respond."

"You sure?"

"Yeah, trust—" Her phone beeped, and she grabbed it off the charging pad. "That's the email tone." She unlocked the phone and opened the email app. "Yep, it's from her."

"Read it aloud for the class, Little Merry."

She gave him a look, then did as she was told.

> *Dearest Meredeth,*
>
> *Please forgive my delay in answering, but I had to spend a bit of time thinking about your last message and doing an evaluation of how I feel about my name. I guess it comes down to a feeling, and like you, I don't feel like Julie Fuchs belongs to me anymore. Also like you, I appreciate you telling me. Maybe I can use that information to track down my relatives. I do realize, however, how difficult I'm making our communications. Go ahead and call me by Ankou's name for me: Michelina.*
>
> *As for how Alex was before Ankou got his hooks into her brain, I can't tell you. We weren't allowed to talk while we were confined to the boxes, and Father's punishments were severe. No one dared to break the silence rule.*
>
> *Except Randall, of course, and look what that got him.*
>
> *And once I earned my way out, I sort of hated her. She ran my ECT programs, and she was vicious.*

Plus, by that time, Ankou had convinced her she was male, so she was kind of a freak.

I have to admit that at the time, I didn't give a crap about what anyone's name was. I was smart enough to realize that fighting Ankou was a fool's errand. The only way to get away was to do what he wanted and hope he didn't see I was only acting. He forced me—all of us—to do things for him. Despicable things. Violent things. Things I won't be discussing with you yet.

As far as I know, I'm the only one to despise him for it. At least consciously.

As for the order, Mack came during my stay in the box, and Lucy came after I was out, but one boy (Carl) came between her and Mack. I also have to admit, however, that the prospect of knowing their real names now fills me with anticipation. Could you please share those names?

Friends?

Michelina

"Well, there you go," said Kevin. "She wants to talk, to tell you things that will help."

Meredeth levered herself out of bed and went for the case binder she'd left on the kitchen table. As she returned to the bedroom, she looked up the names. She set the binder on top of Kevin's dresser, then snuggled down under the covers. "Mack was born Steven Aldridge, Carl was Greg Henderson, and this Lucy was named Stephanie Milneaux. We got at least that much."

"You got more than that, FBI. You have Ankou giving the orders."

"That's at best co-conspirator testimony. You heard the email. Michelina *did violence* for him. That means she killed someone most likely."

Kevin rolled to face her. "Yes, but she was a victim, a brainwashed victim. She said it was the only way to get away."

"Kill once, get a taste for it..."

Kevin grunted. "I don't think so in this case. Of course, I don't know that for sure or anything, but that's what my gut's saying."

"Well, I have to know for sure if I'm going to help her. I can't go into it blind."

"No, of course not." He took her phone from the mattress between them and handed it to her. "What are your goals regarding this next email?"

"First, I have to ask her point-blank about her activities. I can work on getting her immunity once I know that. I also want to know more about her. Where is she? What does she do for a living? Third, I want something actionable to hold over Doe's head. Finally, I need to pump Michelina for information about Mack and Lucy since she says they are likely next." She opened her email app. "I'll dictate this one. Sing out if I botch something, okay?"

"Sure."

"Here goes: 'Dear Michelina, Of course we are friends! I'm happy to help you out if I can. Where did you say you were living? What—'"

"Hold on, Mere. Too much, too fast. Go easy."

"Right. 'Dear Michelina, Of course we are friends! I'm happy to help you out if I can. It sounds like Ankou's techniques couldn't strip away your morality, which speaks to the inborn strength you must have. I admire that.' How's that?"

"Good. Go on."

"Next paragraph: 'It must have been hard breaking away from the only thing you'd known for so long. You'd have needed a job and a place to stay. Did you stay in the Yoagoh area? What do you do for a living? I ask because I'm curious. I'm not trying to profile you, I promise. Well, at least no more than I do everyone else in my life, ha-ha.'"

"Keep going," said Kevin. "You're doing fine."

Meredeth nodded. "'Part of helping you is to take away Ankou's power over you—at least in my opinion. To that end, can you remember any details of what he made the others do? Victim names and dates (even approximations) would help a lot. Also, if you can say which kid was assigned the victim, that will help me build a picture.'"

Kevin rolled onto his back and stared up at the ceiling. "Also, good."

"Okay. Continuing: 'If you can include your own acts on his behalf, I can work on getting you into protective custody and then into Witness Protection. I'll also lobby the US Attorney's office for a grant of immunity. They may not go for a full ride, but anything they are willing to do will be better for you in the long run.'"

"I don't know," said Kevin. "That's worded okay, but do you want to jump right to sentencing with this woman? I'd cut the last line."

Meredeth nodded once and made the deletion. "Here's the last paragraph: 'You mentioned before that the next foe I will face in Ankou's grand plan will likely be Mack (Steven Aldridge) or Lucy (Stephanie Milneaux). What can you tell me about them? Do you know where they are living? Do you know their occupations?'"

"Good," said Kevin.

"Then I'll sign it like this: 'Well, it's getting late for me, so I'll cut this short. Sorry for the direct questions—that's just the kind of woman I am. I meant what I said about helping you, Michelina. I hope you will trust me to do that. Your friend, Meredeth.'"

"Ship it," said Kevin. "That's a good one."

Meredeth let her arms flop to the mattress and relaxed her neck. "Whew. I'm really beat now." She let go of the phone and nudged it onto the charging pad.

"It's a good thing we're in bed, then," said Kevin with a snort. "Go to sleep, Mere. Get some quality rest."

"I'll try to squeeze that in between the ninety-five wakeups."

Kevin chuckled softly. "Want to come into the station a little tomorrow? I could use the help on a few things."

"I don't know, Kevin. The thought of it alone makes me want to take two naps before I go to sleep for real." Her voice was low, throaty, and a little muzzy.

"Well, I do have the comfortable couch in my office. What do you say? Is it a plan?" The only answer he heard was Meredeth's soft snoring. Smiling, Kevin rolled onto his other side and closed his eyes.

CHAPTER 13

STACK THEM EIGHTS

Yakima, WA

TRAFFIC ON I-82 was usually better than other Interstates, which was why the trucker preferred it. He was ahead of schedule and driving a little aimlessly. He had a Seattle delivery from Las Vegas and a subsequent pick up scheduled for the next day, so another detour on US 95 in Idaho had made sense. He'd left Idaho in his mirrors as he picked up US 12 and crossed over into Washington state, the memory of leaving the little Ford in flames a few weeks prior singing an aria in his mind

Unlike some drivers, he didn't mind taking his rig off the Interstate network. He enjoyed the surface roads, and far more often than not, they afforded him opportunities to feed the darkness at his core. He'd followed US 12 until Kennewick, then jumped on I-82 in the interest of making up lost time. Usually, I-82 was great for that purpose, but on that day, traffic was murder.

He glared out the windscreen at the parking lot the northbound lanes had become. It was near quitting time, but it wasn't like Yakima, Washington had a gridlock problem. He glanced at his GPS for the first time since getting on the Interstate, saw construction icons peppering the freeway between the next two exits, and decided on a little detour. He'd take 24 to Birchfield, which turned into Gun Club Road, then north on 41st Street, turning west on Terrace Heights Drive, then rejoin the I-82 past all the construction nonsense.

His lips curled a little with pleasure. He enjoyed the navigation part of his job—he liked finding his own solutions to problems. Like when Randall had been killed all those years ago. *Anyone* could stab the boy. Or beat him to death with a hammer, even. But Randall's death had been elegant. His grin widened as he slid down the offramp onto 24.

He really didn't mind driving a big rig through town—it was the only thing he ever drove, and he was used to its proportions. Even the fifty-two-foot trailer seemed natural, but then again, he'd started in the industry when he turned nineteen (three months after "graduating" from his father's training regimen) and with the exception of a few days when he was too sick, he'd driven a truck every single day—whether he had a load and destination or not.

And he drove with what he considered to be perfect consideration of his fellow drivers. He always signaled, and he always kept to the slow lanes in town unless he had to be in a turn lane for a left-hander. He never ran a yellow light unless the mass behind him forbade stopping in time, but those instances were rare and far between. He *anticipated* the needs of his truck—and the darkness inside him.

The last time he'd fed that particular beast was, in fact, that little orange Ford, and he could feel the hunger, the *need*, nibbling around the edges of his awareness. On the whole, however, his fellow drivers over the past twenty-days or so had been quite courteous, and he made it a point to only kill those that deserved it.

Anyway, his darkness didn't seem sated after a purely random killing. One thing his father had inspired in all of them was a strong pragmatism. "Do what works for you," the man had always said, and he'd listened.

He enjoyed Ankou's company. There were no games, no talking behind your back, no lies, no tricks. That sounded strange, given his upbringing, but he understood his father had done what was necessary to make him the best man he could be.

But thinking about his father was a solemn activity now that the man was in prison. He'd never see him again, unless, when the time came, he arranged to be captured back in New York. There was no link between them—at least no *legal* link the authorities could use to keep them separated—and he liked to imagine the two of them together again. Maybe even sharing a cell. After all, he had no delusions about the inevitability of his capture if he followed his father's plan to the letter—hell, even if he ignored what the plan needed and instead gave it only what *he* wanted to give. Some smart analyst at the FBI would put it together eventually, and once they did, all they'd need to hone in on him was to recognize his somewhat unique method of signing his crimes. Speaking of which, there would be an opportunity in Yakima. The location was right, he just needed a target.

His revery was broken by a horn blast behind him. The trucker glanced at his sideview mirror and saw a purple Dodge Challenger driving aggressively through the light traffic. "There's no reason for all that," he murmured, frowning. "What's your hurry?"

The Dodge leaped out of the fast lane with another angry blast of his horn, goosed the accelerator, and sped past the old lady in her minivan who clearly wanted to turn left. The purple Challenger raced along in the slow lane—coming right up on Mack's donkey before letting loose with another blast of his beeper.

With a curt nod to himself, the big rig driver lifted his foot off the accelerator and let the truck slow even further. The bridge over the Yakima River was coming up, and push come to shove, it was close enough to mile marker thirty-three to assuage his need to sign his kills.

The Dodge weaved back and forth in the lane behind him, filling first the driver's sideview, then appearing in the passenger's side. The Pete's driver tutted and shook his head. Not only was the driver being extremely rude, but his antics bordered on dangerous. "What if you lose control of that rocket?" he asked the image in the mirror. "What if you go off the bridge into the water?"

Almost as if in answer, the purple car swung wide to the left, his passenger side tires inches from the stone curbing as if the driver intended to pass him on the left, which the trucker couldn't understand since the fast lane was wide open. But the bridge was close, and there was no shoulder on it.

He hoped the kid driving made his move. The bridge had concrete barriers and an iron rail on the sides, but he knew a trick to pop cars up and over those barriers when conditions were right. Mack slid his foot to the brake pedal and slowed even further, earning him a fresh barrage of horn. "Come on by, bozo. Let's make this your last sunset."

He could almost taste the desire to do the driver of that Dodge a helping of vehicular violence. The guy had lessons to learn, and the truck driver was not shy about dishing out lessons. The only thing that might ruin what he had planned was if the Dodge driver didn't get on the Interstate. That was where mile thirty-three was marked in Yakima, just past the upcoming onramp. The Dodge didn't have to end up there, but it would make everything much more powerful if the lesson *started* and ended close to the thirty-third lollipop on I-82.

He let the rig glide toward the dashed white lines separating the slow and fast lanes, giving the pass-on-the-left temptation more teeth, but the Dodge driver must have known the bridge was coming. With an almost desultory beep of the horn, he changed to the fast lane—*finally*—and roared past, giving him plenty of room though it meant clipping the double yellows with his driver side tires.

The Pete driver released a pent-up breath and almost laughed at how tense he'd become. He forced his muscles to relax. Driving tense was a sure way of being sore in the morning, not to mention the increase in fatigue. "Easy come, easy go," he said, then chuckled.

As Terrace Heights became Yakima Avenue around the bend just after the bridge, he heard the Dodge's horn ahead. Peering into the setting sun, he could barely make out the purple car weaving from lane to lane behind a pair of citizens who chose to drive the speed limit.

Mack's grin was akin to that of a Great White shark as he accelerated a skosh—just enough to tickle the legal limit. He wanted to see the show, to tally the count, to judge the man as if fate were on his dashboard, staring right at the guy.

He cruised along as the Challenger's driver continued to show his ass to the world, and his grin grew and grew as he counted the offenses. His face blossomed with a huge predatory smile when the Dodge's turn signal came on a block from the I-82 onramp, and the trucker closed the distance between them, allowing the speedometer to creep past the posted speed limit, getting into position.

With a final, petulant blast of his horn at the two cars who'd stymied him, the Dodge driver peeled off onto the onramp, and when he did, the powerful Peterbilt 389 was right behind him. The trucker was ready, and he knew *exactly* how he wanted it to go.

A voice in his head kept repeating: *The river. The Yakima River*, and he could see it, not three hundred yards to the onramp's east side. There would be another chance on I-82 itself if things didn't go as planned, but Mack had confidence they would.

He downshifted and unleashed the power of his modified compound boost setup—a small turbo feeding a large turbo to one hundred and fifty pounds of boost— enjoying the shriek of the turbos, the ugly growl of the diesel engine using every square inch of air the turbos could cram into it, the wet-sounding rasp of his tires on the asphalt, the mechanical whine of the transmission. The rig ate the distance between the Dodge's purple rear bumper and his chrome heavy-duty bull bar. With a savage howl, he blew his air horns a few seconds before the impact.

The rear of the Challenger caved in as if it were tin foil and the big rig was an M1A1 tank. He kept his foot mashed into the mat, lifting the back end of the Dodge and shoving the whole car toward the shoulder. He didn't ease off for the curve ahead, nor did he lift when the purple idiot-car nosed into the guard rail at close to seventy miles per hour.

The momentum Mack had built up slammed the Challenger into and through the guard rail with a horrible scream of metal tearing, driving the posts set in the asphalt to break free of their moorings, allowing the guard rail and the Dodge to marry as the car slid to the left, gouging great furrows in the wet earth. He continued plowing straight ahead, and the car speared down the embankment toward the empty parking lot of a Mexican restaurant, while truck and trailer followed behind with all the grace of a drunk elephant on ice.

At the bottom of the slope, he downshifted again to bring his revs up, and the truck leaped straight toward the driver's door of the Dodge. The driver's face was a bloody mess, and he seemed out of it, but that was nothing to the Pete's pilot—it just made his task easier. He slammed into the car with the force of a derailed locomotive, pounding the car across the parking lot, across the two-lanes of the Yakima Greenway, and toward the edge of the rocky embankment opposite that descended into the Yakima River with gentle grace.

He slammed on the brakes and powered the air brakes at the last second, and his rig came to a skidding halt, but the Dodge rambled over the rocks, tipping, tipping, then rolling down into the river, pinballing from tree trunk to rock to tree trunk, then splashed into the river like a cannonball. It came to rest with its tires aimed at the sky, and Mack whooped at the luck. He sat there a moment, watching the river for signs the driver had gotten out, but there were none.

The rush hit him then, the ecstasy, the release, and he squeezed his watering eyes shut and moaned. He knew he couldn't luxuriate for more than a few seconds, though. He'd already taken a monstrous risk, which only grew more and more grave the longer he sat there, his truck still, the license plate there for anyone with working eyes to note the number.

That didn't worry him much, though. He had other plates, other registrations for both the tractor and trailer, and he was very practiced in getting the old plates off and the new ones on. He'd drilled and drilled the process.

Even so, he opened his eyes and took one last look at the purple car, one last scan of the banks, one last look downstream, and then was satisfied the driver was done breathing. Still feeling the rush, he flicked on his left blinker and cranked the wheel to match, heading north on Yakima Greenway. He could pull to the side of the road and change plates in a few minutes when he was out of sight of any witness and inspect the front end for damage. The impacts had been bone-jarring, and he worried the bull bar had taken damage.

No matter, he thought. *I have spares.*

CHAPTER 14

SEAT COVER LIFE

Hanable's Valley, NY

FRUSTRATION AND ANNOYANCE warred for dominance within her, and Meredeth had to squeeze her eyes shut against a throbbing pain that was bouncing back and forth between her left and right eyes. That part was new, and it was something she needed to discuss with Darren Taber. She got up and took yet another tour around Kevin's house—maybe the twentieth or thirtieth circuit she'd made since he'd gone to work.

Time was not her friend. Waiting was anathema to her, and at her last appointment, Dr. Atallah had given her a date for the reversal of the ileostomy—two weeks in the future. She didn't know how she'd survived the previous six weeks, or how she'd survive the wait until the surgery. She wanted the damn bag off her flesh that very moment. She wanted to erase the ileostomy from her belly, from her mind, from her life.

But instead, she had to *wait*.

Since Bobby and Big Dave had traded media attention for a full confession from the Baltimore Brawler (also known as Hyena) everyone was happy—including Meredeth. But the end of their case meant she didn't even have that to think about anymore.

She was antsy. She was bored. She was crawling out of her skin. She sat in the La-Z-Boy but sprang back up for another tour of the house almost immediately. *I'm going to lose my goddamn mind!*

Kevin had offered her things to do at HVPD, but with the bag swinging like a pendulum from her waist with every step, she wasn't comfortable being out among people. He assured her no one could even see it unless they knew to look for it, but with the shirts two sizes too big, and the only comfortable shorts being of the athletic variety with the waistband rolled down, she felt like a bum. A fat bum, at that.

And the diet... They called it a low residue diet, but as far as she could tell, it was a typical teenager diet: no fiber, no vegetables, no fruit, no seeds or nuts, no vitamins, no prebiotics... She ended up with multiple versions of potatoes everywhere that they went to eat, and even then, she had to be careful as she couldn't have the potato skins. Other than that, she could have anything she wanted—which amounted to almost nothing after six weeks on the damn diet.

She huffed out a breath and crossed her arms. She knew better than to perseverate on things she had no control over but found herself a little helpless. The television was off and would remain off. She'd seen enough of it in the past six weeks to know there was nothing she had to see. That left surfing the web or hitting up social media, but both seemed a big waste of time to Meredeth. For a while she'd gone on a texting spree, but that had grown old fast.

And what made her boredom even worse was that Michelina hadn't emailed for three or four days, and Meredeth found herself worrying about it any time she thought about it. She'd thought they were good after the last exchange, but so far, no reply. She'd checked her spam folder, she'd checked her inbox, she'd even called the Bureau tech support line and had them check the status of her email account, and the answer was the same. She had no email because Michelina hadn't written it yet, and she might never do so.

She went back to the recliner and plopped down into it. She had an interesting book to read, when she could summon the willpower to block out her naysaying thoughts long enough to get into the book. In the past three days, she'd also refamiliarized herself with all the details of the kidnappings that occurred in the nineties. Michelina's homelife hadn't been good, even before John Doe had kidnapped her and killed her mother, her younger sister, and her mom's dirtbag boyfriend. Still, Meredeth thought the woman was *smart*, and she had no doubt the girl would have escaped the squalor on a full academic scholarship to a good school.

Her Bureau phone rang, and she made a lunging grab for it off the coffee table and accepted the call. "Hello?"

"Hey, Mere," said Bobby.

"Oh, hey, Bobby. How's life in the limelight?"

"That's all faded already. I'm back in the office, though, and that's good."

"You didn't like Big Dave?"

"No, Big Dave is fine, but he's no Meredeth Connelly."

"Ha, I bet. No headaches, no surly attitude."

"No incredible leaps, no profiles I can learn from. When are you coming back?"

"My reversal surgery is in two weeks, but the doc said it's much easier in terms of the actual event, and the recovery, than the first surgery."

"Well, I'd hope so. You were kind of swirling around the drain by the time they figured out what they wanted to do."

"Nah, they stabilized me first. I remember that part."

"Swirling the drain, I say. Anyway, what does 'easier' amount to?"

"Well, the first surgery was five and a half hours. He said this one would take thirty to forty-five minutes. He said I'll be able to come back to work within two or three weeks."

"That's great news!"

"Yeah, it is...*if* I can stay sane until the surgery."

"You've got to stay positive, Mere. I know how hard that is to hear. When I was recovering from my Afghanistan wound, people said it to me almost every day, and it made me want to choke anyone who was foolish enough to get close to the bed. But once I set my brain to receive and forced a positive outlook, I started making huge strides in my recovery. I know it's different, but—"

"It is different, but only because your wounds were much more serious than this."

"How do you know what my injuries were?"

"I'm FBI, Van Zandt. When McCutchins recommended you as my new partner, I looked you up. Your actions in that last battle over there earned you a Bronze Star, did it not?" Bobby said nothing for the space of a few breaths, and Meredeth was content to wait him out.

"Just try to have a positive outlook instead of negative. Think you can do that, or do I have to call you multiple times a day and remind you?

"I can do that," she said in a quiet voice.

"Good."

"Did you call to tell me that?"

"No," said Bobby. "When I was back in Baltimore, McCutchins tasked me with reviewing a few ViCAP entries that had one of our crime analysts feeling antsy."

"Oh?"

"Yeah. She didn't know whether it was random MVAs or something more sinister."

"And what did you find?"

"Here's the thing, Mere. All these accidents occurred at mile marker thirty-three, but none of them occurred on the same roadway."

Meredeth bit her lower lip. "Going back how long?"

"I sent the analyst on a deep dive into ViCAP, and I think we need to send up a flag for any MVAs around mile marker thirty-three."

"What does Jim say?"

"I haven't spoken to him yet. It's only been a few days and getting Hyena's confession was priority one for a couple of those days."

"He won't give you much slack with something like this."

"I figured."

"But if you tell him now, he'll give it to someone else."

Bobby clicked his tongue. "Mere, maybe it needs to go to someone else. People are dying."

"What's his frequency? Is he on a cycle or are these truly random?"

"I can't say for certain, but I think they are completely random. Like that hitman who worked for the Cartels. The one that flipped a coin to decide who lived and who died."

"Then we don't know if anyone will die before my reversal surgery. The doc said I'd recovery quickly. It may even only take a few days."

"I'll make you a deal, boss. I'll hold off filing my report and blame it on you. I'm going to send you the ViCAP entries and ask you to develop an initial profile. You can take as long as you need up to the next murder. If it happens tomorrow, I file. Does that sound fair?"

"Yes," said Meredeth. "Send me the reports, including your draft, and I'll work up a profile. Tell Jim that's what we're doing before he calls you in to see why it's taking so long."

"Ten-four."

"Good." She tugged her lip a moment. "So, tell me how it felt."

"How what felt, Mere?"

"Swinging Hyena around and getting the confession."

"To be honest, at first, I felt pretty sleazy. That role—the bigot only out for himself, is hard to play."

"But as it started to yield results?"

"Then it got easier. I could see the benefits of the role."

"And you used them well. How did it feel when Hyena extended that pseudo-demand?"

"About confessing in exchange for a little press time? I wanted to get up and dance. But, I'll tell you what, I still don't understand why he'd go from a short beef to confessing just to get his picture on television."

"That's easy. Whatever justification he drummed up for the crimes, he's a serial killer to the bone. He *wanted* everyone to know how dangerous he is. He wants the rep in prison, the infamy."

"That seems..."

"Crazy? Yes, it does, but remember the dark triad and its implications."

"Well, narcissists boast about their conquests."

"And everything else. But think about what all three personality types have in common."

"Obviously a lack of empathy and stunted or no emotions, but I don't imagine that's what you mean."

"No. If I put you on the spot and ask you which of the three personality types best match Hyena, what would you say?"

"He shows a marked preference for manipulation, exploitation, and deceit. And obviously the lack of empathy and emotion."

"Okay. What else?"

"He showed a high degree of confidence. He jumped right on Big Dave rather than fleeing when he suspected he was a cop. He seemed pretty cock-sure during our interviews with him, too."

"That's to be expected of all three. Have you heard about the Dirty Dozen?"

"Great flick. Lee Marvin was such a bad ass."

"Um, not that Dirty Dozen. What I'm talking about is an instrument first proposed by Jonason and Webster. It's a twelve-question test."

"Nope. What are the questions?"

"The first four measure Machiavellian traits: 'I tend to manipulate others to get my way,' 'I have used deceit or lied to get my way,' 'I have used flattery to get my way,' and finally, 'I tend to exploit others toward my own end.'"

"He's definitely a manipulator and a glib liar. He didn't seem that inclined toward flattery, but I think he's solidly in the exploitation camp."

"Rate them on a one to seven scale, where one means 'strongly disagree' and seven equates to 'strongly agree.' With that done, total them and that will give you a sense for how well Machiavellianism fits your suspect. The higher the total, the stronger the tendencies."

"Seven, seven, four—which I assume is neither agree or disagree?"

"Sure."

"Okay. Seven, seven, four, and a six. Twenty-four total."

"Twenty-four out of twenty-eight possible."

Bobby whistled softly. "That's pretty high...ninety-six percent."

"The next four questions are: 'I tend to lack remorse,' 'I tend to be unconcerned with the morality of my actions,' 'I tend to be callous or insensitive,' and 'I tend to be cynical.' Before you start answering the questions for Hyena, between psychopathy and narcissism, what's being measured by these four?"

"Easy one. Psychopathy."

"Right. What's your total?"

"Seven, seven, seven, and seven. One hundred percent."

"Okay. The last set measures narcissistic traits. The four questions are: 'I tend to want others to admire me,' 'I tend to want others to pay attention to me,' 'I tend to seek prestige or status,' and 'I tend to expect special favors from others.'"

"Woah. That's another hundred percent, but that's okay, right? He can rank highly in all three as well as just one?"

"That's right, Bobby. The instrument is designed to tell us how strong the tendencies are bent toward the Dark Triad. Hyena definitely exhibits enough of these tendencies to merit a diagnosis. Where I go from there is the DSM-5 to decide between ties. Just look up Narcissistic Personality Disorder and Antisocial Personality Disorder. That will give you a firm sense of the man."

"Okay, I'll find a copy of the Diagnostic and Statistical Manual around here somewhere."

"Top left drawer of my desk."

"That's cheating, Mere. You never told me—"

"I can't give you all my secrets all at once, Van Zandt. It would make your head explode."

"Is that so?"

"Absolutely, Bobby, absolutely. Send me those ViCAP cases right away. I'm *bored*."

"I will, Mere. Don't you worry."

CHAPTER 15

WALLY WEAVER

Hanable's Valley, NY

WHEN KEVIN ARRIVED home, Meredeth looked up from her laptop and checked the time. It was after seven in the evening, and she hadn't eaten anything since breakfast. His eyes crawled over her face, then zipped to the insulated bottle he'd set out for her before he left.

"Is that the same drink I gave you this morning?"

Meredeth felt the flush on her face and couldn't meet Kevin's gaze. The surgeon had told them both how important it was for her to keep hydrated since her colon could no longer reabsorb the water that went with digestion. "Um, I don't remember."

"Meredeth..." Kevin shook his head and closed his mouth. "You're a grown-ass woman, Meredeth. You don't need me to chew you out for ignoring the doctor's orders, but let me ask you this one question: Do you want EMS to rush you to the hospital because you're so dehydrated your kidney's fail?"

"I..." She grabbed the bottle and drank the half that remained. "You're right," she said after she caught her breath. "I've been irresponsible, but I've been working on—"

"*Working*? The next words out of your mouth better be 'a puzzle' or 'a game.' If it's anything else, you might see the angry-Kevin face."

She dropped her gaze to her lap and watched as one thumb tried to pick the old nail polish off the other. "I'm just doing an initial profile for Bobby. He's—"

"I'm going to kill him."

"Kevin, it's not his fault. I wanted to do something, and I..." She risked a quick peek at Kevin's blood-suffused face. "I volunteered to do this. I didn't want McCutchins to give the case to someone else, so I had to make a deal with Bobby—"

"What goddamn case, Meredeth?" he hissed at her.

"Don't be mad, Kevin. I know I've been off in Meredeth-land all day, and—"

"Your bottle's empty. I'll go refill it with Gatorade." His voice was flat—calm and emotionless, with no sign of the seething anger he'd just expressed. He stepped toward her, but she flipped the lever on the arm of the La-Z-Boy and stood.

Too fast, as it turned out, and the room swam around her. She squeezed her eyes shut and fell back into the recliner.

"What? What's wrong, Meredeth?" Emotion filled Kevin's voice as he crossed the room to her in three long steps.

"Just a little dizzy."

"Dammit, Meredeth! That's a sign of severe dehydration." His cool fingers landed on her wrist. "Your pulse is a little high, too. Not a lot, but a little."

"Is that another—"

"Yes. Let me look at your feet."

"My feet?"

"Shut up and show me, FBI." She did as he bid her, and he grunted. "You're not swollen. How about muscle cramps?"

"No, nothing like that."

"Headache?"

"Well, I always—"

"I don't mean your freaking migraines!"

Her shoulders twitched in the merest suggestion of a shrug. "Then, no."

"Dry mouth? Cough?"

"No, Kevin."

"Everything all right with your plumbing?"

"My plumbing?"

"Are you peeing, FBI?"

"Yes."

"And the color?"

"Normal."

He glanced through the pass-through into the kitchen and made a noise of disgust. "Your lunch is still there on the counter. Did you eat today?"

"I was so absorbed in—"

"Goddammit, Meredeth," Kevin said in a voice that sounded exhausted and beat down.

"I know, Kevin. I'm *sorry*." She felt her eyes tear up, felt the ache in her throat, but she fought for control and won. "I got distracted, which is something I desperately needed. It's... I *needed* to do something, Kev. *Anything*."

"I suggested you come into the station with me."

"I know, and maybe I should've, but..." She shook her head. "It's probably vain, but I don't want to be seen like this. I don't want to go out where people can stare at me...or *smell* me."

Kevin sighed and sat on the couch. "Meredeth, no one can smell anything."

"I can, Kevin. And if I can, so can others."

"You can because your nose is only a few feet away from that vented bag. If anyone else gets close enough to smell it, I may shoot them."

As if on cue, her small intestine released sonorous, noisome methane into the ostomy bag, and Meredeth blushed a deep crimson. "And there's that."

"Meredeth..." Kevin shook his head and stood, then grabbed her bottle and walked into the kitchen. "You say you don't want me taking time off, that I should save the time for when we can do something fun. I get that, FBI. But then you go and do this." In the kitchen, Gatorade gurgled into her bottle.

"I know, Kevin. You have every right to be mad at me. I..." Her voice threatened to crack, and she closed her mouth on the rest of what she'd planned on saying.

"I'm mad, but only because this is serious, and when you do something like this..." He sighed as he returned to the living room. "Drink it. All of it."

She took the bottle and let a huge gulp of Gatorade fill her mouth.

"I've got more right here"—Kevin held up another pint-sized bottle—"so finish that entire cup."

"That's thirty ounces, Kevin."

"Yes, it is, and it's thirty ounces you should have sucked down at about nine this morning. The surgeon spelled it out, right? I remember him saying around one hundred and eighty ounces per day. So far, you have maybe thirty-five ounces in you."

Meredeth hung her head. She knew Kevin was piqued with her, and she deserved that, but he was also disappointed in her, and that she didn't know how to deal with. She picked up the YETI bottle and tossed back half of what remained. Gatorade wasn't her favorite drink in the world, but Dr. Atallah had said she needed a lot of electrolytes. She swallowed and took another gulp, then dropped her gaze to the floor. "I'm sorry, Kevin. I'm not used to this."

"None of us are, Mere," he said. Some of the anger had left his voice. "But look, what's done is done. We have to get on with our evening. We need to eat, and you need to drink four more of those thermos bottles of liquid."

"Coffee is liquid," she said and stole a peek at his face. She saw the smile flicker, but it didn't last.

"And a diuretic—the absolute last thing you need tonight."

"Gatorade it is, then," she said. "I... I really am sorry, Kevin. This is just... It's how I work. Full focus on the issue. You know that."

"I do, Meredeth, but that has to change as of now. Maybe not permanently, but at least until your insides are back on your inside."

"Deal."

"You promise?"

"I do, Kevin. I will do my best."

"I'm not sure that cuts it, FBI. Promise me you will do what I ask—not your best."

"I..." She shook her head, not knowing what to say. Usually, Kevin thought her best was good enough.

"This is *your life* we're talking about, Mere. This isn't whether you're going to remember to call me when you get back to your hotel. This isn't whether you're going to hydrate and eat to combat the migraines. This is about you not killing yourself by allowing your kidneys to fail. This is serious stuff, FBI."

"I know," she said softly. "I promise I *will* do better. I *will* keep track of my hydration."

"Okay, then." He turned back toward the kitchen. "Let me see what we have in the freezer."

"Maybe..." Meredeth bit her lower lip, then pushed herself to her feet. She stood there swaying a moment, eyes closed.

"Maybe you need to eat quicker than I can cook up something?"

She nodded gratefully. "The diner?"

"You want to come with me? You can tell me about this thing Van Zandt is working on."

"Sure," she said. "It'll do me good to get some fresh air."

"Let's go, then. I don't suppose you want to eat there?"

"Inside?"

"They have pie," he said, eyes twinkling.

"That's dirty pool, Saunders," she said, then laughed. "You're not ashamed to be seen with me?"

"Are you kidding, FBI? You're the prettiest girl in this one-horse town. Throw your hair in a ponytail and let's go."

"Can I borrow one of your caps?"

"Of course. You don't even need to ask."

"Give me five minutes to get ready. I want to cover my hairy legs with pants."

"Let someone say something..." Kevin growled.

She grinned at him, then went into the bedroom to find a pair of sweats that wouldn't hurt her stoma or any of the surgical sites. She did opt for a loose ponytail and a black cap with HVPD emblazoned across the front.

The ride to the diner took them all of four and a half minutes, and they saw only two other vehicles—one HVPD cruiser who blipped his rotating lights at the chief's car, and a fancied up big rig, set aglow with maybe all the chrome in the world and a million lights. Meredeth was glad the ride was a short one—something dug into the wafer holding her ostomy bag to her skin the entire four and a half minutes.

"Tell me what Bobby is into."

"Right. A Bureau crime analyst found a disturbing pattern in the ViCAP data. It may be a serial, but if it is, he's unlike any other on record."

Kevin arched a brow at her. "Yeah? Another one like Ankou?"

"These deaths could be felony hit-and-runs, vehicular homicides committed by drunks, except for one thing."

Kevin opened the door and held it for her. She gave him her prettiest smile as she walked by him, then stood next to the little sign saying, "Please wait to be seated." Kevin walked right by it, then stopped and turned toward her.

"That sign isn't for us," he said.

She arched an eyebrow. "It isn't?"

"No, hon," called a rich baritone from the passthrough to the kitchen. "We tried and tried to get the chief to obey the rules, but...well, you know him as well—or better—than we do."

She laughed and stepped toward Kevin.

"And if I can say so, I was sorry to hear about your injury and all that. If this were a just world, nothing like that would happen to you guys who stand between the rest of us and the worst the world has to offer."

"Thank you," said Meredeth.

"Johnny, are you hitting on my woman?" growled Kevin, though his eyes twinkled, and he was having a hard time keeping a grin off his face.

"Shoot, no, Chief. I don't want twenty or thirty parking tickets a day!"

Kevin lost the fight with the grin. "Okay if we take the back booth? We've got some business to talk over."

"Suit yourself, Chief. It's slow tonight, though, so you can probably sit anywhere you want."

"That back booth, then."

"Know what y'all want?" asked Johnny.

"Give me a damn second to look at the menu, you pushy cook!"

Johnny laughed, and it was one of those larger-than-life laughs that made Meredeth want to join in. "Hey, Johnny?" she asked.

"Yes?"

"Was it my imagination, or did you just y'all us?"

Johnny laughed again, then nodded. "Yes, I did. You got a problem with that, Ms. Special Agent?"

She grinned at him. "That's something I don't hear much in these parts. You must be an immigrant."

"Like you, you mean? Sure. I'm a Texan, born and bred, and I can't help it if folks up here can't talk right."

"I'm from Georgia, myself."

"A Georgia Peach? I should've guessed that already, pretty as you are. What are you doing way up here? And with the chief to boot?"

"Let's see," said Kevin. "I wonder if I can get the town council to make unpaid parking tickets a felony..."

The three of them laughed as Kevin and Meredeth took the closest booth to the double doors that led to the kitchen. Kevin looked at her across the table and smiled. "He's right, you know. You are as pretty as a peach."

Meredeth grinned despite the warmth blossoming on her cheeks. "That's sweet. I can't repay you for the kindness at the moment, but I'll remember. *All* of the kindnesses."

Kevin blushed, then cleared his throat. "Go on with what Bobby's got you doing."

"Like I said, there's a pattern in some of the ViCAP entries that could be the result of random traffic accidents except for one thing."

"What's that one thing?"

"They all happen near a mile marker thirty-three."

Kevin arched his eyebrows. "On the same road?"

She frowned. "Unfortunately, no. They're spread all over the country, but always thirty-three miles from the start of the road or the state line."

"That's... I'd have a hard time believing that's not significant."

"Right? I did some digging through ViCAP and found similar accidents at the same marker. More than the crime analyst found. A lot more."

"This isn't sounding good."

"No," she said and grimaced. "And Bobby wants a profile to include in his report."

"Want to try it out on me?"

"You don't mind? Even though working on it..."

"That's over, FBI," said Kevin with a gentle smile. "You heard my concerns and are addressing them."

"I am," she said firmly.

"Then let's hear this profile."

"Understand that this is guesswork."

"Aren't they always?"

Meredeth grinned. "Don't look behind the curtain, sir. Yes, profiles are guesswork, but they're *educated* guesswork. In this case, I'm making a lot of assumptions— the biggest of which is that there is actually a serial killer behind these deaths. The most recent happened near dinner time, and a lot of people saw an eighteen-wheeler smash the car through a guardrail and down into a river. The local police searched but didn't find the right truck, though they found several that matched the various descriptions. They also mentioned the driver of the car was showing his ass to God and all the saints. He was driving in a hyperaggressive manner, blowing his horn, harassing people who wanted to drive the speed limit."

"Hmm," said Kevin. "A vigilante?"

"A mission-oriented serial killer would be my guess."

Kevin inclined his head to the left, then straightened it. "Okay. Tell me."

"Some of it is boilerplate. White male, twenty to forty years old. Specialized education in the form of a class A commercial driver's license. He's a loner who drives a lot based on the geographic disparity between the cases we've found. He takes good care of his vehicle, and he's probably customized it to a high degree. He might not have a home other than his semi. The truck is a flashy color—red or orange, something like that. He—"

"What did the wits report?"

"Red and orange were the highest percentage, but also yellow, green, and black were reported. The license plates reported in some of the cases don't match. They aren't even registered to the same trucking company."

"What about previous crimes?" asked Kevin.

"Probably nothing on his record. This one's never been caught doing anything. He's convinced his methods are the best, and it looks like he's probably right—with a significant amount of luck, the chances of tracking him down are very slim. He's flown under the radar for at least eleven years—that's the oldest case that *might* match."

"Celtic knot?"

"Nothing so far."

"Then he might not be one of Ankou's victims."

The bell above the door tinkled, and Kevin turned to see who was entering the diner. Meredeth glanced over as well. A big man stood just inside the door. He was lean but muscular and wide-shouldered. He looked like a player for the NFL. His hair was clipped to an eighth of an inch all over and looked self-done. His gaze flicked toward them, and he nodded. He pointed at the sign and raised his eyebrows.

"*Johnny!*" yelled Kevin. "You've got a customer." He turned his back on the newcomer and waved Meredeth onward.

She drew a deep breath in through her nose and held it a moment, then released it all at once. "It's possible Doe had nothing to do with this unsub, but he's made it no secret that his plans involve challenging me." She smiled ruefully. "This is challenging." Her gaze drifted toward the counter as Johnny came out of the kitchen wearing white pants and a white chef's tunic. He ushered the big guy to the counter, and the man glanced at her again, this time narrowing his eyes at her scrutiny. She gave him a quick flash of a contrite smile and turned her gaze on Kevin.

"I understand that, Mere, but you captured Delamort six weeks ago. That should—"

"Seven weeks."

"I stand corrected. That should have triggered the next one on the hit parade, no?"

Meredeth shrugged. "I have no idea how this is supposed to work. I should ask Michelina." As she said the name, she caught a flicker of movement in the corner of her eye, and when she looked, she thought the newcomer had just looked away in a hurry. "Maybe we should save this for later."

Kevin glanced over his shoulder. "Little ears?"

"I think saying that name shocked him. I believe he looked over here, then cut his gaze away when I looked up."

"Believe or know?"

She shook her head. "Believe." As she said the word, her phone pinged—another email. She opened the app, then looked up, first at the man at the counter, then at Kevin. "From my sister."

"Go ahead a read it," said Kevin. "You can fill me in later."

Meredeth gave him a curt nod, then turned her attention to the phone's screen. The email read:

> Dear Meredeth,
>
> I'm flattered by your admiration. If it's genuine—I don't mean to call you out, but I know a little about law enforcement negotiation tactics. I'm unreservedly happy that we're friends—that

makes baring my soul easier in a way. But before I do that, I need some assurances.

For instance:

1. You said you would work on getting me immunity and protective custody. I'll take the immunity, of course, but protective custody is a non-starter. I know how Ankou and his collection of killers think. I'm far safer protecting myself.

2. Everything I tell you must be sealed as tight as an FBI agent can. I don't want one of my so-called siblings using the Freedom of Information Act to find out I'm helping you.

3. I'm going to need transactional immunity for everything I tell you, or I can't speak about my personal experiences.

If those three things are doable, I will tell you all about my part in Ankou's family. Until then, however, I'll keep my secrets.

I know Ankou tested Alex with a bum in a Jonodot alleyway. She beat the old guy to death with a hammer. As a reward, Ankou took her on the raid that netted me. Murder, more murder, and kidnapping. That should do you fine for leverage, Meredeth.

As to Mack and Lucy, I can only help with the latter. I haven't heard anything about Mack in *over a decade—even before I broke away. He was just gone one day.*

Lucy, on the other hand, is somewhere out west. Sacramento, California, last I heard. Be careful of her, Meredeth. She's like an angry snake most of the time, but when she's friendly toward you, you are really in trouble. Don't ever turn your back on her like you did Alex.

Let me close with answering your other questions as best I can at this point. I live on the eastern seaboard, not too far from the ocean. I work for the government like you, but I sit in a cube and deal with large datasets every day. I'm a techie nerd.

Yours,

Michelina

Meredeth raised her eyes and met Kevin's direct gaze. She gave him a slight nod, then glanced at the counter, and again, she caught the big guy looking away. "He's watching me, Kev," she whispered.

He nodded and stretched. "So? How was she?" he said in a loud voice.

"My sister? Oh, you know. A little paranoid, a little reserved, but you know how it is—a woman in the tech field working for the government."

"Tell me when he's looking," Kevin whispered. "Are you so sure it's her who is paranoid?"

"Let me send her a quick reply, hon," she said. She leaned against the booth's padded back, raised her phone to eye-level, and turned on the camera. After a few moments, the man turned his head and stared at them. "Well, *I* wasn't being paranoid," she said with a laugh.

Kevin chuckled. "You never are. I've got to use the facilities. Don't leave without me."

"I'll wait right here."

He slid out of the booth and got to his feet, then turned toward the other side of the diner where the restrooms were located. He adjusted his utility belt, so it rode a little easier on his hips. Then, he started across the restaurant, but when he reached the man at the counter, he stopped and leaned down to whisper in the big guy's ear.

"Hey, I'm just waiting on my to-go order. You're the only people in here. I didn't mean to make the lady uncomfortable."

"Well, that's fine. Please stop staring at her."

"Yessir," said the man. "I'm sorry." He turned toward Meredeth, but his eyes didn't land on hers. "I'm very sorry, ma'am. I didn't mean anything. I was just curious about your cap."

"It means, 'Hanable's Valley Police Department,'" said Kevin in a cold tone, "and *this* is Hanable's Valley. That means she can arrest you."

The man smiled. "Does it? I'd think she'd need your approval"—the man peered at Kevin's uniform—"Chief Saunders."

"Well, see? That's where you'd be wrong. In fact, the way things are, I'd need *her* approval."

The man arched his eyebrows. "Statie?"

"I was. She isn't."

"Oh. Fed?"

"Why is that your business?" demanded Kevin.

Johnny picked that moment to burst through the double doors to the kitchen, a brown sack in one hand and a big cup of coffee in the other. "Say..." He scanned up to Kevin's face. "Problem, *Chief*?"

"Hey, man, it's not my business. I'm a curious person, that's all. I'm sorry I stepped on your toes. I'll take my meal and go if it's all the same to you."

"I've never seen you before."

"No, and you're not likely to see me again. I'm just passing through."

Kevin nodded once, took a step back, and raised an open hand toward the door. "Have a good night, sir," he said in a friendly voice, though his eyes were still hard, and his right hand stayed close to his holster.

"You, too, Chief." The big man smiled at Johnny and slipped him two twenties.

"No, that's too much," said Johnny. "Your bill was—"

"Keep it." The man turned toward the door and crossed the intervening distance in two large steps, shoved it open and held it with one hand, then glanced at Meredeth and winked. "You have a good night, Ms. FBI," he said, and then he darted out the door and jogged toward the opposite corner.

Kevin moved toward the door, but Meredeth called him back. "It's probably nothing, Kevin," she said. Then, as he came back to the table, she asked, "What did you whisper to him?"

Johnny stood behind the counter, his gaze flipping back and forth between their table and the door. Kevin shrugged and slid into the booth. When he was comfortable, he said, "I told him I was taking his leering at you personally."

Johnny cleared his throat. "If I'd known he was harassing you, Agent...uh, ma'am, I'd have got after him with my cleaver." He frowned instead of chuckling as Meredeth expected he would if what he'd said were a joke. "He paid cash, so I don't have nothing official, but he said his name was Carl."

Meredeth's eyes widened.

"That mean something to y'all? I don't cotton to people harassing my good friends."

"It's over now, Johnny," said Kevin without turning. "Are you sure about that name? Not Earl? Not Mark?"

"Nope. Says it right here on his order. C-A-R-L."

"Coincidence?" Kevin asked her in a low voice.

"Maybe," she said with a shrug.

"Well, your food's almost up," said Johnny. "I apologize if there—"

"No need, Johnny," said Meredeth. "He was just staring at me. I'm a little sensitive right now."

"Yes'm. I imagine you might be. But, at the risk of earning a bunch more parking tickets, let me tell you that you look *good*, ma'am."

Kevin sighed and started to slide toward the end of the bench, and Meredeth laughed. "Now, boys, let's not fight over little old me. And, Johnny?"

"Yes, ma'am?"

"You call me ma'am one more time and I might have Kevin arrest you. My name's Meredeth. Meredeth Connelly."

He beamed at her. "Johnny Chornikvulyts." His last name came out sounding strange in his Texan accent. It sounded like *chore-nik-vullets*.

"I see why you go by only your first name." Kevin winked at Meredeth.

"We can't all have *boring* names like Saunders."

"And that's another parking ticket," said Kevin in a mock-severe tone, but also with a smile. "Now, where's *our* food? You waiting for us to pass out from low blood sugar so you can steal my ticket pad?"

Laughing, Johnny returned to his kitchen.

While they waited, Meredeth told Kevin about the contents of Michelina's email. "She wants the grant of immunity up front. I'm not sure I can get an Assistant US Attorney to do that without a proffer."

"And she turned down the protective custody? What about witness protection?"

"She said a protective detail would put her in more danger than her own measures. I'll ask her about witness protection since that will come after the case is wrapped up. Sealing the case file is easy enough. It'll just take a conversation with Jim McCutchins."

"Well, that's two things you can do right away. Guarantee you won't sign her up for a protection detail and then get McCutchins to seal the file on her."

Meredeth nodded. "Let me reply to her real quick."

"Yeah, no problem. I think Johnny needs me in the kitchen." He grinned at her as he got up.

After watching him for a moment, Meredeth opened her email app again and hit the reply button.

> *Dear Michelina,*
>
> *Thank you for letting me know your general geographical area and giving me an insight into what kind of work you do. Big data, huh? The Bureau has analysts who work with giant data sets—ViCAP is probably the biggest. Or at least, one of the biggest. And don't sweat the cube farm. I think that's government-wide in this day and age.*

As to your three requests, two are easy, and I'm here to say that I won't put you in for a protective detail unless you change your mind. You should consider witness protection for after the case, however. The program has a terrific track record. I am in the process of getting your case file sealed, even within the Bureau, and though I'm not in the office at the moment to ride herd, I am sure it will be done as soon as possible. The last, though, will be hard without a proffer. I will pursue it, but it will take time. Also, I probably need to know the state and area you live in so I can approach the AUSA for your region.

Let me take a moment and assure you that my admiration is genuine. I do lie from time to time when interrogating a suspect, but I consider you a friend (not to mention a cooperating witness), and as such, I have no need to trick or lie to you. You have my solemn word on that, Michelina.

Quick question about Alex's test. You said she assisted Ankou's attack on your family? I assume, then, that Alex's test with the homeless man took place before you joined the family. Did you learn about it by gossip? If so, that won't be usable in court, as valuable as it is for working through what he put you all through.

I'm also assuming you were tested, and that your test was something like the one he put Alex *through. Were all the kids tested with violence? Mack? Lucy? Carl? I don't think it's going out on a limb to assume all the tests involved murdering someone (yours included). To help me sell all this to the AUSA, can you give me an idea of how many crimes you were forced to commit before you could escape?*

Please don't think there is any judgment in this. I have no basis for judging you, Michelina, and I doubt many do. And it's not as if he wasn't holding a metaphorical gun to your head the whole time. When the order is. 'Kill this person or I will kill you,' judgments become moot in any case.

I'm going to start putting things together for the AUSA—I'll email my prep files to you in a day or so if that's okay, and you can add specifics and outline what you can personally testify to and what you can't. I'm also going to have your case file sealed by the time you read this (unless you are Michelina-on-the-spot).

Oh, and back to something to hold over Ankou, can you tell me a story about something that happened that you witnessed directly? Anything else will be hearsay, and while it does help to educate me, it won't stand up in court if it comes to that. Ankou will know that. If it's easier, just highlight such a memory in your content for the proffer letter.

Until next time!

Your friend,

Meredeth

Once she hit send, she sent an email to McCutchins, cc'ing Bobby, explaining the need for the sealed file. As she put her phone down on the table, Kevin and Johnny came out of the kitchen double doors, and each of them held a tray of food. Meredeth's mouth started to water as soon as the scent of the food hit her nostrils.

CHAPTER 16

CUTTIN' YOU DOWN TO SIZE

Western New York

HE WAS GLAD he'd decided to come back to the right coast for a month or so—even though it had meant deadheading the trip. His profile in the Pacific Northwest was getting hot, and he'd been pulled over because his truck matched one used in his dealing with the purple Challenger more than once. Of course, those stops meant nothing, and he'd changed plates after each one. The cops had nothing—a poor description of a truck of various colors, including red, he imagined. Maybe even a partial plate.

In any case, a change of scenery had seemed best, so he'd used I-80 to cross the country from one ocean to another, then made his way back to where he grew up. His truck wasn't known in New York, and he felt safe. And to cap it off, he'd driven through Hanable's Valley, driven by the police station, then the chief's house, and happened to cross paths with the chief's cruiser as it crossed town. He followed them to a nice little diner with a very friendly cook.

He shook his head, feeling louche because of his ham-handed actions in the diner. He'd done something to alert Connelly and her pet police chief. He hadn't meant to stare, but evidently, he had. *Oh, well. Nothing can be done about the past.*

He flicked on the satellite radio. Usually, he listened to comedians, or the comedians on channel nineteen of his CB radio, but he felt like he had to get his brain back in the game. He twisted the dial until he found a twenty-four-hour news station, then sat back and unpacked his dinner.

"Hey, Nancy, I have something here that might be interesting."

"Yeah? What's that, Frank?"

"I have it on good authority that law enforcement officials are searching for a man dubbed the Highwayman."

"And what does this Highwayman do? Rob people?"

"No, Nance, he's a cold-blooded murderer. Perhaps a vigilante."

The trucker smiled at that. He wasn't at all threatened by the news. The story no doubt originated in Yakima, but it didn't really matter where it came from. He couldn't be identified by his crimes.

"Sometimes I wonder if we should just legalize vigilantism."

"How can you say that?"

"Law enforcement is obviously having a hard time. Maybe empowering citizen militias would help them."

"Oh, no. I'm not going to get drawn into that argument again."

"I'm just saying that—"

"Next, Nancy, we have a story of interest out of Florida."

"The Passe-A-Grille Killer case?"

"That's the one."

The Highwayman perked up, leaned forward, and turned up the radio, his BLT forgotten in the Styrofoam box resting in his lap.

"What has that woman...or man, or *whatever*... What's it done now?"

"It, Nancy? That's—"

"Yaddy," said Nancy. "Don't hit me with your limousine liberal crud tonight, Francis. I'm not in the mood."

"But, Nancy, if this Sonya Sargent or Alex Delamort is a true transgender person, then we owe it to—"

"Hogwash, Francis. It is a serial killer, plain and simple. I don't care what gender it's decided to be."

A shiver of recognition, of fear, rambled through the Highwayman's belly. *They caught Alex already*? *How did I miss this*?

"Uh... Send your emails, as always, to 24-hour News Studios. Make sure you quote Nancy in your letter."

Nancy chuckled. "And that's if you're with me *or* against me. Now that we've got that out of the way for the evening—"

"In record time, too."

"—maybe you can get on with the story?"

"Happy to, Nancy. As our listeners may recall that Sonya Sargent was the alias Alex Delamort used to perform his duties as the Assistant District Attorney for Pinellas County in Florida. Today—"

"Is that near Disney World?"

"Um, closer to Bush Gardens, Nancy. It's on the west coast of Florida."

"Ah. Go on."

"Right. Today, acting as his own attorney, Alex Delamort filed an injunction against the Pinellas County District Attorney and the DA's office, claiming bias on the part of the District Attorney himself, and by extension, the entire office."

"It doesn't mess around, does it?"

The trucker growled, at the disrespect shown to Alex.

"*He*, you mean."

"We've covered this, Francis. You call it what you want, and I'll do the same."

"Well, if you are comfortable with me cringing every time you say something, I'll—"

"What else is new, cupcake? Come on, Frank. Get on with it—there's real news to cover."

"Uh, right. We asked our legal consultant, Becca Mosa, to review the filing, and she has. She's on line five, if you'll bring her in."

"Becca!" said Nancy with what sounded like genuine joy.

"Hey there, Nance. How's it going tonight?"

"Libtard Frank is up to his tricks, as usual."

"Francis Carpenter!" said Becca. "Are you stirring the pot?"

"Hardly, Becca. Nancy is insisting on calling Mr. Delamort 'it' every chance she gets."

"Ah, and that offends your delicate ears?"

"I just think that as a fellow human, he's entitled to our respect."

"And I think he's a no-good serial killer who's entitled to a needle in the arm. Does Florida still have the death penalty, Bec?"

"Yes, Nancy. Capital punishment is a legal penalty in Florida."

"Good. Maybe they'll be smart enough to use it in this case. Then there will be no confusion about whether it's a boy or a girl or neither."

Frank sighed. "Becca, what is your opinion of the brief?"

"I think it's good enough to get Delamort a change of venue."

"Of course!" said Nancy. "Ship it somewhere else and let them deal with it."

Anger thrummed in the Highwayman's belly, in the veins and arteries in his neck, behind his eyes, and deeper still. He rolled down the window and chucked the very good BLT out into the grass. He could no more eat than fly. He switched off the radio, making a note of the station on his 'do not waste your time' list. Then he fastened his seat belt, put the truck in gear, and released the air brakes.

As if it could sense his mood, the truck seemed eager to get out of the little town of Hanable's Valley and onto the open road. He turned the truck to the northeast, toward his second childhood home. He wondered, what with Father in prison, if any of the others had come home.

His mind twisted back to the disturbing fact that Alex had already been caught and frowned at the stygian darkness beyond the nose of his Peterbilt 389. He was to go next, to start marking his victims with the Trinity Knot his father had chosen for the project. He was supposed to *advertise* that he was one of the original cohort of Branch farm siblings, and he didn't know what he thought about that. His methods were superior to anything the others had come up with, and if he were careful, he could go on and on and on, though he would no doubt have to change his methods as law enforcement twigged to his methods.

And if I dispense with this symbol crap, he thought.

Bright blue-white light stabbed through the darkness on the curve half-a-mile ahead, but the Highwayman paid it no mind. His speed was just at the marked limit for the road—his habit when he wasn't hunting. Avoiding complications like speeding fines and location information that went along with them was in his best interest.

I can't believe Connelly caught Alex so quickly, he mused. *I wonder what she did to corner him. His cover was perfect.* He pursed his lips. *I bet it was his temper.* He thought back to the way she was dressed at the diner, the paleness in her face, her greasy hair shoved up into a cap, the baggy clothes. *I also bet he almost got her. She's injured, there's no doubt about that, but injured how?*

The bright lights ahead resolved into a pair of LED headlights and a light bar, mounted way up high as one would on a semi-tractor. Whoever it was, he was booking along at quite a clip...and weaving from side to side in the lane. Mack grabbed his mic. "Hey there, westbound, how about you?" He waited, mic in his right hand on the wheel, but no answer came, the lights didn't dim. *Too snooty for me, westbound?* As the other truck drew closer, he could see there was no trailer behind the rig. *Bobtailing it home, are we?*

As they closed the distance between one another and the lights grew to eyeball-scalding levels of bright, he grew irritated. He flashed his high beams and the lightbar he had on top. "Hey, good neighbor, want to dim those lights for me?"

After an especially egregious swerve toward the shoulder, the truck veered across Mack's lane onto a side road, and the Highwayman slammed on the brakes, adding the jake brake and the air brakes for good measure. He cut the wheel to the left, hoping to go around the drunk idiot, but the brakes on the cab *and* the trailer locked up with twin screams of burning rubber, and he found himself skidding out of control, dancing on figurative ice. "Jesus!" he shouted, pumping the foot brake in a vain attempt at regaining traction. He white-knuckled the steering wheel, cranking it to the right.

The moron in the bobtail rig went on his merry way without so much as an apology on the radio. A beer can whistled from the cab to the gravel on the shoulder. The Highwayman's Pete came to a halt at the white line that separated the travel lane from the shoulder, amid a cloud of swirling tire smoke. With a low growl, he switched off the jake and air brakes, then wrenched the truck into gear and put the accelerator to the mat. He followed the other truck down the narrow side road, chasing his weaving brake lights into the darkness.

"This is a sign," he muttered. "Time to play my part."

CHAPTER 17

ROAD PIZZA

Hanable's Valley, NY

MEREDETH HEARD KEVIN get up, heard the subtle rattle of his phone on the nightstand as he picked it up, heard the door to the bathroom close with a slight click, then turned her head toward the other side of the room and tried to go back to sleep. She had no idea what the time was but was intimately familiar with the muzzy-headed-middle-of-the-night feeling she had. It was early morning, if she had her guess, probably four or half-past four. Curiosity pricked her mind. *Is he getting called out to a crime scene?* she wondered. She turned her head back toward the bathroom door and opened her eyes, straining to hear Kevin's side of the call.

The door swung open, and Kevin stepped out of the bathroom's black maw. Light from his phone screen danced across his cheek as he moved silently toward the bed. "Meredeth?" he whispered in such a low volume she almost thought it was her mind playing tricks. But Kevin didn't get back in bed, just stood there watching her for signs of wakefulness.

"What is it, Kevin? Are you getting called out?"

"No. It's Van Zandt. I'd let you sleep, but he has news about the road rage cases—specifically about a fresh one very close to here. He wants us to pack up and run."

"The hell with that," she said as she stifled a yawn. "Who's the local contact? I want to go to the scene."

"I don't think that's a good idea, Mere," said Kevin. "Neither does Bobby."

"How far away is it?" She swung her legs out of the bed and pulled on her shorts. "I have to empty the bag, and I should take some supplies in that little bag the ostomy supply company sent me, rather than lugging the crap around in my purse."

"Didn't you hear me, Mere?" asked Kevin, a note of annoyance in his voice.

"I did, but I need to go there, Kevin. This guy's long gone. That's in his MO."

"Maybe, maybe not." He removed the phone from his ear and turned on the speaker phone feature. "Bobby wants to say something direct."

"That's right," said Bobby, his voice tinny. "Listen, Meredeth Connelly, you are on medical leave. Alex almost killed you, and now we have this suspicious move from the Pacific Northwest right into Kevin's backyard."

"That's right," said Kevin. "It's just north of Browncroft, about fifteen miles from here. That guy last night might be the unsub, Mere."

"What guy last night?" asked Bobby in a sharp, no-nonsense tone.

"Some guy in the diner who stared at me a little too much. But he apologized and left when Kevin confronted him."

"That's not good," muttered Bobby. "Especially since someone was murdered at another mile marker thirty-three."

"Come on, Bobby. Don't jump at shadows," said Meredeth. "The guy—"

"Gave me a case of the hinkies," said Kevin.

"Look, you guys, my reversal surgery is in a matter of days now. I can't go into hiding."

"You could," said Bobby. "You could delay the surgery."

"No," she said flatly.

"Be reasonable, Mere. If it's a matter of life and death—"

"But it *isn't*, Bobby. We have no credible evidence that the person committing these crimes has anything to do with Ankou. And, even if we assume that he is, there's nothing that says he's out to do me harm. Besides, I'll have surgery in Florida."

Kevin gave her his severest cop-frown. "I don't know... Call me crazy but I consider the events of seven weeks ago to be pretty credible evidence that your life is in danger with these brainwashed victims of John Doe."

"There's that," said Bobby with a chuckle. "Come on, Connelly! You have to admit the man is right."

"That could've been a one-off. Doe never says he wants me dead. In fact, he says the opposite every time I talk to him. Until his master plan is done, he wants me around to experience it. He wants to pit his brain and the brains of his so-called children against ours. That's where he is having his fun. If he wanted me dead, he could have done it on that first case. He could've just pulled the trigger instead of chewing me out and ordering me down into the basement. He didn't do that."

"Maybe not," said Bobby, "but Delamort sure didn't get that memo."

"I'm an FBI agent and have been for going on twenty-four years. Danger is part of the job, but my tenure proves I'm careful, that I take adequate precautions. I've never once needed to go into hiding, and I don't now. Kevin is here, and you'll be here tomorrow—unless I miss my guess."

"No, you didn't miss," said Bobby. "I want to be at the scene while it's still fresh."

"See there?" said Meredeth. She turned a pleading gaze on Kevin. "I need to be in on this."

"Don't you remember our agreement?" asked Bobby. "I said I'd sit on the report unless there was another murder."

"Sure, and I agree, but you shouldn't turn it in until you've had the chance to see this scene. After you do turn it in, we can lobby McCutchins to assign the case to you."

"Me?" asked Bobby. "But until you're back recovered and back at work, I'm just a junior agent flapping in the wind."

"And there's no reason for that. Part of your development to senior agent includes taking the primary role on cases. Let this one be the first."

Kevin gave a sour chuckle. "And what are you going to use to bribe *me*, FBI?"

"I'm not bribing him, Kevin. He's ready to take the lead, and he should do so."

"It just seems convenient timing."

Meredeth shook her head. "And maybe it is, Kevin, but I want to be on this case! It's going to be difficult, even for Bobby and me. We can't let it wallow in the wind in the hands of a less capable team."

"And if I won't take you to the crime scene?"

"Then I'll rent a car and drive myself."

"Are you up to that?" asked Bobby.

"I have no idea, but if Kevin refuses to take me, we'll find out together."

Kevin took a deep breath and puffed his cheeks out with it. "Let's ignore the fact that you have no valid basis for entry to that scene, and that you can hardly get dressed in your business suit and go flash your badge. If—"

"I'll find a way to—"

"*If you are going in any case, I might as well go with you—*"

"Thanks, Kevin," she said with the beginnings of a smile.

"*—to protect you from yourself, FBI,*" Kevin finished, raising his voice to talk over her.

For a moment, no one spoke. Meredeth and Kevin had their gazes locked on one another—at least until Meredeth dropped her gaze to the floor. "If you really think it's too dangerous for me to go to the crime scene..."

Kevin heaved a sigh. "Mere, I know you're capable of handling almost any threat—when you're healthy. But you aren't right now. Maybe you don't recognize the fatigue, the malaise—"

"Trust me, I do. I haven't felt right since before Delamort stabbed me."

"Well, there you go," said Kevin passionately. "Even you admit you're not at your best."

She walked around the bed and stood in front of him, looking up into his eyes. "That's why I need you with me, Kevin. Bobby can't get here until noon or later, most likely. I don't want to wait for him."

"Gee, thanks, Mere," said Bobby with a laugh. "It's nice to know where I stand."

"You know where you stand with me, Bobby," she said in a gentle voice. "This is about logistics, not worth."

"I know it."

"What do you say, Chief Saunders? Do you feel up to stepping in as my Personal Protection Detail until Bobby can catch a flight up here?"

"Longer than that," he murmured, putting his arms around her shoulders.

"Mom and Dad, quit talking dirty," said Bobby.

"Hurry up and get your flight details sorted out, Van Zandt," said Meredeth with the crackle of command in her voice.

"Yes, Mom."

"Call when you know."

"Will do. Saunders?"

"Yes, Bobby?"

"You've got the ball, Chief. Don't drop it."

"Count on it."

"I am, Kevin," said Bobby. "All right. Promise to call if anything comes up."

"Yep," said Meredeth.

Bobby hung up, and Kevin dropped his phone on the bed. "I guess we're getting dressed now?"

"Yeah. I want to *get out there*."

"It'll take you longer to get ready than the drive, so try to relax, FBI."

She smiled at him, then headed toward the closet to find something halfway presentable to wear. She settled on a pair of black warm-up pants, but though she tried it, she hated the way her silk blouse lay over the ostomy bag.

It was like a billboard that screamed her medical condition to the world with blinking neon lights.

"Wear the shirt if you want. You can borrow one of my LEO windbreakers and keep it half-buttoned up. You may get warm, however."

She shook her head. "I'm afraid something that tight will cause problems."

"Want one of my dress shirts? Or an HVPD uniform shirt?"

"How about a white button-down?"

"Sure. Right there by my suits."

Dressed in sweatpants, a man's dress shirt, a man's windbreaker, and a ball cap, Meredeth examined herself in the mirror and sighed. She adjusted the ostomy bag, trying to make it less obvious and failing.

"Listen, Mere, no one can see that. If they do catch it, no one will know what it is, okay?"

"They'll catch my greasy hair and my mismatched clothing."

"Let them. This isn't a fashion show, and the deputies out there at the scene will be approaching the end of a graveyard shift. None of them will be looking their brightest, either. And, if they give you any trouble, your Personal Protection Detail will kick their ever-loving asses into the dirt."

"You say the sweetest things sometimes, Saunders."

"Shut up and get in the car before I change my mind."

With a smirk, Meredeth brushed past him out of the closet, but her hand trailed across his belly, and she let him catch her hand in his own. "Oh, I forgot the supplies bag. Just a second." She went into the bathroom, opened the linen closet, and pulled out the Amazon box that held her ostomy supplies. She rooted around within until she felt the small canvas bag and pulled it out. It was like a cross between a cheap purse and a bookbag that was too small to carry books. It was dark navy blue and had several zipper pockets around an internal pouch with yet more organizational compartments. She pushed a few pairs of nitrile gloves into the center, along with a spare wafer and a spare ostomy bag. She added a two-inch stack of gauze four by fours, a tube of adhesive paste, a wax ring for sealing the base, adhesive remover wipes, and skin prep wipes. "What am I forgetting?" she muttered. She added a package of flushable wipes, then nodded. "That's it."

She turned to find Kevin leaning against the doorframe and grinning at her. "I packed up some extra clothes." He lifted a small blue duffle bag.

"Thanks," she said. "Why do I have the feeling I'm forgetting something important?"

"Your gun and FBI credentials?" he asked with a smile. "In the outer pocket of the duffle. You don't need to fool with them until we arrive at the scene."

She sucked her teeth. "What would I do without you, Kev?"

"Bully someone else into doing your will?"

She chuckled but looked at her bare feet. "Were you going to mention shoes?"

"Hey, Mere, I was only kidding."

"I know." She nodded once and cast a quick peek at his face. "But I do think I need to wear shoes."

He grinned. "It was a test of your mental state."

"Sure it was, Saunders. Sure it was."

He walked to the dresser and opened her drawer, fished out a pair of white crew socks, and tossed them her way. "Better put on your boots. The area we're headed to is either woods or farmland. Muddy this time of year, either way."

By the time she got her shoes on and they set out for the scene, it was ten minutes after five, and Kevin had already called both Sheriff Jackstral and Captain Morse of the NYSP to let both agencies know their intentions, then he'd called Butch Schweighart and invited him to meet them at the scene. After he grumped about the time, Butch gave in and promised he'd be right out.

Kevin made better time than he'd estimated. He took a couple of backroads and ran his roof lights as he hammered down. They turned north on US 219, approaching mile marker thirty-three with his lights still spinning. He pulled in behind several Cattaraugus County Sheriff's Department cruisers and killed the engine and the lights.

A cabover semi rig sat in the middle of a small field east of the road. Deep tracks ran to the truck, and a set of shallowed ones led back to the macadam. He hadn't lied, the field was mostly mud. A knot of deputies stood on the shoulder of the road, and Kevin waved to them. "You want in there alone?"

"Yes, please," said Meredeth. "At first, anyway. I'll wave when I'm ready for you to come out and save me from the deluge of mud."

Kevin nodded, winking at her, and then headed over to the knot of deputies.

She picked her way out to the older green cabover, her gaze flicking back and forth from the truck to various points in the trees surrounding the field on three sides. She saw nothing moving—neither in the trees nor in the cab—as she'd expected.

She paused ten yards from the tractor, which leaned heavily to the left. She didn't know enough about trucks to see if there was any other damage, but all five tires on the driver's side were dead flat. The sidewalls of each tire looked to have been cut in an almost perfect circle.

When she reached the green truck, she climbed up the ladder, set her phone into flashlight mode, and peered in the driver's side window. A man sat in the driver's seat, and someone had slit his throat for him. Blood had cascaded down his T-shirt and across his ample belly, but the killer had slit the shirt down the middle. "Now, why do that?" she murmured.

She turned her light to the steering wheel and the dash, which was immaculate, and frowned. She cast light on the driver's seat itself, and though it was spotted with a little blood, there wasn't enough blood present for a man with his throat cut from ear to ear to have bled out in the driver's seat. The rest of the cab looked well-worn but also well-maintained.

"So, where did he kill you if not in your truck?" she murmured. "The side of the road? How did he slice your tires up?"

When she was sure she'd seen as much as she could without disturbing the scene, she opened the door and gingerly maneuvered around it as she opened it wide. Gripping the doorframe with her right hand, she leaned in and twitched the edges of the cut T-shirt away with a pen.

A Trinity Knot was hacked into the man's abdomen.

Meredeth muttered an unladylike curse and carefully climbed down into the mud. She stood, arms akimbo, staring up into the open door of the cab, thinking furiously, and her head began to ache. The dawning day seemed far too bright all of a sudden, and she closed her eyes, pinching the bridge of her nose. She felt light-headed and more than a little woozy. She took deep breaths through her nose, filling her lungs, then released each lungful through an almost closed mouth. After a few minutes, when the light-headedness disappeared, she turned and trudged back to the shoulder, keeping her head down and watching where she put her feet. The last thing she needed was to fall face-first into the mud, land on her ostomy bag, and get its contents all over herself.

CHAPTER 18

EYEBALLING BEARS

North of Browncroft, NY

THE HIGHWAYMAN LOWERED his expensive binoculars as Connelly moved away from the green cabover. He wondered what she'd made of his staged scene. He wondered if she'd seen the Trinity Knot, or if that little revelation would come at the postmortem. He thought she'd seen it, though, given the way she'd stood there and stared at the truck.

She'd looked like she was about to puke, and he didn't imagine that would be a good thing for a woman in her obviously poor health. *Still,* he thought, *gotta give her credit for being badass enough to come out here despite what Alex had done to her.* He didn't know the details, but she hadn't looked all that spry the night before. And she'd sat in a way that made him think of an old woman protecting her belly from a savage dog.

I did it, Father, he thought. *I put your damn mark on that crackerhead, and now Meredeth Connelly knows I'm one of yours. I'll keep going as long as I can, then I'll fade into the background and disappear for a while. Maybe after Lucy— or whoever you told to go next—finishes up, I'll start up again. More twisted wreckage, more bodies with the Trinity Knot. It may be pure hubris, but I don't think they can catch me as long as I stick to my rules.* He backed into the dark depths of the woods at his back, watching that clump of pigs on the shoulder, watching Connelly pick her way across the muddy field as he faded away.

He had a bit of a hike ahead of him, and he wanted to get back to the farm at the best possible speed so he could remove the fifth-wheel towing boom he'd used to pull the cabover into place. Then, he wanted to load his gear and shake a leg on the Big Road back to the west, maybe to the Southwest, maybe to Southern California.

Cutting that mark into the rude trucker who'd nearly made him jack-knife made him anxious. He felt like anyone who looked at him would instantly know he was the one that had carved that mark.

He knew it was silly. He knew his father would be disappointed to learn he was letting his emotions rule him. Then again, it seemed his father had done the same thing, letting Connelly provoke him into a silly move that landed him in prison for the rest of his life. To the Highwayman's way of thinking, it would have been better to disappear, to continue to write taunting letters to the

New York Times, to lord his success and his escape over Connelly while the rest of them went to work.

When he was well back from the edge of the field, and when the trees obscured his vision of the cops and Agent Connelly, he turned his back on them and walked through the spring-thick brush and trees, heading roughly due east toward Kuhn Road where his rig sat. He had an hour's drive, then a half-hour to remove the tow-boom and pack it away in his trailer behind the false wall with his spare parts and other necessary items. Then, he'd attach his customized dry box trailer and head out.

Let Connelly try to find me, he thought with a grin. *I'll be halfway to Nevada before she realizes I'm gone.*

CHAPTER 19

FULL GROWN BEARS

North of Browncroft, NY

MEREDETH HEARD BUTCH Schweighart before she picked his bulky form out of the crowd. He and Kevin stood side by side, entertaining the deputies with some story from when Kevin was a trooper, no doubt.

"Christ, Schweighart, you look even bigger in your civies."

Butch spun on the balls of his feet, a huge smile splitting his lips. "You don't look all that dead, Connelly, and from what I read, you probably should. You got nine lives or something?"

"Eight, now," she said with an answering smile. "How are you, Butch?"

"Sexy, strong, and open to my emotions. Tell the truth, Meredeth. How are you?"

"I'm getting there. This is a big step."

"I'll bet." His gaze drifted lazily to the green cabover out in the middle of the field. "But we shouldn't work on empty stomachs." He grinned, first at her, then at the deputies.

"If I can conscript one of Cattaraugus County's finest to serve breakfast around, I brought two boxes of coffee, two dozen donuts, and a fruit basket from Wegman's." A deputy held up his hand, a child's grin on his face, and Butch tossed him the keys.

"Are you not working today, Butch?" asked Meredeth.

He shook his head. "I'm here as a sort-of civilian—thus no uniform. It's no big deal. I work a lot of my days off."

Their chitchat continued in that vein until everyone had coffee, and all but Meredeth and Kevin had either a doughnut or a plastic bowl of fruit.

"You don't want a doughnut, Kevin? Since when?"

"I can't eat any of that," said Meredeth. She approached Kevin and laced her fingers with his. "He's being gallant."

Butch dropped his gaze to the ground. "Dammit, I didn't think of that. I'm sorry, Meredeth." The deputies knotted around them lowered their food as if trying to hide it from her.

She grinned and punched Butch lightly in the arm. "Nah. Even if I wasn't almost gutted like a fish by Alex Delamort, I'd still turn you down. It's morning, and my stomach isn't my friend at this time of day."

His gaze snapped up to hers, his brow wrinkling in confusion, then it jumped to Kevin. "Uh..."

Meredeth laughed—a full belly laugh that made the bag on her stomach jiggle and dance. "No, no, no, Butch! I'm *not pregnant*. It's the headaches."

He looked at her sheepishly. "Sorry, I just thought…"

She shook her head. "Bless you for the compliment, but I'm too old, Butch. Don't let the particular requirements of my gut renovation stop you." She glanced at the deputies. "Any of you. Eat up, gentlemen. I'm not bothered by it." She squeezed Kevin's hand. "That goes for you, too, Chief."

Kevin glanced at her and shook his head. "I'm okay."

"Go on," she said. "Get yourself one of those donuts before Butch eats them all."

"The fruit is my thing," said Butch. "The donuts are for Kevin and any deputies that want them."

"You're sure?" Kevin asked her.

"Yep. Go on, Kev."

He shrugged and walked over to the two boxes of donuts. He picked a raspberry-filled doughnut with white icing layered on top, then took a big bite on his way back to them.

"All right, enough with the small talk," said Meredeth, her grin dissolving. "In that green monstrosity out there, I found the body of a white male, late forties or early fifties. He wasn't killed inside the truck"—she waved a hand at the deep tire tracks—"and it was obviously towed to this field. I saw no evidence of a kill scene."

"Staged?" Kevin asked around a mouthful of sweet dough and raspberry filling.

"Yes. He was killed elsewhere, then the unsub towed the truck here and staged him in the driver's seat. But that's not the worst of it."

Butch arched an eyebrow. "No?"

Meredeth shook her head. "No. His shirt is cut down the middle. There's a unique wound you would recognize cut into his flesh."

"A Trinity Knot?" asked Kevin, his doughnut forgotten.

"You got it in one."

"Postmortem?"

Again, she shook her head. "Judging by the blood from the wound, I'd say antemortem, but not by much. I think the unsub may have surprised him, cut his throat, then carved the symbol."

Butch looked down at his feet for a moment. "What are the chances that this is a copycat?"

"Nil. We didn't even know for sure if the other mile marker thirty-three slayings were homicides."

"Now, I guess you do," said Butch softly. "How many?"

"The count isn't in yet, Butch. Maybe this is a copycat," mused Kevin. "This isn't like the other stuff in ViCAP, Mere. This isn't a hit and run, this isn't a vehicular homicide, this is up close and personal. Cutting someone up is a lot different than ramming them with an eighteen-wheeler."

"I agree with you on that. But it's not a copycat, Kevin. It's a message."

"A message?" asked Butch. "To whom? And what's the message because I don't see what this could possibly mean to anyone."

"It's a message to me, Butch," said Meredeth softly. "And it reads: 'I'm here. Look how close I got to you. I can do this anytime I want.'"

"Uffda. All that?"

"And one more thing. It also proclaims to the world that the unsub is one of John Doe's so-called children. He brainwashed the lot of them, killing the kids who it didn't work on, then sent them out into the world. It's all part of his plan, and it revolves around me."

Butch's gaze dropped to her stomach. "Ever think about taking a desk job?"

"No, Butch, that would kill me for sure."

CHAPTER 20

POWERING UP

David Branch's Farm, NY

WHEN THEY PULLED into the farm's side yard, their father was already waiting on them. His eyes widened as Mack drove the fancy semi-tractor next to the barn, then hopped down, leaving the rig idling. Father's gaze zipped to the Bronco and pinned Alex where he sat. "What's this?"

"This guy almost killed us," said Mack. "He ran—"

"*I'm talking to Alex!*" Father shouted.

Mack took two instinctual steps back even as Alex got out of the Bronco and came to stand before their father. "We were careful. The body is in the sleeper so we can dispose of it in the graveyard tonight."

"Careful." The scorn fairly dripped from Father's words.

"No one saw us, Father," said Mack. "I didn't pick a fight in the center of Yoagoh this time. We were out in the country."

"I trusted you not to lead Mack astray," Father said as if Mack hadn't spoken, never taking his eyes off Alex's face.

Alex shrugged. "You said he was ready for his test."

"I said *perhaps* he is ready." Father took a half-step closer to Alex, his fists clenched at his sides. "But *I* decide, Alex, not *you*. Is that clear?"

Alex gazed up into Father's angry face and cocked his head to the side. "Females are the illogical, emotional barrens of the species. I need you strong, cold, and deadly, Father."

Mack held his breath, ready to run for the truck and get the hell out of there if that's what it came to, but Father only narrowed his eyes for a moment, then the corners of his mouth curled upward a little. "Very well, Alex. That was clever."

"Thank you, Father," Alex said. "You said many things to me once upon a time. 'I have remade you in my image. Your will is iron, and my plan is your plan. You are logical, reliable. You are my right hand. You have great worth; I would have you eclipse me. You are my son—my first son—and heir to everything I've built.' Have you changed your mind?"

It was their father's turn to cock his head to the side, giving up on his solemn pretense and grinning at her. "I did say those things. I meant those things. I *still* mean those things."

"Good," said Alex. "I'm sorry we surprised you—I know you detest surprises. This man deserved what he got, just like the Caddie driver. He almost killed us, and Mack saw a way to make him pay. I let him run with it—as I think you would have."

"Maybe so, Alex." He turned to meet Mack's gaze. "You wouldn't have made it to the tree line, my son. It's good you didn't give in to the impulse." With the heavy atmosphere of potential violence dissipating, Carl and Lucy came around the corner, and Father beckoned them over. He smiled. "Everything is okay." He turned so that he faced the fancy big rig. "Tell me about this, Mack."

"I thought... That is..."

"Go on, Son. There's no reason to be frightened."

"Yes, Father. I thought we might change the VIN or do another title transfer like we did for the Cadillac." He turned to face the truck as well. "But this time, I'd like to keep it."

"*Cool*," murmured Carl.

"Yeah," said Lucy, her eyes on Mack.

An expression of surprise flirted with Father's face, and he glanced at Alex.

"He thought it through in advance," Alex said.

"I think it could be my thing," said Mack quietly. "Driving a truck, crisscrossing the country, feeding my copilot with the deaths of the bad drivers, the wild and crazy ones, the assholes. I think..." He shot a timid glance at his father.

"What, Mack? You think what?"

"I think my actions may never be recognized as murders. I think I'll be so mobile that no one will ever connect me to the crimes."

His father's expression grew solemn. "And the plan?"

"I'd be able to do my part without sparking interests with my own work. I could easily drop a body with your mark on it, then be three states away before the body is found."

"I see you have been giving this some thought. You would need a Class A Commercial Driver's License, and that's not something we can forge—not if this is to be your career."

"But I think I should have multiple CDLs, and I *know* how to drive this baby already. I'd like several different sets of registrations and license plates. That way, if someone *did* see me do something, I could drive away, then change the plates the second it's safe. I might be questioned by the police, but with the license plates not matching, they'll send me on my way."

"I'll look into it." Father turned his gaze back on the tractor. "You will need a trailer, as well. It will need to be modified to hide things you will need: spare parts, extra bumpers, things like that."

"Yes," said Mack, warming to the subject. "I'd want to add power to the engine, too. And as for the bumpers, I'd rather get one of those big bull bar things. I could keep two or three spares in the hidden part of the trailer."

Father nodded, speculation dancing in his gaze. "I commend you on your planning, Mack, but how did you know you'd come across this man—or someone like him—to provide you with the rig?"

"I didn't," said Mack, "but given how everyone drives around here, I figured that given time, someone would volunteer."

His father's face split into a wide grin, and he clapped Mack on the back. "A good plan and recognizing the need for patience. You *are* ready, Son."

Mack froze for a moment, fear an icy lump in his guts. "For my test?"

"Indeed," said their father. "You are ready in every way but one. Get a parts list together for your truck. We'll work on it together, and when the modifications are finished, you will take your test. I'll get you a new VIN *and* a clear title."

"Thank you, Father!"

"Can..." Carl managed to squeak before his throat closed completely around his words.

"Yes, Carl?" asked Father, turning to the younger boy and arching an eyebrow.

"Can Mack get me a truck?"

Father grinned. "You like that rig, eh?"

"It's totally cool," said Carl in a wistful voice. "And what Mack talked about, cruising the open road, looking for trouble...that sounds like heaven."

"Well, we'll have to see. You are not nearly ready for such freedom, Carl."

"Yes, Father," Carl said, dropping his gaze, misery in his voice.

"Which is not to say having a goal like this won't speed you along, Son."

"Yessir," said Carl, cutting his eyes toward Mack.

"When Mack was your age, I wouldn't have let him do this, either."

"You can help us, Carl. You can learn about trucks as we rebuild this one," said Mack.

"A noble gesture." His father turned toward Mack and lifted one pedantic finger. "Parts list."

"Yessir," said Mack. "I... Well, I already started one. All I need to do is match the parts to the Peterbilt."

Father smiled, and for an instant, Mack could have sworn he saw pride in the man's eyes.

CHAPTER 21

DEAD PEDAL

Alden, NY

THE DOORS CLATTERED and clanked behind them, shutting out a warm spring afternoon as they stepped into the interview room once more. Bobby had landed just an hour before and was by her side, while Kevin took up the spot next to the wall behind her. So far, she hadn't heard back from Michelina, so she didn't feel all that confident that she could bend Doe over a barrel (or even threaten to do so).

She spent a handful of minutes trying to find a comfortable position in the hard chair, then gave up and resigned herself to being physically miserable throughout the conversation as well as mentally so. She watched the hall expectantly, drumming her fingers on the table.

"He doesn't get within three feet of her," said Kevin.

"Four," said Bobby. "If he tries, I'll break him into pieces."

"Boys, settle down," she said under her breath. "I'll be fine."

Before either man could explain to her why they couldn't settle down, the door at the far end of the long, glass-walled hallway opposite them clattered open on its tracks. Doe shuffled into the hall ahead of a grim-faced Henedy, the same guard that accompanied Doe on their previous visit. As Doe approached, he never took his eyes off Meredeth, not even to skewer Bobby or Kevin with a mocking smile.

As soon as the door to the interview room opened with a groan and a mechanical grinding noise, Ankou entered the room quietly and came over to sit in the chair that was bolted to the floor. He cocked his head to the side, his eyes flickering from here to there across her features, then he nodded. "Alex was not supposed to do this to you. He was always so sure he knew best." He tilted his head back and sniffed like a dog, then a sour expression flashed across his features.

"A failure of your conditioning program?"

A soft grin surfaced on his features. "Even with your guts mostly cut out, you can still mount a good fight."

"That's what Alex learned firsthand," said Bobby.

Doe rolled his eyes. "I imagine you had more to do with that than Old Mare, here. But it's no matter. Alex should not have attacked you at all, Meredeth, let alone in such a grievous manner. I would promise to discipline him, but...well...circumstances as they are..."

"Right," she said. "Do your other children disobey you, too?"

Again, a small smile surfaced on the man's lips. "Hardly. Alex is a special case. I indulged him too much."

"Why? Because he was your first success with psychic driving?"

He lifted his chin and sniffed the air again, his smile seeming more forced than a few seconds before. "I don't know who's been telling you stories, Meredeth, but I assure you they are no more than that. Besides, my children didn't disobey me much more than one or two times."

"Or you killed them," said Kevin in a flat voice.

"No, Chief Saunders, I didn't. The ones who couldn't get with the program, I sent on their way with a hundred bucks and a change of clothing. Where they went after I dropped them in Rochester, I couldn't say."

"It's strange that you'd make that claim," Meredeth said slowly. "I have it on good authority you killed the ones that resisted."

"Good authority, Mare? Are you kidding? Who is a better authority on the subject than little old me?"

"For now, I'll keep that to myself."

"*Of course* you will." He leaned forward, cocking his head as he did so, and looked her up and down. "Are you feeling okay, Mare? You look peaked, and there's an odor… Shall we continue this another time?"

Meredeth flashed a shark's grin at him. "No, no. I'm fine, John, but thanks for your concern." She leaned forward and looked him up and down, the grin turning sly as she mimicked the man. "Want to tell me about Darrell Rogers?"

"Who?" asked Doe, making a show of examining his fingernails.

"Oh, come on, John," she said. "You know the real names of your victims, don't you?"

"I'm afraid I have no idea to whom you are referring."

"Fine. You renamed him Randall. He was the next abduction after Missy Smith's."

"Missy Smith?" he said, looking down at the table and smearing his finger across the shiny surface.

"That's Alex Delamort's real name—as you already know," said Bobby. "And her gender, I guess."

"No, Van Zandt," grated Ankou. "That is not anyone's real name. And Alex is one hundred percent male."

"Except for her genitals," said Meredeth. "Those are one hundred percent female."

"Alex is transgender," said Doe.

"No." Meredeth stared at him, but Ankou wouldn't look at her.

"We can deny transgender issues all we want. They still exist, and the people facing them have enough—"

"Oh, get off your soap box, Doe," said Bobby. "We all know you brainwashed Missy Smith. You *programmed* her to think of herself as a male serial killer. That's not the same thing."

"Isn't it?" asked Doe, his face the very picture of innocence.

"It really isn't," said Meredeth. "You turned Missy Smith, a thirteen-year-old *girl*, into a cold-blooded killer. Not satisfied with that, you pushed further, imbuing gender dysphoria and a false sense of gender identity in her, both of which only made her compulsion to murder stronger, her bias toward violence more intense. Neither of those qualities are seen much in the transgender community."

"Tomato, to*mahto*," said Doe, flipping one hand back and forth. "*Alex* is male at heart, and that's what matters. Missy Smith ceased to be a long time ago. Calling Alex by that name will only enrage him." His mouth settled into a grim line as he sniffed the air again, then he bunched his brows and sniffed his underarm. He shook his head and smiled when he caught Meredeth watching the song and dance. "You see, I am the true master of psychic driving. I've got so much deeper than Dr. Cameron was allowed to consider. There's no coming back from my technique."

"Isn't there?" asked Meredeth in a sickly-sweet voice.

"No, of course not," said Doe. "I broke those kids down to nothing, then built them back up, *molded* them in my own image, and they are all the better for it."

"The lies you do tell yourself, John," mused Meredeth.

"Lies? *LIES*?" He pushed himself halfway to his feet, but in the time it took Meredeth to draw breath, Henedy stepped forward and clamped Doe's shoulder with an iron grip. "Settle down, inmate," the guard grated.

Meredeth didn't so much as twitch from John's display. She was tired from the morning's activities—exhausted really—but even more than that, she didn't believe Ankou would do her harm. Not yet. Not until their battle of wits had lost his interest. "Yes, John. Lies. You and I both know your technique didn't work one hundred percent of the time. We both know you killed the ones who resisted openly, and we both know some of your children have broken away from you."

A slow grin spread across John's lips, and he shook Henedy's hand off his shoulder. He sank into his chair. "Well, now I know who's been telling tales out of school...that ungrateful little *bitch*."

"Uh, I think you've got the wrong impression, John. I've been speaking to a man."

"No, you've been speaking to Michelina—oh, excuse me, *Julie*. Julie Fuchs." He sneered at her.

Meredeth cocked her head to the side. "Who?" She glanced at Bobby. "What was his name?"

"Uh..." Bobby began flipping through his notepad. "The most recent one?"

"Oh! I remember! He said his name was Carl."

Doe broke into a harsh cackle. "Oh, my dear Meredeth. The lies you do tell."

Meredeth shrugged. "That's the name he gave us."

"No," said Doe, shaking his head. "You will meet Carl soon enough. And though I give you credit for the attempt, Carl would no more speak to you than he would walk into a police station and give himself up."

"That's not far from the truth," said Bobby.

Doe sobered, and an expression of concern distended his face. "What are you saying, Van Zandt?"

"Carl got himself pinched, John," said Meredeth in a quiet voice. "He's trading information about you and your grand plan for years off his sentence."

Brows furrowed, John stared at her for almost a minute, then his expression relaxed, and he chuckled. "You almost got me, Mare."

Meredeth shrugged. "Think what you like. I don't know this Michelina person. Not by any name."

"Yes, you do." He leaned back and showed her a snarky smile. "You'd better talk to her fast and get everything you can."

"What's that supposed to mean? Are you threatening to have her killed in front of two FBI agents and a police chief?" Kevin snorted. "And all this time I thought you had brains."

"You mistake my meaning, Chief Saunders. I merely meant that Michelina is a fickle soul."

"Uh-huh."

"Let's stop wasting time, John," said Meredeth. "Tell me about Mack and Lucy."

"Who?"

Nodding, Meredeth leaned forward and stared into his eyes. "You know who. Steven Aldridge. Victim number four from the original abduction spree. And Stephanie Milneaux, renamed Lucy."

"Original spree?" Doe chuckled. "Are you implying there's been more than one? What evidence do you have to support that?"

Meredeth grinned like the Cheshire cat. "You gave it to us back at the Branch farm, remember?"

Ankou frowned and looked perplexed.

"The young man out by the barn? Remember?"

"I had nothing to do with that."

"You expect us to believe a stranger appeared at the perfect moment to split the party in two and give you the opportunity to abduct me?"

"I expect you to believe the truth. At any rate, that hardly constitutes evidence that *I* kidnapped additional children, now does it?"

"It does," said Bobby with a slick smile. "He was too young, Johnny-boy."

Doe cast an irritated glance at Bobby. "Next time, Agent Connelly, come alone if you want me to talk."

"Oh, I don't think so. Next time, I'll probably be coming to notify you of additional charges and read you your

Miranda rights. *Again*." She cocked her head and leaned back in her chair. "Unless that is..."

"Unless what?" John snapped.

"Unless you start giving us reasons *not* to file additional charges."

"You're asking me to rat on one of my children? Didn't we dispense with that nonsense last time?" His face bore a smile, but his eyes contained only vehemence and anger.

"John, John, John," she said with a sigh. "When you gave your test to Alex, did you expect him to bash that homeless man's skull in with that hammer, or did you expect him to balk?"

"I never gave Alex a test," he said in a firm voice. "By the time he was who he is, there was no need to test him."

"Oh, that's right. You tested *Missy*, didn't you?"

"No. By the time I tested any of my children—and I'm not admitting the methods you claim I tested Alex with have any relation to the truth of the matter—they no longer thought of themselves by the names their horrible mothers gave them."

"Fine. What name was Missy going by at the time of her test?"

John shrugged and grinned at her. "Alexis, of course."

"Uh-huh," said Meredeth. "And after she killed the man in the alley, you took her to Julie's house, and she helped you murder Julie's family? She did what *you told her* to do?"

Doe spread his hands. "Oh, Mare, I almost feel sorry for you. If this is all you've got, you don't have anything to threaten me with." He laughed, his eyes dancing as he shifted his gaze from hers to Bobby's and then to Kevin's.

Meredeth waited, counting to two hundred in her head, and the silence fell across the room like a blanket of snow in the wake of a strong blizzard. When she spoke next, she smiled wide and widened her eyes. "What makes you think that's all I've got?"

John's whole face twitched, almost like an involuntary reaction to getting poked in the eye, and the mirth left his expression *tout de suite*. "What else?" he demanded, all pretense of happy-go-lucky Ankou discarded like the foil top on one of the juice cups they served prisoners at Wende.

"Why would I share information with you, John? You're giving us nothing. Tell me about Mack, Carl, and Lucy. Tell me about their roles in the plan, and I'll consider telling you what I know."

"*Little bitch!*" John muttered. "Duplicitous little bitch!"

"Oh, you cut me, John," she said with a snicker.

"Not you!" he snapped crossly. "Michelina!"

"Back to that, John? Really? I told you it was a man calling himself Carl, and I told you why he's willing to talk."

"Is that so, Old Mare? If what you said is true, you can tell me which city Carl resides in."

"He was picked up in San Diego for possession," she said, and by the genuine smile that spread across Doe's face, she knew she'd screwed it up.

"I don't think so, Agent Connelly. No, I'm sure Michelina is the traitor. You know what happens to snitches, don't you?"

"Again with the threats?"

"Not at all," said John, spreading his hands as wide as he could with them shackled to his waist. "It's a common sentiment. 'Snitches end up in ditches.'"

"Great, we can add another murder to your sentence if this woman is killed."

"Oh, I assure you I will have nothing to do with it. Many people view snitches as traitors, as people not worth saving. I'm sure someone will sort her out."

"Someone like Carl? Or maybe Lucy?" she all but snapped.

"My dear, you just told me Carl is in custody in San Diego. Why would I expect him to do *anything*?"

Meredeth's head ached and ached, and the damn urge to cough had resurfaced. She glanced at Henedy. "Could I get a bottle of water, Officer Henedy?"

"I can't leave him unsupervised. I'm sorry."

"I'll go," said Kevin, and the door behind her buzzed, then slammed shut.

"Listen, John," said Bobby. "As much fun as all this is, would it be so crazy for you to give us a hint about your plan?"

"What is it you think Mack or Lucy or *Carl* has done?"

Meredeth covered her eyes and massaged her temples. Each breath seemed to bring her closer to vomiting all over the table.

"Mare? Are you unwell?" asked John in a parody of concern. "Henedy, I think Agent Connelly needs assistance."

"No, I don't," she said. "I'm fine, John."

"You don't look it."

"The water will fix me right up. Which of your victims uses a semi to commit murder? Has he or she always killed with that semi? Did you buy them the truck?"

"Semi?" asked Doe, but Meredeth thought she saw a touch of fear in his eyes.

"Sure. The one he's been using for years to run people off the road and kill them."

"My, my," muttered John. "And you're sure one of my *children* is responsible for all this?"

Meredeth watched him closely, tracking his micro expressions. "You are a good liar, John. You probably fool most people."

"But not you?" He smiled at her sweetly.

"Sometimes I think you might pull it off one day, but not always. Today is one of the latter varieties."

"And not with respect to this mad trucker and his vile activities?"

She shook her head in the negative.

"Oh, my, my, my, my, my." He lowered his head so that he could drum his fingers on his lips. "You mean I'm giving everything away by talking to you? Maybe I should refuse your requests for an interview from now on."

"Sure, you can do that," she said with a shrug. "You will lose any opportunity to help yourself, but it's your choice."

Doe threw back his head and laughed, his cackles reverberating around the small room. "This is why I talk to you, Old Mare. You can be so funny, so entertaining. You might not know this, but prison is *boring*." He turned a little in his chair and speared Officer Henedy with a hot glare. "Few people here can carry on an intelligent conversation."

"Do you know why I talk to you, John?"

He returned his attention to her face, his eyes narrowed a little. "Because I'm so charming?"

"I talk to you, John, to learn about your family. That's what you want, isn't it? To gain recognition for your accomplishments with psychic driving?"

"That's not bad, Mare." He treated her to a snide half grin. "A little clumsy on your part, but the sentiment shows you are not entirely composed of vegetable matter like Van Zandt."

"Why, thank you, John."

"I believe in giving credit where it's due. Of course, such ham-handed appeals to my vanity will get you nowhere, but at least you tried something new."

"John, I'm just trying to give you an excuse to do what you so clearly want to do."

Ankou tilted his head to the side and scrunched his brows. "Oh? And what is it I clearly want to do?"

"You want to impress me with your intellect, your cold heart, your dedication to your plan and ideals."

He raised both eyebrows and tilted his head to the other side. "You could be a worthy opponent after all, Meredeth."

"Thank you, John. You are very generous with your compliments today."

"As I said...credit where it's due."

"What is it you want me to know about Mack, Carl, Lucy, and Michelina? I'm here to listen."

"Then why come in here with your vacuous threats, your clunky intimidation tactics?"

"I had to establish my baseline, didn't I?"

"Oh, I see. We're to engage in a little behavioral analysis, are we? That's a two-way street, Agent Connelly."

"Yes, I understand that, John. I imagine that every time we speak, you learn about what makes me tick."

He inclined his head, and when he raised it again, he was smiling. "At last, we dispense with the fencing."

"John, I'm a mere FBI agent. Yes, I have over two decades of experience in tracking serial offenders, but at the end of the day, I only have the tools the Bureau trained me to use. And I admit I didn't like you very much after the incident back on your farm. I—"

"Please allow me to interrupt. By implication, are you admitting you now enjoy my company? And, by the way, you are hardly a mere FBI agent. We both know that."

"Do you think so?"

"I wouldn't waste my time otherwise. For example, I wouldn't talk to Van Zandt on his own."

"Don't sell him short, John. Your view of Bobby and Kevin is skewed by your own psychological needs."

Again, he flashed a one-sided, snide smile. "And what needs are those?"

"Come on, John. You said we were dispensing with the fencing. You know what I'm referring to."

Doe waved a hand. "My need to control, to dominate."

"Of course," she said with a nod. "Would it be crazy if we stop pretending that we don't understand each other?"

"You don't understand everything about my character."

"That's true, of course, just as you don't have a complete understanding of mine."

He inclined his head once again.

"With that as our basis, what is it you want to tell me about...oh, say Michelina. Julie Fuchs."

John glanced at Bobby and Kevin, then met Meredeth's gaze. "She's a duplicitous person. She lies like you and I breathe. And she's hardly an innocent babe in the woods. If you knew what she'd done, you would break off all contact with her."

Meredeth shook her head. "John, I'm not in contact with anyone named Julie Fuchs. I told you we've been speaking to a male victim of yours."

"*Child of mine*," he grated

"Potato, po*tah*to," she said with a grin.

"Touché." Though he returned her grin, his expression wasn't entirely friendly. "But, come now, Meredeth. You don't expect me to believe you spoke with Carl."

Her grin widened. "You can't blame me for trying, John. It's not as if I can freely tell you who we're speaking to. You'd have him killed."

John shrugged. "I am cut off from the world, Mare. You saw to that. No internet, remember? How would I orchestrate this assassination?"

"I'm sure you are in contact with your...*children*."

He nodded and smiled. "Thank you for not saying victims."

"There's no reason for animosity between us, John. I hope you'll tell me if you disagree?"

"At this time, I agree."

"The last time we spoke, you said my nature and yours dictate that we fight, and that our fight had only just started."

"That is all true." He assumed a more comfortable position, hampered only by the shackles on his wrists and feet. "Can we have done with these restraints?" he asked idly.

"I see no harm in it," said Meredeth.

"Good. Let's get them off so I can be comfortable."

"Give us something, first," said Bobby. "Anything about one of the children Meredeth asked you about."

Doe's gaze never left her own, and she gave him a curt nod. Tilting his head to the side and rolling his eyes, Doe said, "*Fine*. Mack has the capacity to elude you forever, Mare. He has nothing permanent in his life. No home now, not even the farm. He will never go back there. Not now, not with me in prison. He's totally free—no ties to anyone or anything."

"That's helpful," said Meredeth, nodding to Officer Henedy. "Please remove the cuffs on his hands."

The guard made a face when Doe turned toward him and lifted his cuffed wrists, but he stepped forward and took off the bracelets. "These can go back on just as fast as they come off, Doe."

"Yes, yes," said John in a longsuffering tone.

"With no home, Mack must get very tired of couch surfing. How does he relax?"

John chuckled. "I asked him once. He told me he relaxes by driving. He always had an affinity for road trips. He said it's the only thing he's ever truly loved." With a shrug, Doe winked at Meredeth. "Of course, we both knew killing was something he loved more."

"Speaking of his love for murder, what's his method?" asked Bobby.

"His method is so far off your radar, that if I tell you, Van Zandt, you'll accuse me of lying."

"We happen to be tracking a string of cases that have us a little stumped," said Meredeth. "That's why we're asking you so many questions about your...your family."

"Ah," Ankou said with a gravedigger's smile. "Tell me the details, and I'll see if I can help."

"The press is calling him the Highwayman. He kills in a very impersonal way—with a semi—and there's no way he can return to the bodies, or even the scenes—at least, not without drawing a lot of attention to himself," said Bobby. "I can't figure it. What would someone like you get out of a sterile murder with no real contact between you and the victim?"

"Well, I don't know about *someone like me*, but I can tell you that *I* would get nothing from it. I am not motivated by biology, Agent Bobby."

"Okay, leaving aside that your answer was complete bullshit and everyone in this room knows it, which of your children would get off on what I described?"

Doe sniffed and looked at him. "Mack has this thing. Like me, he hates rudeness. Mack also hates poor driving; he hates aggressiveness and road rage. Carl is a different sort. His motivations are definitely biologic. He enjoys blood and fire. Both are motivated to assuage his own needs, like everyone else."

"Between the two, which would be most suited for such impersonal killings?"

Doe spread his hands. "That, I don't know."

"Why doesn't he stage the scenes?" asked Bobby. "It almost looks as if he's trying to hide the crimes, rather than call attention to them."

"That's the thing with your narrow views of serial murder," said Ankou. "You always assume the murder, the ritual, is the most important component of the crime. That isn't always the case. I instilled a pleasure response in my children derived from staying off the radars of people like you. From the way you describe it, it sounds like the Highwayman takes that sentiment to the extreme. And I think I might know who he is, but it's all mere speculation. If you share the details of the crime, perhaps I can do better than guess."

Meredeth glanced at Bobby. "Do you recognize something in what we told you so far?"

Ankou nodded, a fox's grin on his lips. "One of my sons once told me he could go on and on, killing people who've wronged him, and no one would even know he was committing murders on a regular basis, let alone be able to tie the crimes to him."

"Then a lack of signature is sort of his signature?"

"You could say that," Doe muttered. "But I know him. You give me a list of suspected crimes, and I can tell you if it's my boy or not."

"I thought you were loyal to your children," said Bobby.

"I am. I always am. But, Van Zandt, you will never catch this boy, so I can tell you everything you want to know about him. He doesn't mind. He's so far above your vantage he can afford to look down, watch your antics, and laugh."

"I'm having trouble with this, John," said Meredeth. "He's a mission-oriented killer, then? Highly organized? Power and control motivated?"

Doe flapped his hand as if shooing away flies. "Serial killers defy classification by their very natures, Meredeth. You know that."

"I'm not sure I do, John. For example, none of you feel guilt or empathy toward your victims."

"Michelina does. I imagine we all do to some extent."

"And thrill-seeking behavior? Arrogance? Lack of or shallow emotions?"

A lopsided smile surfaced on Doe's face. "Just because you don't understand how we experience emotions—or how they affect us—doesn't mean that we don't experience genuine emotions. Not all serial killers are motivated by excitement, either. I'll give you that we tend to more than our fair share of hubris."

"That's interesting, John. You told me once that you were a new breed of serial offender. That the world had never seen anyone like you."

"I did?"

"Yes, you did. Do you not feel that way?"

"Oh, I do, I just don't remember sharing that feeling with you."

"What exactly do you mean by a 'new breed?'"

"Leg shackles first," he said with a grin.

Meredeth nodded to Henedy, whose grimace reached epic proportions before he knelt by John's side and removed the leg irons.

"Ah, that's better," said John. "It's nice to be able to stretch out, to be comfortable. I'll probably give you more information than I intend to as I relax, but thank you for doing the decent thing."

Meredeth's shoulders twitched up and down. "What did you mean by a 'new breed?'"

"My own crimes—the murders, the kidnappings— served a greater purpose than my own basic needs. In essence, I am a moral serial killer."

"I'm not sure I get it," said Bobby.

"He's saying that his crimes serve the greater good. How is that, John? How does what you've done set you apart?"

"My actions were mere steps taken toward a better future for all."

"How's that?" blurted Kevin.

"Our culture is crippled by its own weakness, therefore what you blindly accept as ethics are nothing more than a method of control. Those in control aren't subject to them. The majority of the population needs to wake up, to assume the mantle of self-guided morality and do away with those leaders."

"How does murder—"

Meredeth held up her hand to stop Bobby, then said, "And where do I fit in to that goal?"

"Two ways: First, you have to realize how your own personal controllers have impacted you and those around you."

"Those around me... You mean Kenny?"

Doe nodded. "You told me you had no choice in the matter, but I think you did. No one used sleep deprivation or ECT on you, Agent Connelly, and you're missing the first ten years of your life—or were until we met."

"I'm sure I was medicated with hypnogogic drugs. I might have even been hypnotized."

Ankou shrugged, a mischievous gleam in his eye. "Those are both probably accurate guesses, but hypnosis requires tacit approval to work. Don't you agree?"

"I've never thought about that."

"The 'Manchurian Candidate' effect requires the tacit cooperation of the person in question. We know that for a fact. Otherwise, the attempt is destined to fail."

"Is that why you abandoned hypnotism in favor of psychic driving?"

His smile was slow but broad. "Very good, Agent Connelly. Your intelligence and instincts do you credit."

"How many children did you attempt to hypnotize before giving it up?" asked Bobby.

"You are always after quantifiers, Van Zandt. That's the sign of a weak mind. In answer, I'll tell you that I made sufficient attempts to verify the conclusions about so-called 'Manchurian Candidate' sleepers."

"And that's what you need, isn't it?" asked Meredeth. "Sleepers. Your children might feed their own demons, but they do it safely—as Alex did—until you need them. Does it require contact? Do you have to speak to them to activate your sleepers?"

"Not at all," said Doe. "They know what I need from them and when."

"And when they start killing to serve your plan, they begin to mark their victims with your Trinity Knot."

John lifted his hands from the table and spread them wide. "How would you know the credit for those kills is mine, otherwise?"

"Walk me through how this is going to change society," said Kevin. "Because I don't see how these isolated incidents will effect anything."

"They are pebbles rolling down a mountainside. Each examined in isolation is nothing more than a pebble, but when viewed as a whole, those little pebbles become a landslide."

"If you say so," said Kevin.

"Have faith, Chief," said Ankou, and he grinned his death's head grin.

"Okay. That's your overall intention," said Meredeth as she rubbed her temples again. "Why am—"

"Excuse me, Meredeth," said Doe. "Are you unwell?" He sniffed the air. "By the odor, I'd say Alex's knife lacerated part of your digestive track."

"Never mind that, you—"

"It's okay, Kevin," Meredeth breathed. "To be honest, John, I haven't been my best since Alex revealed himself to me. I tire easily, and I'm not back to work yet. But what I'm feeling now is a combination of fatigue and a migraine."

"Oh, poor girl," said Doe in a flat voice and with an expression that contained no human warmth. "We should stop here, in that case. I can't take advantage of your injury. Come again when you've fully recovered. We can pick this up when you are more fully yourself."

"No, it's okay, John, but I do appreciate the thought. You said earlier that the Highwayman has the potential to elude me. What traits or skills did you train into him that give him this advantage?"

With a smile, Ankou said, "That's clever, Old Mare, but I said *Mack* has the potential to elude you, not your Highwayman." He peered at her, a slight frown on his face. "But I think my assessment of your condition was accurate. I'll answer this last question, but that is all." He turned toward Henedy and snapped one of the bracelets on his left wrist, then held his right out toward the guard.

"And it's less something that Mack has as something he lacks. Unlike me, Mack has no need of an audience. He doesn't care if you or I or anyone else knows what he's doing. He's doing what he wants, by methods of his own devising, and once he leaves his victim, he stops caring about them at all. You see, Mack lives entirely in the moment. In that way, he's like a wolf, attacking from stealth, making his kill, then fading into the night without looking back."

"I see," said Meredeth. "Humor me with one more question. What—"

"*No!*" snapped Ankou. "I'm done for now, and if you have any common sense, you'll return to your home and deal with your ostomy. You will clean yourself, Meredeth, so you no longer smell of manure. And you look like death warmed over. Get some rest. Once you've recovered, we can talk again, but not until then."

"It's just one more—"

"*I said no!*" he shouted. He stood, even though Henedy hadn't finished securing his feet. "We can finish this in the hall, Henedy." Without waiting for Henedy's response, Doe walked out of the room and stood facing the concrete blocks that lined the hallway leading deeper into the prison.

Henedy muttered a curse, then flashed an apologetic smile at Meredeth. "Feel better, Agent Connelly." Then, he too was gone.

CHAPTER 22

GREASY SIDE UP

Alden, NY

MEREDETH LOWERED HERSELF into the passenger seat of Kevin's cruiser, then sighed with relief. Her belly was sore, the constant movement, the sitting upright, the waistband of her pants all contributing to her general misery by applying constant pressure to the wafer that held her ostomy bag to her belly. As Bobby slid in behind her and Kevin closed her door and walked around the rear of the car, she said, "Tell the truth, Bobby. Can you smell me?"

"Not even a little, Mere. He was antagonizing you."

"You're not fibbing to spare my feelings?"

"No. I'd tell you if I could smell anything."

"Good. Kevin has enough to deal with."

Saunders opened the driver's door and got in. He started the cruiser with a flip of his wrist. "Home?" he asked.

"No, let's go to the station. We can set up in—"

"That's a non-starter, Mere," he said in a gentle voice. "Doe wasn't lying. You don't look so good."

"I'm *fine*, Kevin, and we need to—"

"He's right, boss," said Bobby. "You need to rest. If you wear yourself down to a nub, your surgery will get postponed."

She rubbed her forehead with her thumb and index finger. "Look, guys, I'm a grown woman, and I—"

"Should have learned to listen to good advice long before now," Kevin finished for her. "You, Meredeth Lynne Connelly, are going home to rest. You've had a long day."

"But it's not even two o'clock!" She hated the whiny quality of her voice. *I must sound like a petulant child*, she thought and rolled her head to lean her forehead against the passenger window. "I'll rest on the ride."

"I'm still taking you home, then I'll run Bobby back out to the crime scene if he wants."

"Usually, I just stand around and keep the local cops occupied while Mere does her thing. I don't really need to see it if Meredeth has."

"And we have work to do," said Meredeth. "We need to discuss what Doe said and did, what he told us about the Highwayman. We need to—"

"As I said, Meredeth: You need to go home and rest, sleep if you can. We can discuss everything after you have recovered some energy. Remember what Dr. Atallah told you."

"Yeah, yeah," she grumbled.

"Come on, Mere," said Bobby. "Don't be like that. If anything, the way you are acting should show you how right Kevin is."

"I know," she said, "but I'm sick and tired of..." She shook her head and clicked her tongue against her teeth.

"Sick and tired of being sick and tired?" asked Bobby with laughter in his voice.

"Yeah." She couldn't help but smile.

"Well, the treatment for that is having your surgery as soon as possible, not working yourself half to death and having Dr. Atallah say you are too rundown for the surgery. Keep in mind how much the first surgery took out of you. Remember the constant napping, all that. It's better to rest when you need to *now*, rather than go through that again, isn't it?"

"That was because the first surgery lasted five and a half hours. They had to use a lot of anesthetic, and that takes time to clear out of your body."

"Maybe in part," said Kevin. "But we both know that exhaustion lasted much longer than it takes for your body to metabolize the drugs. Darren said as much."

"I know," she said in a little girl's voice. "But—"

"Meredeth, I'm not going back until tomorrow. We can talk after you've rested. And while you are sleeping, Kevin can fill me in about the scene—and how surly you've been."

She chuckled at that. She wanted to be irritated, but Bobby was...well, he was *Bobby*, and he had the gift of making her feel better, no matter what.

"You've got until I get you home to discuss Doe," said Kevin. "Once we're there, you're taking a nap."

"Yes, dear," she said with a grin.

"Do we believe him?" asked Bobby.

"That he can't reach out to his victims with instructions? Not at all. There are myriad ways to sneak instructions out of prison. A buddy who has access to the library computers. A guy about to get parole. Coded letters, ESP..."

"What about that stuff about his kids?"

"I believe that Ankou believes what he said. I'm not sure how objective he is. As for his purposes in doing what he's done, I don't buy his explanation. It sounded too much like justification to act how he wants. He makes it sound like a noble mission to 'wake society up' to the dangers of our culture, but in the end, he murdered people, he kidnapped God only knows how many children, and he tortured those poor kids to turn them into his pet psychopaths."

"And he murdered the ones who didn't play along."

"That's right. Where's the morality in all that?" She snapped her mouth shut as her phone pinged.

"Your deep-throat contact?" asked Bobby.

Meredeth looked at her email client and nodded, then began to read aloud.

Dear Meredeth,

I'm writing because I just had an epiphany. Or maybe I broke through some programming Ankou set in my brain. Either way, I think I have something that will help.

Mack stole a truck a short time before he left the farm. And that's a euphemism for killing the owner and taking ownership of the semi. Ankou helped him fix it up. Carl was also intensely interested in the thing, and for a while, he idolized Mack and what Mack had done with Alex on the way to Jonodot had elevated them both to walk-on-water status in his young eyes. Mack taught Carl all about trucks, both mechanically and how to drive one. They were both infatuated with semi-trucks, and both had plans for keeping themselves out of trouble by travelling constantly.

The Highwayman could be either one of them. If I had to decide right now, my guess would favor Carl, but full disclosure, I had a crush on Mack.

I hope it helps. Maybe you can ask Ankou about them?

I know I owe you a longer email, answers to your questions, and I promise to find time to write you soon. I just wanted to put this out there in case you visit him in Wende.

Yours,

Meredeth sighed and rubbed her eyes. "Well, there you go. We've just narrowed down the suspect pool to two individuals, both of whom are victims of John Doe."

CHAPTER 23

FULL BORE

David Branch's Farm, NY

THE TRUCK WAS a work of art, a real thing of beauty, and Mack was proud of it. It hadn't been easy—neither he nor his father really knew the details of how a big diesel engine worked, and he'd had to spend at least as much time studying how the truck worked as he had working on it. But, at the end of the day, it had only made him better equipped for the life he envisioned for himself. And, it had been fun to take Carl under his wing.

Between the three of them and a couple of internet forums, they'd managed to rebuild the old engine and retuned it for a little more power, a little more torque. In addition, they'd added the thick bull bar his father had suggested and had beefed up the already heavy-duty suspension and brakes. It was more tank than semi-tractor, but it would still haul freight.

He was ready...ready to hit the open road, ready to set out on his own, to live his own life. There was only one thing left to check off his mental list.

The test.

He'd tried to speak to his father about it, tried to wrangle a little information from the man, but he should have known better. Beyond tight-lipped smiles, his father hadn't responded to any of his questions. Alex had told him to relax, that the tests were always easy, and better yet, *fun*. Mack was still nervous, however. Failing one of his father's tests was a sure way to end up in the box for more sleep deprivation—or worse yet, ECT.

Michelina stood beside him in the fall sun, looking up at the giant truck, a small smile playing on her lips.

"Do you like it?" he asked.

"It's a thing of beauty, Mack."

"I hope Father agrees."

"Of course he will. He's been helping you every step of the way."

"I'll be leaving soon if he does," he said and was surprised by the stricken look that passed over Michelina.

"You'll be leaving soon *when* he does, Mack. It's not like he's done all this work only to keep you here for another few years. Trust me, you'll face your test, pass it, and be gone." She glanced at him shyly. "I only wish..."

He gave her his full attention. "You only wish what?" he asked, though he thought he knew. "That you could come with me?"

She blushed but nodded.

Mack felt heat in his face. "But you know the plan. We're all to separate, to go our own ways."

"Yes," she said, averting her gaze and keeping her face pointed toward the ground. "The truck is lovely, Mack."

"Thanks." *Why is she acting like this*? he wondered.

She turned and almost ran back up to the house. Mack watched her every step of the way, his thoughts awhirl. He climbed up into the cab and started the big rig, letting it idle to warm up the oil and engine components. His father would be out any moment, and when he came, he'd want to leave. He hadn't told Mack where they'd go, only to make sure the truck looked its best and had full fuel tanks.

Mack fiddled in the cab, adjusting the seat again and again until he felt comfortable, until he could reach the plethora of switches and push buttons on the dash. He knew exactly what each control did and when he should use them, but even so, he studied the layout again. He needed to know it like it was second nature to him. He couldn't give any onlookers any reason to doubt he was fully licensed. He couldn't give any police officer any reason to pull him over.

Father had fixed the VIN and obtained both registrations and class A CDLs that would return real data if a police officer ran the number. Each set of registration,

CDL, and license plates bore a different name—and he had enough of them that he could switch plates as many times as he liked, and no one would be the wiser. Now, all that was left was proving himself to the man who'd raised him, who'd saved him from a banal life filled with shifts at the knife factory back home and too many beers drank late into the night.

"Ready to go?" asked Alex. He stood on the ground outside the open driver's side door, looking up at Mack with a strange emotion in his eyes.

"Just waiting for Father to tell me what I need to do."

"I wish I could change places with you. Hell, to feel what you're feeling right now, and what you *will* feel later..." Alex sucked in a breath. "I wish I could go back in time, knowing what I know now, and enjoy my first kill. At the time, I thought it was something I had to get through."

"And now you know better?"

"Sure. But this isn't your first in any case. Even so, savor the time with Father, and listen to everything he says. Sear it into your memory."

"I will," Mack said. As Alex nodded and turned to go, Mack jumped down and caught him up in a big bear hug. "Thank you, Alex. Thanks for everything," he whispered.

"We'll see each other again, Mack. This isn't goodbye."

Mack nodded, but he knew Alex was wrong. If he succeeded in passing his test, he'd be gone—gone on to his life—the open road, hauling freight, bad drivers, rude drivers, dangerous drivers. And if he didn't, after all Father had spent on the truck, he didn't like his chances of coming back with him to try again. He released his littler older brother and thumped him on the shoulder with a closed fist. "Follow your dream, Alex. Get that law degree. It's a perfect cover."

Alex gave him a rare, full smile and tossed him a wink. "You'll come to visit. We'll hang out, and it will be like it always was."

"That's right," said Mack.

At that moment, their father came out of the house. He wore steel-toed boots, blue jeans, a western shirt, and a trucker cap. "Is everything ready, Mack?"

Mack nodded. "Yessir."

"Good." Father turned his gaze on Alex. "You're in charge until I come back. It might be a few days, or it might be later tonight."

Alex threw a quick glance at Mack, then nodded. "Everything will be fine, Father. I've got the new ones in hand, and the rest are progressing nicely."

"I know." He turned away from Alex and jerked his chin at the truck. "Show me how you drive this thing, Mack."

With a grin that stretched from ear to ear, Mack turned and jogged to the truck. He leaped up into the cab and pulled the door shut behind him. As he waited for Father to walk around the truck and climb in, he glanced up at the second-floor windows and caught a glimpse of Michelina's teary face before she dropped the curtains.

Mack didn't understand her. They'd used each other's bodies more than once, but it seemed to mean something to her that it didn't to him. He stared at the window a moment, lost in thought about her strange behaviors. It was almost as if she were faking being cold and hard.

He shrugged. He'd never faked anything, and he'd made her no silly promises they could never keep. For a moment, he considered telling Father about the strange dichotomy in her behaviors—one set for Father, Alex, and the rest of them, another set for Mack.

No, he decided. He didn't have much empathy, but he didn't want to see Michelina suffer. He didn't want to be the cause of her suffering, either.

Father yanked open the passenger side door and climbed aboard. "This beauty sounds ready. Are you sure *you* are, Mack?"

That confirmed Mack's feeling that it was do or die time, but the fact of the matter was that he *was* ready. More than ready. He'd learned everything Father had instructed him to learn. He'd listened to all his lectures, his talks, his silences, and he'd extracted the principles and techniques that allowed him to concoct his slightly-off-center approach. His gratitude toward the man was as big as the truck and trailer combined. "Yessir. I'm as ready as I'll ever be. It will either be enough or..." He let the sentence die as he met Father's direct gaze.

Father lifted his chin half an inch and returned Mack's gaze, the picture of calm, the eye of a hurricane. "You understand what's at stake, Mack. I see it in your eyes. Alex is smart and picks up things quickly, as are you and as do you. But in many ways, you have the advantage over him. The minute details never escape you. You have been a great student and will make a great man, a great soldier in the plan. I have every confidence you will pass this final test. This *graduation* test."

Mack nodded.

"You will be the first to graduate. I'd thought it would be Alex or Michelina since they started before you, but neither of them has grasped what I have to see before graduation."

"A plan of our own devising," said Mack.

"Yes."

"Father, Alex has a plan. And it's a great one."

"Then why hasn't he voiced it?"

"He thinks you need him to help manage the barn."

Father lifted an eyebrow. "I appreciate you telling me. Perhaps Alex will join you in the world sooner than I thought."

"He wants to study law," Mack blurted. "Then become a prosecutor. I think it's a perfect cover."

Father's lips turned up in one of his rare smiles that reached his eyes. "It is a very good plan." Then he faced forward. "Take us off the farm, then head through Yoagoh."

"Yessir," said Mack as he wrenched the truck into reverse and performed a perfect J-turn despite the fifty-three-foot trailer. He didn't look back at the barn as they passed it, so he didn't see Carl watching them go with envy written across his face. Nor did he look at the house—he didn't want to catch Michelina doing whatever she was doing. His gaze was on the future.

His future.

CHAPTER 24

SLEEP MAKES YOU OLD

Hanable's Valley, NY

KEVIN HAD MADE it very clear that he expected her to *rest* while he and Bobby ran some "errands," but though she lay in Kevin's bed, she had two pillows stuffed behind her head and had her phone's browser open to Google. She was searching for motor vehicle accidents involving fatalities at mile marker thirty-three.

Her phone buzzed in her hand—the distinct pattern of vibrations she'd assigned to incoming emails—and she flipped to the app and saw a new email from Michelina. She opened it and started reading, a knot of anxiety in her belly that grew directly from John Doe's incredibly accurate guess of who had fed her information.

Dear Meredeth,

Thank you for the kind words in your last email, especially the bit about judgment. You do seem to understand the situation I was in—"Do it or die." In essence, my proffer for the AUSA is insider information on Ankou and his soldiers, including the crimes performed at Ankou's demand that I personally witnessed (including my own). I know I will have to give you details on my crimes, I'm just loath to even think about it.

I live in Virginia. Garrisonville, to be precise. That should be enough to move forward. Please make sure that information is sealed from everyone not involved in the case. Ankou's children exist in all walks of life, including at least one in law enforcement. Father would be very upset with me, and when Father's emotions are in control, things get terrible very quickly.

While I still have the nerve, let me tell you that I've committed three murders. I've been an accessory to five others and accessory after the fact in at least ten. I've honestly started to forget all the times Ankou woke me in the middle of the night and commanded me to start digging a grave.

Oh! Let's add that to my proffer. I will draw you a map of every grave site I can remember. That should give you plenty to hold over Ankou's head. You are right about the gossip about Alex. I have no direct knowledge of any of that, but I do have direct knowledge of other things, and I will both share that knowledge with you and provide a sworn statement to the AUSA.

Come to think of it, I do have direct knowledge of a couple of things that may help you get Ankou talking. One night, about two and a half years before I "graduated" and was able to get away from my "family," Ankou, Mack, and Alex left around midnight. Usually, that meant a new sibling would show up in the barn the following morning, but that particular night, the trio were only gone for about twenty-five minutes before they returned. They left in Ankou's old Ford and returned with both the Bronco and a seventies era Cadillac Fleetwood. That was one of the nights I had to get up and go dig a grave. A few months later, Alex and Mack left to pick up supplies in Jonodot. When they came home, Mack had a semi-tractor. They (Mack, Carl, and Ankou) worked on both vehicles, restoring them, altering the VINs, whatever. The car was sold, I know. The last time I saw the truck was the last time I saw Mack. He drove it off the farm with Ankou in the passenger seat—ostensibly on the way to Mack's test. Only Ankou returned, and it was without the truck. I bet you could track the vehicles down by disappearances in the area.

I am sure about the Cadillac. I think the truck was a Peterbilt. Something with numbers. Mack was wild about it.

I'm happy to add all that to your paperwork for the prosecutor's office. All I want in return from them is transactional immunity as we already discussed. All I want from you is your word to keep me out of the public eye.

And, yeah, you could say ViCAP constitutes big data ;)

I'll be watching for your documents and any emails you care to send.

Thank you, Agent Connelly, for your understanding.

Yours,

Michelina

P.S. Did the information about Mack and Carl help with your interview?

Meredeth read through the email a second time, wanting to ensure she hadn't missed anything. In her opinion, the proffer was coming together in a form the AUSA would accept. The map of the grave sites was huge, and the familiar old excitement danced in her belly. She tapped the reply button with her thumb and began typing.

Dear Michelina,

Thank you for your trust. You have my word that your location will never appear in any public documents. I am very concerned, however, at your revelation that one of Ankou's brainwashing victims works in law enforcement.

Please let me know who and the order in which this person was kidnapped.

Oh—your email arrived just as we were leaving Wende, but it helped us confirm a few things we extracted from Ankou during our interview. It will also give me ammunition for the next meeting.

The information you are offering the AUSA will tempt him to the extreme, and I honestly think you have a shot at full transactional immunity— but be forewarned, the AUSA for Eastern Virginia almost always requires testimony in court cases, should this come to that. I have no idea if it will. On the one hand, your information could topple Ankou's house of cards—especially with details like the two you shared about the vehicles. On the other, he's smart, and he knows that if he goes to court and your testimony is required, he will have the opportunity to cross-examine you.

I'm blown away you live in Garrisonville. I know exactly where that is! I'm just to the west in Tacketts Mill. Small world!

Thank you for your honesty about your involvement in so many crimes. I have my own hard information to pass on: Ankou's first reaction to me mentioning Mack, Carl, and Lucy, was to blame you. I believe we convinced him he was in error—that our informant was a male. If you can pass along a name of a man that might fit the bill, that would help solidify things for Ankou.

I'm very sorry about everything that happened to you. I'm not sure you are aware, but I worked on your kidnapping case back when it happened. I failed to close the case, I failed to rescue you, to save you from that torture. I'm glad to see that you've managed to pull away from the brainwashing.

I'll be traveling south tomorrow in anticipation of a second surgery. I'll have some time on the plane to finish up the proffer document for the AUSA and get it to you when we're at our hotel. I'll cc my partner on the email as I'll be out of the loop for a few days, and Bobby can help you get everything finalized. You can trust him, Michelina—he's a good man.

Please stay safe,

Meredeth

She went back and forth on the line "I believe we convinced him he was in error." The problem was, she didn't have any idea what Ankou had walked away believing. It was hubris to assert they'd convinced him of *anything*, but she could hardly say that and expect Michelina not to disappear forever. She felt guilty about the lie, but more so about not managing Ankou properly. She should have given more thought to a plausible story of where the information had come from. Her thumb alternated between hovering over the send button and the side of her phone case.

She *needed* Michelina's help. She had to send the email and try to convince the woman to take protection.

She'd just pressed send when Kevin opened the door as quietly as possible and peeked in on her. His face folded up like an old baseball mitt when he saw her sitting up and using her phone. "Have you rested? At *all*?"

"Kevin, I—"

"We have to fly *tomorrow*."

"I know."

"Then your surgery is the day after!"

"Yes," she said, meeting his gaze with a calm one of her own. "But I've been resting for weeks, and there are things that require my attention."

The war to suppress his anger played out on his face, but when he spoke next, his voice was gentle. "Michelina?"

"Yes, and trying to track down the Highwayman." She told him about the contents of Michelina's last email, and he whistled at the amount of potential information the woman had to offer. "You see? I have to get her proffer paperwork done so she can add the details and we can submit it as soon as she gets it back to us."

"I guess things are what they are with respect to your health. Nagging you doesn't seem to make an impact, so I guess I'll give it up."

"I'm tired, Kevin, but it's a good kind of tired."

He nodded, but he didn't smile.

"Besides, it's like that song says: 'Sleep makes you old.'"

CHAPTER 25

GRANNY LANE

Orlando, FL

AS KEVIN PULLED the rental car into a space near the hospital's entrance, he reached over and took her hand. "It's going to be fine," he said. "I checked Dr. Atallah out, and the man is the real deal. He's double board-certified and completed the Harvard Medical School Surgical Leadership Program. He's *pioneered* a couple of surgeries, including the robotic thing he did for you in St. Petersburg. You were lucky he was in town for that seminar and was willing to take on your case."

"I know. He's brilliant," she said. "And I'm not really nervous about the reversal—Dr. Atallah can do this with his eyes closed. Plus, I'm ready for this damn bag to go in the trash. I *am* worried about the recovery, though."

"It takes as long as it takes, Mere."

"Yeah, but it's going to take too long."

"Meredeth Lynne Connelly, it will take as long as it takes. Don't make me call your grandmother."

"You enjoy threatening me a little too much, Saunders," she said in a mock growl. "Besides, Grandma would be on *my* side."

"That's not what she told me last night. She said—and I'm quoting her here—'Don't let Meredeth wind herself up in knots. She's prone to that kind of thing. You'll have to take her in hand, Kevin. She's going to complain about the recovery. She's going to try to go back to work immediately. You can't let her do that until she's ready.'"

"When did you talk to her?"

"You were in the shower doing the antimicrobial thing. She also told me there's no sense trying to convince you to rest and recuperate. She said even as a child you resisted rest."

"Well…"

He grinned at her. "Nothing to worry about, Mere. It was just two people who love you commiserating about what a pain in the ass you can be."

"You love me?"

"Of course I do, FBI. Why else do you think I've been nagging you to keep hydrated and to rest? If you were any good at this profiling thing, you'd have known I fell for you almost immediately during the Ankou investigation. I've loved you for a long time, I was just too chicken-shit to come out with it."

She smiled at Kevin and gave his hand a squeeze. "I love you, too, Kevin Saunders." She glanced at the clock on the car's dash. "But, if I don't get inside, they're going to do the surgery without me."

He grinned, and they got out. They walked into the lobby and approached the reception desk.

"I'm Meredeth Connelly," she said to the woman behind the desk.

"You're here for surgery?"

"Yes, with Dr. Sam Atallah."

"Very good." The woman turned her attention to Kevin. "I assume you'll be waiting for your wife in the surgical waiting room?"

Meredeth flashed a one-sided smile at him. "Yes, he'll be staying close by."

The receptionist smiled. "I'll need your ID, sir, so I can print your visitor badge." She turned her attention back to Meredeth. "You can have a seat, and someone from the admitting department will be right out."

"Okay." She turned and took a seat that looked out the floor-to-ceiling glass on the parking lot. She heard Kevin's pleasant patter with the receptionist and grinned a little. She'd told him she wasn't nervous about the surgery, and that was true, but she *was* anxious—she wanted everything to speed up. She wanted to be done with the prep and to have propofol and go to sleep so she could wake up without the damn ileostomy. She wanted the surgical wounds to heal, she wanted to be on a regular diet, and she wanted to be independent, to take a shower on her own, to dress in her *real* clothes instead of the two-sizes-too-big crap she'd bought off Amazon. She just wanted it over.

Kevin joined her with a smile and a fancy printed sticker on his chest. "She admires you for keeping your own name."

Meredeth grinned. "I suppose we'll have to get used to people making assumptions. We're too much like an old married couple to expect anything different."

"I can think of worse things than that."

"Me, too."

"Maybe we should—"

"Ms. Connelly?" asked a young woman holding a clipboard.

"That's me."

"I have a few forms here that require your signature. Once we've handled that, a nurse will be out to take you back to the surgery waiting room."

"Okay. Just show me where you need my John Hancock."

"The first one is giving the hospital permission to treat you. It's standard."

"Fine," said Meredeth as she scrawled her signature on the line the woman pointed out.

The woman went on to explain the three other forms in excruciating detail, while Meredeth bit the inside of her cheek to avoid shouting at her to hurry up. Once she'd signed everything and the woman returned to the admissions department, she rolled her eyes at Kevin.

"I thought you might stab her with that pen," he said with a big smile.

"The thought did cross my mind." She returned his smile, then leaned over and grabbed his hand. "What were you about to say?"

"Just that with all this going on, I've really gotten used to you being around. Maybe we should—"

"Ms. Connelly?"

With a rueful grin, Meredeth held up her hand. "That's me."

"I'm Amanda, and I'm here to take you back now. Do you have any luggage or personal items?"

"Kevin will bring them in once I'm in my room."

The nurse nodded. "You'll be staying the night."

"At least," Meredeth said, getting up.

The nurse was short but pretty, with dark hair pulled back in a French braid and wearing lavender scrubs. "I just meant you wouldn't leave from recovery."

"Oh, sure."

"If you'll follow me, then?"

With excitement burbling in her stomach, Meredeth did so, and Kevin held her hand until she was transported to the OR itself.

CHAPTER 26

HAMMERING DOWN

Mt. Bellamy, NY

THEY ARRIVED IN the sleepy little town of Mount Bellamy from the southwest, and the road they'd taken deposited them in the downtown area at close to seven in the evening. Mack brought the truck to a smooth halt at the stop sign and glanced at his father.

"Left and then right at the light."

Mack nodded a single time and did as he was told.

"Second street on the right," said Father.

"Yessir." Mack turned just before the Walgreens onto Sallington Street. He drove slowly down the street, breaking through a shelterbelt of trees to find a trailer park all mixed up with a working farm. He arched an eyebrow at his father.

"Last road on the left. It's called Lunds Lane. There are five streets off Lunds Lane, two on the right, three on the left. The streets to the right are dead ends, the three on the left are looped together. You will pick one on the left and turn down it. Then, you will ready yourself to accelerate at my word. You will do exactly as I say, without questions, without balking."

"Of course, Father," said Mack. That was the real point of the graduation test, he figured. After all, he'd already killed three people, so it couldn't just be about committing murder. He imagined his father would pick a very sympathetic target—not that Mack cared at that point. He'd run down Alex, himself, for a chance to get off the farm, to get out of New York, and to start his life. He followed Ankou's instructions to the letter, choosing the first road on the left—Gardenia Street—and idling down it.

Beside him, his father leaned forward, squinting into the gloaming beyond the reach of the headlights. "There," he finally said, pointing at the silhouettes of four kids on bicycles. "Get them all. Go, Mack! Go, now!"

Mack downshifted and put the hammer down without a single moment's hesitation. The big, beautiful truck responded as he'd imagined it would—the addictive shriek of compound turbocharging, the roar of the exhaust. The truck accelerated quickly with its empty trailer, and he was on the quartet of boys before they'd recovered from the abrupt tumult. He never lifted his foot from the accelerator, not even as the weight of the tractor crunched the four bicycles and smashed the boys' bones to gravel.

"Very good," was all his father said.

Which was okay because Mack knew what had to happen next. He continued down Gardenia until it became Pork Hill Lane, then slowed and sedately retraced his path back out East State Street, then pointed the nose of the truck east.

"There's a fuel stop near I-395. You can change your plates there."

"Yessir."

He drove to the fuel station, which was on the opposite side of the road, and pulled into the wide asphalt apron around the convenience store and the fuel pumps. He brought the truck to a smooth stop behind the building, then jumped out, new plates in one hand and a screwdriver in the other. He changed the plates as quickly as he had in practice, then jogged to the front of the truck to check for damage but found the bull bar had done its job.

He jumped into the cab, and said, "Now what, Father?" He glanced over, but the passenger seat was empty. He cranked his head around and checked the sleeper compartment, then looked out the front window.

His father stood near the corner of the building, his profile turned to the truck. He lifted a hand, then turned away and walked into the store.

A sudden panic erupted in Mack. He was done. He'd passed, and that meant he was on his own. He sat for a moment, then put the truck in gear and set out on his great adventure.

CHAPTER 27

LOLLIPOPS

Hanable's Valley, NY

MEREDETH FELT MUCH better. She hadn't realized how poorly the ileostomy had made her feel—tired, rundown, almost sick—until it was gone. Dr. Atallah had sent her to their hotel the second day after the surgery, and after a day of resting and eating whatever she wanted from room service, she and Kevin had returned to Hanable's Valley.

She had gotten up early—her eyes just opened, and she was wide awake. She'd gone to the kitchen to allow poor Kevin to sleep in. She had her Bureau laptop out and was searching ViCAP, digging back ten years, trying to spot Mack's pattern in the sea of data. She reached for her mug of coffee without looking away from the screen and brought it to her lips before she realized the mug was empty. Grinning at herself, she got up and crossed to the coffee machine and refilled the cup.

As she took her seat, her Bureau phone rang, and she picked it up without looking at the caller ID screen. "Morning, Bobby," she said.

"How are you feeling today, Mere?"

"Like a million bucks. I woke up at my normal time—no alarm or anything."

"Poor Kevin."

"Nah, I let him sleep. I'm in his kitchen drinking coffee and going blind looking at ViCAP. How do the analysts do it?"

"I'm not sure they're entirely human. I couldn't sit at a desk all day and stare at a computer screen. Has it been a fruitful search, at least?"

"I went back a decade and tried to find this guy's MO. There are—"

"The cable news channels have discovered our investigation into these crimes. Probably tipped off, but by whom, I have no clue."

"Awesome. The unsub will know we're looking for him, not just local law enforcement."

"Maybe not. I doubt he gets cable in his truck."

"True, but as soon as the cable news outlets start blabbing, everyone follows them."

"Even if he hears about it, he may not realize it's about him. So far, the only thing they have is that there is a potential serial killer working the interstates."

"We need to find that leak, Bobby. Especially if the source is Bureau."

"I'm on it."

"Good. I'll keep searching ViCAP."

"Why? Michelina told you he's been committing these crimes for ten or eleven years, right? Why do we need to know them all?"

"When he was just starting out, he wasn't as polished as he has grown to be. I want to examine his raw behaviors, not the ones he's adopted to obscure what he's doing."

"Are you having any luck?"

"I've got three so far."

"And?"

"And I only found them because they occurred at mile marker thirty-three. Each of the three victims had their skull caved in with a blunt cylindrical object. We only know there was an MVA involved because their cars were mangled before the unsub pulled them out and went to work."

"Brutal."

"He displayed a lot of pent-up rage. I'd like to question Ankou again.

"To what end?"

"I'm curious if he did something during his psychic driving to heighten the unsub's rage."

"And you think he'll tell you?"

"Probably not."

"Then…"

"How else can I find out?"

"Didn't Michelina say that Alex did a lot of the training?"

"She did," said Meredeth. "Are you suggesting we turn around and go back to Florida?"

"We might get more there than we will with Doe. Alex clearly doesn't have as much control as Ankou does."

"Well, we should have some leverage to use on John. Did Michelina get the documents back to you?"

"She did, and I submitted them to Brienne's office yesterday afternoon."

"Good. It's ironic we're using a Jane Doe agreement to protect Michelina from John Doe."

"I told the AUSA's office that you'll be the contact person. I hope that's okay."

"It's fine. The way I'm feeling, I'll be back at work in the next day or so." She took a sip of coffee.

"You're looking into the old crimes. Want me to liaise with local-level agencies to track MVAs near the thirty-third lollipop?"

"Lollipop? Did you hit your head recently?"

"It's CB slang for mile marker, boss."

"That's a good idea. Put out a call for information for hit and run or road rage incidents resulting in a fatality within the last…oh, say three months. Ask to be updated on any new incidents for the foreseeable future."

"Check."

"Once you've got that out, book a flight up here so we can take another stab at Ankou. I'll call the warden and set up an interview for tomorrow afternoon."

"Sounds like a plan. I can tell you're feeling better."

"How so?"

"You're back to being bossy."

"Oh, I wish you would've waited to say that until we were in the same zip code."

"Do you think I'm insane? No thank you. I'll make all my snide comments with the buffer of six or seven hundred miles."

"That's fair. Track down the Cadillac and the semi-tractor Michelina mentioned. She said in an email she thought it was a Peterbilt. Given the timeframe she mentioned, it would have been twelve to thirteen years ago in Livingston County, New York." She grinned a little, then said, "How was that for bossy?"

"Pretty good, Mere. It's like you have practice at it."

"Don't let me see you up here without some information we can use against Ankou, or I might have to slug you for all this tomfoolery."

"Yes, ma'am."

"That's better."

"Oh, my, Kevin has really spoiled you, hasn't he?"

"Get to work, Van Zandt, before you piss me off."

CHAPTER 28

THROUGH A FOGGY NIGHT

Needles, CA

THE EVENING CURLED up and died in a blaze of yellow-gold, red, and bloody orange. The death of the sun was a beautiful time of day but not ideal for a westbound route of travel. On top of the ever-present glare scorching his retinas, he thought he'd gotten a bad meal somewhere in his rearview, and his stomach didn't feel quite right. The Highwayman had known I-40 would be an annoyance at this time of day, but if he wanted to keep moving, there was nothing for it but to grit his teeth, squint a lot, and do his best to keep the rig on the road.

To that end, he was driving slightly below the posted speed limit but was keeping to the granny lane and showing as much courtesy to the other drivers on the road as he knew how...which was not to say that other drivers returned the favor. He'd already had multiple four-wheelers go screaming by in the hammer lane, only to cut over into his lane the second their bumpers cleared his own. They weren't cutting him off, not even making him brake hard, but they were dancing precipitously close to the line.

He was doing his best to let the stress and anxiety roll over him like a wave, leaving calm, smooth water in their wake, and everything was going fine until he saw the black Mercedes Benz coming up fast in his mirrors. He could make out three silhouettes inside the vehicle, and each one looked male to his experienced eye.

He watched his side mirror, trying to gauge the speed of the Benz, trying to assess the driver's state of mind. I-40 was one of the less common routes to and from Las Vegas for the residents of Southern California, but it was a handy route to know when I-15 was overloaded. Vegas regulars knew of it, and he often saw carloads of guys in a rush to lose their money heading east and carloads of guys in a rush to get back to the real world in time to scrounge enough money for food and rent. He judged the Merc to fit in the latter category.

As the black car drew closer, the truck driver frowned at the thin, tinny sound of the horn coming up behind him at speed. The car raced up into his donkey, then cut the wheel and almost lost the rear end as the car jerked into the left lane for a high-speed pass. The Benz rocketed past, the horn blaring, the motor shrieking, then cut back into the right lane, and the Highwayman had to stand on the Pete's brakes to avoid hitting it.

His blood boiled, and that only made him feel worse. The sun dropped below the horizon as he downshifted and put the hammer down. His turbos screamed, and his engine growled as he put all twenty-one hundred foot-pounds of torque to the pavement, and the truck surged ahead.

He had no real chance of staying with them on the upslope that served as his landmark for the western edge of the Mojave National Preserve—and the Needles Freeway's mile marker thirty-three. He had to catch them before that or give up the chase. Luckily, the road had either none at all or very little gradient until that point, and he could run the Cummins engine flat out, and he switched to the hammer lane to do so. The black Mercedes Benz was speeding, but now that he'd unleashed the beast, the Peterbilt grew closer with each passing second. He flicked on his headlights and the fifty-five thousand lumen light bar on the roof, and the traffic parted before him as though he were Moses standing on the shore of the Red Sea.

He caught them at the overpass for Kelbaker Road—a mile and a half or so from the incline into the mountainous region southeast of Barstow. A desert fog had rolled in as they approached the mountains, and with all his lights burning, he must have seemed like a charge of angels in the rearview mirror of the Benz because they switched into the slow lane. With a grin, he pulled abreast of the three men in their fancy car, and as he did so, the driver laid on the horn. Grin widening, he reached up and blew a long, sustained blast of his air horns.

The Mercedes seemed to squat, then leap forward, attempting to accelerate away from him. With an almost lazy twist of the steering wheel, the trucker changed into the slow lane, almost catching the rear bumper of the car on his bull bar. He downshifted and stood on the accelerator, causing the engine to roar and the turbochargers to whine like grumpy banshees.

The Benz jerked into the left lane, almost losing the rear of the car to a slide. Chuckling, the Highwayman followed them with a statelier lane change and stood right on their bumper. The black car swerved to the small shoulder separating the travel lanes from the median, then shot across both lanes to the shoulder on the other side of the right lane, and he followed yet again.

His truck couldn't handle like the Mercedes Benz, but so far, they hadn't been able to evade him. Red lights flashed—the Merc's brake lights—but the Pete's pilot didn't slow a whit. With a thump and the sound of metal distending, bending, sheering, he smashed into the back of the Benz, his foot still pinning the accelerator to the mat. The car jittered to the left, then back to the right with a screech of tire rubber.

He jerked his big steering wheel and moved into the slow lane, dancing at the very edge of control. He pulled alongside the German sedan, then blew a blast from his air horns and jerked the truck toward the car, catching the Merc with the side of his bull bar. He turned into them, using all thirty-five thousand pounds of momentum to shove the black car's back end almost ninety-degrees to the direction of travel, and they ended up facing the dusty median strip.

The moment his bull bar lost contact with the car, the Highwayman cranked his wheel to the left and stood on the go-pedal once more. When he smashed into them broadside, he hit square with the bull bar and shoved the Benz down the road sideways.

He flicked on the work lights on the passenger side of the truck and saw only desert stretching away to the right, accented by a small mountain range. The desert was filled with mini dunes that would be fun to push the Mercedes up and over, but there was no way he could get his truck back out of all that loose sand if he did. Then a gleam of something ahead caught his eye, and his grin became vicious, savage.

He steered a little to the right, the custom tow hooks on the chrome bull bar bringing the car along for good measure. The vehicles drifted first to the edge of the slow lane, crossed the solid white line and the rumble strips that marked the left shoulder, and then they drifted past even those. The Peterbilt's passenger side tires dropped off the pavement one by one until he had the car pointing right at his target.

At the last minute, he cranked his steering wheel to the left and slammed on his brakes, chewing the inside of his lip as the lag between his hydraulic brakes and the initiation of the air brakes ticked away. The call box pole gleamed in the brilliance of his forward-facing lights, drawing closer by the second. The trucker stiffened his body, gritting his teeth against the impact.

Reckless! Why did you push them at a fixed object?

But then the tow hooks pulled free with a scream of metal, and the cab lurched to the left while the Mercedes continued to slide with a slow rotation to the right. When the black car struck the pole, it sounded like one of the seven trumpets to him as the pole ripped the Benz nearly in half before stopping the car's motion—cutting through the metal like a hot knife through butter.

As soon as he had enough control, the Highwayman brought the rig to a stop then sat for a moment, catching his run-away pulse and breathing. His nostrils flared with each inhalation, and his vision seemed a thing of magic. Everything was clear despite the night, despite the fog. He opened his door and climbed down to the asphalt. He stopped at his toolbox to grab his crowbar and a hammer. He had a feeling he might need both to get at the Benz's passengers.

As he walked back on the shoulder, he peered through the car's windshield. The driver sat with his head back against the headrest, but the front passenger was half-in, half-out of the car, his head having shattered the passenger window. The man in the backseat was a bloody mess, as that's where the car and the pole had made their acquaintances.

He peered at the man with his head back—the only one who might live long enough for the Highwayman's purposes. He smelled like trust funds and old money to him. By the glint of the hazard lights blinking away in the truck, the man was conscious and watching his approach, and he gave the man a wild predator's grin.

In the time it took him to walk back to the car, several other cars and trucks had passed by in the travel lanes. Hopefully, the darkness combined with the water vapor clogging the air would mask the truck driver's features and the license plates of the truck. He could—and would—change the plates before he moved away, but there was nothing he could do about his features.

He came to a stop at the front of the destroyed car, and his gaze met the driver's. He tapped the hood ornament with the crowbar, performing for an audience of one, then sent it spinning off into the desert with a single swing of the hammer. Then he moved around to the driver's side door. The driver wasn't moving, but he followed the Highwayman with his eyes.

"Quite a pickle you've got yourself into," said the trucker. "I'm willing to bet your poor driving and obnoxious road manners contributed to your accident. What do you say, fella?"

The man closed his eyes in a long, slow blink, but though his throat worked, and his larynx bobbed up and down, no words formed. He closed his eyes in another glacial blink, then moved his eyes toward the passenger side of the car.

"Pretty sure both your friends are dead," the Highwayman said through his smile. "The guy in the back is basically pulped, and your passenger friend tried to get out of the car by smashing his skull through the window. You don't come back from that." He shook his head. "Of course, if you had been content to drive the speed limit, maybe he'd still be alive."

A single tear slid down the man's cheeks.

"Hey! I've got an idea," said the Pete driver. "Maybe you can help me with the implementation. You up for that?"

The man closed his eyes.

"Great!" the Highwayman said as if the man had agreed. He tried the door and found it locked. He lifted the hammer, almost casually, and smashed the window. He reached inside and hit the unlock button and grinned at the solid-sounding *thunk*. "German engineering, huh?" He tried the door again, and again, it wouldn't open. "Oh, dear. Buddy, I'd say your car is totaled. The door is stuck, but don't worry." He hefted the crowbar and waved it in front of the driver's closed eyes. "My little friend here will help out."

He set the crowbar in the crack between the front and rear doors, then threw his body weight against it. The door creaked and groaned but didn't spring open the way car doors always did in television shows and movies. "Well, maybe not." He withdrew the crowbar and tapped the roof twice. "But it's no matter. I can do what I need to through the window." He leaned in and set the pointy end of the crowbar in the crease between the man's thigh and torso. Smiling, he maneuvered his other arm through the window and tapped the end of the crowbar—just enough of a tap to make noise.

The driver's eyes were very wide as the Highwayman lifted the hammer and let it fall in earnest. The Benz driver found his voice at last. His incoherent shrieks were music to the Highwayman's ears, and the crowbar was providing enough blood to make his mark on the hood.

CHAPTER 29

MAMA BEAR

Buffalo, NY

FOR AT LEAST the hundredth time, Kevin glanced at her. "Still fine," she said, and he returned his attention to his driving. "I'm so much better, Kev, since the reversal. I can do this."

"Are you sure about that?"

"Yeah. And I already promised to let you know when I tire out."

"Dr. Atallah recommended you take the whole week."

"I know, but in light of the nasty business on the Needles Freeway, I need to be working. And hey, I didn't insist on going out there, did I?"

"Thank God for small favors," said Kevin in a dry tone. "You did send Bobby, though. And I seem to recall you insisting we pick him up at the Buffalo airport so the three of us can spend the rest of the day bandying words with a serial killer."

"I know," she said again. "But I don't know how to find this one, Kevin. I have no ideas that are worth the air it would take to speak them aloud. Ankou can help us, and with the information Michelina used as her proffer to the AUSA, we finally have some real leverage."

"Right, because he responds so well to threats."

"Yeah, but to be fair, he doesn't respond well to *anything*. At least this information will give us a chance. A lack of self-interest has never been one of his weaknesses." She looked out the front window of the cruiser and pointed. "There's Bobby."

Nodding, Kevin pulled his cruiser to the curb in front of Van Zandt and popped out to help get Bobby's luggage in the trunk—not that he had much. Meredeth rolled down her window and said, "You boys don't go talking about me, now."

"She thinks she's the center of the universe again," said Bobby. "That's a good sign."

"That's because you don't have to live with it."

She shook her head and grinned at Kevin in the sideview mirror. "You love it, mister."

"Yeah, I know. You've told me several times."

They put Bobby's small bag in the trunk, then both men climbed in on the driver's side. "Now, tell me the truth, Mere," said Bobby. "How are you feeling?"

"I feel *good*, Bobby. I never realized how bad I felt with that damn bag on."

"Well, you did get stabbed and nearly gutted like a fish."

"That's true, but Kevin has nursed me to within an inch of my life between then and now."

"Are you sure you don't want to wait until tomorrow to go see Doe?" asked Bobby.

"Nah, I'm good. Tell me about the SoCal scene."

"A difference of eighteen hours won't affect the chances that Doe will say anything reasonable. And the Highwayman probably won't strike again this soon. We've got time for you to rest this afternoon."

"Van Zandt, if I do anymore resting, I'm going to explode. Kevin doesn't deserve that."

"Well, thanks for that," said Saunders. "The surgeon told her it would be best to rest the whole week."

"That's not exactly what he said, Kev. He said, 'If you can, holding off getting back to work until Monday would be better than if you can't.'"

"Same difference," said Kevin with a shrug, but his glance said he knew they were going to Wende, and that for all his bluster about getting enough rest, he didn't object too much. Once again, he drove toward Alden, NY without further comment.

"Tell me about it, Bobby," said Meredeth.

"It was pretty gruesome. The car was rammed off the road and into one of those metal call box poles, and at a speed sufficient that the car was almost cut in half. The coroner reckoned that two died with the impact—the front passenger was partially ejected through the side window, and the guy in the back was pulped by the pole. The driver survived long enough to be tortured. The coroner thinks the wounds might have been made with a chisel or crowbar."

"Ugh," said Kevin. "And you're sure it's the same guy?"

"Pretty much," said Bobby. "He used the driver's blood to paint that damn Trinity Knot on the hood of the car."

"You know, I've been thinking about all these hit-and-runs. What if there is more than one unsub?"

"But they're all at mile marker thirty-three, Mere," said Bobby. "That's pretty much the only thing holding them together as a serial group."

"I know but hear me out. What if it's more than one of Ankou's abductees? What if there are multiple guys out there driving a truck and leaving messes on the side of the road?"

"So, neither Mack nor Carl alone, but *both*? The only way you'll ever know is if you catch someone, ascertain his guilt beyond the shadow of a doubt, and then the killings continue. Even then," Kevin said with a shrug, "it could be a copycat or another abductee working to make the one you've caught look innocent."

"Besides," added Bobby, "it doesn't really matter. We have to track the crimes the same way."

"That's true," admitted Meredeth. "How can I suggest it to Doe without coming right out with the theory?"

"The question is: Do you *want* to tip your hand to this man?" asked Kevin. "You might give him ideas he hasn't thought of. And if he has a way to communicate with his accomplices outside the prison, any idea you give him, he can put into play."

"That's also true, but how can we know, otherwise?"

"Even if you do bring it up, there's no reason why Doe won't lie to you if he thinks it will make his plan more challenging. Remember the garden path he led you down on the Pass-A-Grille Killer case."

"It wasn't as much a garden path, Kevin, as the truth wrapped up in misdirection. I mean, he gave us the key to the case, and we missed it."

"That's not fair," said Bobby. "He let us think he was giving us a clue as to why the victims all looked alike, and I guess he was, but not the way he made it seem. He said we had to find the person Alex was killing by proxy, that once we had, we would solve the case. It was pure guile, plain and simple."

"But it was also true. We mistook his meaning—we thought the person causing Alex to hate was a woman who'd hurt or rejected him, but it is his physical body he hates. Listen, gents, we can't expect Ankou to come right out and tell us the identities of these killers, nor can we expect him to spell out how to catch them. We have to analyze everything he says with two guiding principles: First, part of him wants to give us hints, but another part of him wants us to fail, so he's going to give us hints wrapped in lies obscured by artifice. Second, he wants me to survive until the plan's endgame, but we know I can be injured severely, so we have to find the traps before we blunder into them."

"And as far as that goes," said Kevin as he turned north in Alden and headed toward the Wende Correctional Facility, "he doesn't give half-a-shit if Bobby and I get wiped from the face of the Earth. He knows the death of either of us will hurt you, will cause you to abandon logic and work from emotion, making his job easier."

"Bobby is too ornery to get killed, and you're too pretty." Meredeth lay her hand on his forearm. "Plus, I'd take either one of you in a fight against one of Ankou's kids."

"Thanks for the confidence, at least," said Bobby. "And I'm prettier than Kevin."

"Nuh-uh," said Meredeth with a grin for the chief, "but you are ornerier."

"Yeah, yeah."

"What we have to do differently this time is to expect his answers to have some truth to them, but at the same time, we have to expect the sly misdirection. We have to assume that though there is truth in his statements, he's obfuscating it with lies or deviousness. It's our job to weed through it all, to investigate each statement rather than accepting it at face value."

Kevin grunted as he turned in at the gate of the prison and flashed his badge. "Chief Saunders from Hanable's

Valley. These two are FBI. We have an appointment to interview John Doe."

The guard typed on his computer for a few moments then came back to the window. "You're Agents Connelly and Van Zandt?" he asked while looking at Meredeth.

She and Bobby held up their IDs and badges, and the guard nodded and waved them through. Kevin found a space near the building, and they all got out.

Meredeth looked more professional for this visit, able to wear a soft pair of khaki pants, an FBI polo shirt, and comfortable shoes. Her hair was shiny and glowed in the afternoon sun as they got out and headed into the "officials only" sally port. As the warden had promised her, everything was set up in advance, and Doe was already on his way as they signed in and were buzzed into the interview room.

Doe came up the hall as they took their positions, and a small smile played at the corners of his mouth. He watched, sharp-eyed, as she laid out her things—her laptop, her pad, and her pen. He stopped outside the door, saying nothing, only staring at Meredeth and waiting to be buzzed into the room. Henedy stood behind him, and when he saw Meredeth looking at him, he gave her a little shake of his head that she took to mean that Doe was in a mood. She nodded to Henedy, then returned her gaze to Doe and treated him to a friendly smile.

The guard in the control booth hit the buzzer, and Doe pushed into the room and took his seat, immediately holding up his shackled wrists. "Let's start off with civility between us, Meredeth," he said. "You look much better than the last time we spoke, and I can't detect any skatole at all. Congratulations on having your whatever-ostomy reversed."

She couldn't help but narrow her eyes slightly, though she was able to keep her smile loose and friendly.

"What the hell is skatole?" demanded Kevin.

"It's the organic compound that most FBI agents lack."

"What?"

"You know, Chief. Their shit don't stink, and the lack of skatole is why."

Kevin sucked his teeth. "How in the world do you survive in here, Doe? With that mouth, I'd think one of the other inmates would have crushed your puny little head by now."

"Kevin," Meredeth said softly.

"Oh, Chief, I think you're expressing your repressed desires again. But to answer your question, haven't you ever heard a prison referred to as a gladiator academy? Some have tried, and the others learned by their mistakes. There have been no more attempts for months, now the first few are off their ventilators, at least."

Meredeth lifted her gaze to Henedy, who grimaced and nodded. "You should be careful, John. You don't want more charges."

Doe laughed raucously. "You think more charges scare me, Old Mare? I'm in here for *life*, remember? Having to go to Buffalo for a trial would be a relief of the constant boredom. That's why the administration of the prison won't charge me for the minor things I do to the other inmates."

"Eventually, you will go too far, and you *will* be charged," said Henedy.

"Ah, the Great Sage speaks!" Doe turned and shot the guard a dirty look. "You get to run your gab at me all the time, Officer Henedy. Let someone else have a turn."

Henedy returned Doe's stare stone-faced. After a moment, he twirled his finger, and Doe obediently turned back to Meredeth.

"At any rate, Meredeth, you do look better. You are starting to get some of your color back, and though the usual bonfire in your eyes is missing, there are sparks—omens of things to come."

"Thank you, John," she said. "Alex will be quite disappointed."

"Oh, no doubt he will. He never learned to accept failures with any degree of grace. You're lucky he's incarcerated. Speaking of which, I hope they didn't put him on the men's side of the jail. Biologically, he's still one hundred percent female—as you mentioned last time."

"I don't want to get off track this time, John," said Meredeth. "So, let me assure you Alex is in adseg in one of the state prisons with no contact between him and other prisoners—male or female."

"That's probably for the best," said John. He looped his arm over the back of the chair and slumped a little, putting his legs out straight under the table.

"Agreed, but we're not here to talk to you about past successes."

"Successes? That's what you call missing out on the great beyond by a stroke of luck and Marine Corps training?" He nodded his head toward Bobby.

"We are here because we have specific questions on the active case we spoke of the other day."

"I assumed as much."

"Last time, we agreed to dispense with the verbal fencing. Do you recall?"

Doe tapped his temple with his index finger. "I never forget anything, Meredeth. *Never.*" He hissed the last word as if she'd started to argue.

"Good. For my part, let me start by saying we suspect one or more of your...*children*...of the crimes. Specifically, the ones you dubbed Mack—who was Steven Aldridge when you found him—and the one you called Carl. Greg Henderson, by his birth certificate."

"Yes."

"What are you willing to tell us about Mack?"

"I believe I shared that with you last time."

"And you don't care to recant your denial that you bought him the truck?"

"Absolutely not, Meredeth. I did no such thing."

"Okay, then *repurposed* the rig of one of your victims?"

"I didn't do that, either." He cocked his head to the side and looked at her shrewdly. "And, if you stop a moment to think, you will realize that I can hardly admit to anything that will put me in jeopardy of additional federal charges— such as accessory and conspiracy. I like it here at Wende. Plus, even if I had provided him with the truck—and what I just said aside, I did not do any such thing—he would have a different one by now."

"Yes, probably," she said. "He left your farm, what, eleven years ago?"

Doe shrugged. "When you have a large family, it's hard to remember specific dates."

"And how large is your family, John?" Bobby asked. "I'd like an *exact* head count for your file."

"Ham-fisted and clumsy, as ever, Van Zandt," Doe said without lifting his heavy gaze from Meredeth's face. "And I made no promise not to fence with *you*, so let the adults speak in peace."

"I have it on good authority that Mack left your farm eleven years and three months ago."

"Ah, that dratted Carl is telling tales again?" He said it with a sarcastic twist to his lips and in a mocking tone.

"That's right. At least, he gave his name as Carl to the locals out there. Maybe it's another of your success stories subsuming Carl's identity."

"Carl *what*?" asked Doe. "Surely, the cops insisted on a full name. What last name did he give them?"

"Strangely enough, he gave them Carl Doe as his full name. Where do you think he got that idea?"

"Meredeth, if you are not going to keep up your side of the no-fencing agreement, why should I? We both know the person providing you with your so-called information is Michelina. Where does the dear girl live these days? Is she around here somewhere? I always assumed she'd come to her senses one day and come crawling back to her family."

"I have no idea," said Meredeth. "I've never spoken to anyone called Michelina." She turned to Bobby and held out her hand. He laid a commercial truck registration document in her palm.

"Oh, my," said Doe. "Show and tell? I didn't bring anything!"

"This document is the registration of a 1987 Peterbilt 359."

"A fine vehicle," said John. "But what does it have to do with me?"

"The name listed on the registration is Wayne McGovern."

"Is all this supposed to mean something to me?"

"Both the truck and the driver disappeared a little more than twelve years ago. The last known destination was Jonodot, NY. We know he stopped for fuel in Angelica. The most direct route from Angelica puts him traveling right past that farm you stole, through Yoagoh, and then on to Jonodot. He never showed up in Jonodot, so that implies whatever fate had in store for him, he met it near you."

"Hardly. State Route 15 is a better route than Old State Road, but I guess that doesn't match your theory so it must be false."

"Then you deny having anything to do with Mister McGovern's disappearance?"

"Categorically. Run me through a lie detector at your leisure. I've never heard that man's name before, nor did I see him in life."

"That's a strange way to put it, John," said Bobby. "Did you see him after he died?"

Doe rolled his eyes toward the ceiling. "Can't you control your child, Meredeth? He wearies me."

"Even so, John, it is a *great* question. Add to it, what happened to his Pete?"

"My, my, aren't you up on all the trucker lingo..." Doe sighed and dropped his gaze to the table. "Hypothetically speaking, if one of my sons—say Mack, for instance—"

"Yeah, let's say Mack because we know he was behind McGovern's disappearance," said Kevin.

"—did come up with a semi before he left my care, the *only* way he might have gotten one is to steal it. And my children don't leave loose strings behind them that any ambitious police chief might pull on."

"I see. And would Mack have brought a body back to the farm for disposal? *Hypothetically* speaking, of course."

"There's no telling what a teenaged boy may do."

"I'll take that as a yes. And did you see Wayne McGovern dead, then?"

"Hypothetically speaking, I would have seen any bodies brought back to the farm. Leaving the hypothetical behind, nothing like what we've been discussing ever happened."

"No, of course not," said Bobby, his tone sarcastic. "Or if they did, you had no knowledge of it."

"Exactly, Agent Van Zandt. But don't take my word for it. You have the registration. What happened to the vehicle? Surely if I'd given it to Mack, there would be records, registration and plate renewals, insurance, etc."

"The truck fell off the face of the earth, just like the kids you abducted," said Kevin sourly.

"Now, now, Chief. Let's keep it civil," said Doe. "I thought we established that I *freed* those children from a life of drudgery and misery stacked upon misery."

"John, talk to *me*," said Meredeth. "But, as Kevin said, there are no records for that truck after this registration, and it's hard for a semi rig to disappear."

"That it is," said Ankou. "At least on its own."

"What if it were stolen and the VIN altered? Would that make it disappear so thoroughly?"

Doe shrugged, the picture of innocence. "I'm sure I would have no idea."

Meredeth held her hand out toward Bobby once more, and he placed an automobile registration card face down in her palm. "That's unfortunate, John."

He narrowed his eyes at the card.

"You see, that wasn't the only vehicle that disappeared near your farm in roughly the same timeframe. Want to guess what this registration card belongs to?"

"I'm sure I have no idea." His expression soured, and the corners of his mouth turned down in a grimace. "I don't like this game, Meredeth. I thought we agreed to dispense with the verbal combat."

"We did, John," she said in an even tone. "I'm happy to abide by it, but when you say things we know are false, well then, I have to nudge you back inbounds, don't I?"

"This game of twenty questions is how you nudge me?"

"Look, John, it's like this. This car"—she waved the registration card—"and this truck"—she waved the document in her other hand—"disappeared within months of each other. We really don't know what happened to the truck, but we have found this car. It now belongs to a collector from the City. I've seen it on video, and you, Carl, and Mack did a great job restoring it."

"Carl, Mack, and I?" he asked in a toneless voice.

"Yes, John. We have sworn testimony to that effect."

"Add to that the fact that this Fleetwood had its VIN changed, and according to the buyer, he bought it from—and I quote—a big man and a big kid on a farm near Yoagoh," said Kevin.

"Well, you got me, Chief," said John.

"Yes, John," said Meredeth. "We know you have experience altering VIN codes, forging registrations, and driver's licenses. We're not interested in charging you with chicken-shit, but if you force our hands..."

"Yes, yes!" snapped Ankou. "Threat received!"

"It's not a threat. Think of it as a motivator."

"Motivator!" scoffed John.

"Let's get back to the '87 Peterbilt 359, shall we?"

"Why not?" grated John.

"I'll ask you again, John. When you altered the VIN for Mack, did that allow him to register it under his own name?"

"Well, it would, wouldn't it? Along with a bill of sale from a fictional owner."

"But what about the title?" asked Kevin.

"A smart forger would use an out-of-state title—say Pennsylvania or Texas or Florida."

"I see. And you'd just forge all the documents, including the signature of the seller—in this case, a dealer from one of those states?"

"Yes. The verification process is quite easy. You simply print up a letterhead for the fictious dealer and 'verify' the VIN is valid. That's all there is to it."

"I see. And would Mack have traded the old 359 in on something?"

John frowned and shook his head. "I doubt it. Mack loved that truck. So did Carl." He snicked his tongue against his teeth. "Hell, so did I."

"But you said the other day Mack doesn't have a home. Where would he put it?"

John shrugged and examined his fingernails.

"You realize if I get the NYSP to grab another warrant for that farm, and we go execute that and find the Pete, you might face those charges you mentioned earlier—accessory after the fact, conspiracy, like that?"

John sneered at the table. "And what's that to me?"

"Well, John, if you get enough federal charges, you'll be moved to a federal facility—maybe even the Supermax," said Bobby. "Say buh-bye to Wende."

"And what's that to me?" Doe repeated.

"It won't be this comfortable for one thing. You'll be in some other state, far away from everyone you know."

He flashed a one-sided smile at them.

"When we find this truck, John," said Meredeth softly, "we will dust it for prints. Are we going to find yours?"

"After all this time?"

"Then you admit you—"

"No, Van Zandt, I admit nothing! But Old Mare said it was over eleven years ago when the truck disappeared. Plus, if I did help Mack get it back in top shape and he drove it for five or six years, any evidence would be long gone."

"That's true, John," Meredeth said in a calm, even voice. "But finding it at the farm is a fingerprint in itself, is it not?"

Doe held his arms out to his side. "I can't see how. I'm in here"—he pointed at the table with both outstretched hands—"am I not?"

Meredeth nodded. "You are, but come on, John... Let's go back to all that 'hypothetical' nonsense. If you were going to alter the VIN on a Peterbilt, how would you do it? Fabricate an entire VIN plate?"

"Hardly," scoffed Ankou. "There are much easier methods."

"I can't think of any. Help me out. Please, John?"

"An enterprising soul would go to a semi junkyard and lift a couple of VIN plates from some old hulks. VINs are coded for the year of manufacture, so you'd need the one from the vehicle you want to change, or at least from a wrecked vehicle of the same year. Then, it's just a matter of cutting and welding the plates to make a new VIN."

"And no one would notice the welds?" asked Bobby.

"They would if you didn't carefully TIG them, grind the welds down, then restore the painted parts, but once you've done that, the only way to detect the change is to compare the VIN to official records from the manufacturer of the vehicle." His brows bunched for a moment, and he glanced at the ceiling. "I suppose in this day and age, one could hack into the manufacturer's database and insert the new number, and then it would truly be undetectable."

"And this is how Mack got his first truck?"

Doe pursed his lips, then gave her a slow nod. "It *might* be."

"And how the Cadillac seller might have done it?"

"You understand I still have no desire to be indicted for such ridiculous charges?"

"Of course. I imagine you have no more desire to be charged as I do to do the required paperwork to charge you. We aren't recording this, John."

He grinned and pointed at Bobby, then Kevin, then Officer Henedy, then at Meredeth, herself. "I count four law enforcement officers present, and since your testimonies count as two people in court, that makes it eight to one. I don't stand a chance."

"Well, that's true." Meredeth frowned down at the table. "Let's leave those two vehicles a moment. You said Mack would have purchased something new. How would he have done that? Would the truck be registered to him or a company?"

"If it were me, it would be registered to a company that exists in a state that views company registrations and documents as private. All you need in some states is a virtual address—a post office box at one of those private mailbox places."

"I see. And would Mack go with another Peterbilt?"

"Unless Hell has frozen over, I'd imagine so." His tone was droll, but his eyes were decidedly unamused.

"All these MVAs," Bobby said in a broody tone.

"Yes, Agent Van Zandt?"

"How would the Highwayman keep the damage his truck sustained a secret? Most states require body shops to report accident damage."

"Ah, that's the beauty of the way my children think. To a one, they were taught to know in advance what might occur in any situation and to prepare for those eventualities."

"What does that mean in this context, John?" asked Meredeth.

"The Highwayman would armor his vehicle."

"Armor it? You mean with bulletproof glass and thick steel plates in the doors and things?"

"No, don't be such a silly girl, Old Mare. Think about it. What kind of armor would a rolling mass of thirty-five thousand pounds need against a regular car?"

"He'd have to protect the grill," said Bobby. "Maybe reinforce the frame and suspension."

Doe glanced at him and shrugged.

"And carry spare headlights, brake lights, running lights. Also, spares for any trim pieces," said Kevin. "But even if he did all that, one wrong move and he's got buckled sheet metal or broken fiberglass. How does he fix those?"

"If it were me," Doe said with a mischievous glint in his eye, "I'd make sure I didn't make any wrong moves. And I'd make my kills when I was deadheading, so the truck would handle and accelerate at its best."

"But he'd pull the trailer?"

"I would. That adds mass and momentum but also adds braking power and stability in the form of eight extra tires and wheels."

"I see," said Meredeth.

"And power?" asked Bobby.

"Trucks are full of it," said Doe with a shrug.

"Sure, *pulling* power—torque," said Kevin. "But there would have to be some instances when you'd need to chase a car down."

"Very true," said Doe with a grudging nod.

"How would you handle that? Gasoline engines make more horsepower than diesels, and the cars are lighter by a factor of ten. That's a serious obstacle."

"I'm sure."

"So..." Meredeth flipped open her pad to a fresh page and picked up her pen. "We're looking for someone in a late model Peterbilt with something to protect the grill and a modified engine."

"And a built-up transmission," said Bobby. "On the engine side: turbochargers, cam shafts, injectors, possibly internal engine parts. Something like one of those big bull bars they run in Australia could probably protect the grill against anything he'd hit."

"Except maybe a tree," added Kevin.

"Frame modifications?" Bobby asked Ankou with a quirked eyebrow.

Ankou merely lifted his shoulders and let them drop. "I wouldn't waste the resources, but anyone committing these crimes as long as you say would obviously learn by doing."

"Yes," said Meredeth. "Can you think of anything else necessary?"

"Power boosters for the CB," said Doe. "He'd want to be able to hear things coming his direction from a long way off."

Meredeth nodded and jotted it down. "Now, John, I'm hoping you will help me with my profile. What would drive a man to hunt the highways and kill with a semi? It's so impersonal, so..." She shook her head.

"Sometimes, Meredeth, I think all your schooling gets in the way of your common sense." John sighed and rolled his head on his shoulders. "I can't speak to your unsub, but some of my children took rude behavior directed at me as a mortal insult. For my part, I hardly noticed, but they *did*, and some of them were driven to act."

"Yes, but this person isn't around you," said Meredeth.

"At least not anymore," said Bobby.

"As you say." John rolled his head again. "I'm getting stiff. Let's continue this another time."

"John, I need your help *now*, not later."

"I know you do, Meredeth, and I *am* pleased you have finally realized you need my help. But I'm getting stiff, and worse, still: bored."

"Tell me this one last thing."

"Why target people on the road? Haven't you ever heard of mission-oriented behavior?"

"Yes, of course."

"Then?"

"You are saying the Highwayman believes he's on a mission to rid the world of bad drivers?"

"Rude drivers, *aggressive* drivers, maybe," said John. "The one I suspect always had a white knight streak, and I couldn't break him of it. Instead, I incorporated it into his new personality."

"Ah," said Meredeth. "He's making the roads *safe*."

John laughed. "If you could see your faces..."

"I'm sure we are quite amusing."

"Yes, you are when you're flailing around. But in this case, I think you're right. Your unsub is trying to make the roads safe for the polite drivers. For the people who don't cause him trouble, who are courteous."

"I see. Unfortunately, I don't see a way to use that information to bring this unsub to justice."

"Why do you think I'm sharing in such a free manner?" said Doe, quirking a smile at her. He half-turned in his seat and held up his hands. "Come, Henedy. I'm ready to go home."

Henedy raised an eyebrow at Meredeth.

"*Don't look at her!*" hissed Ankou. "*I'm the decision-maker here!*"

Acting as if he hadn't heard a word John said, Henedy waited until Meredeth flopped a hand over in the air and nodded. Then, he stepped close to Doe and slapped the bracelets around his wrists and cinched them tight. He bent and did the same with the leg irons. "There, inmate. You are ready to travel, though why you'd rather sit in your cell and draw your pictures, I'll never know."

John rolled his eyes and stood. He turned and walked to the door, then stopped and glanced at Meredeth over his shoulder. "I'm glad to see you doing better, Old Mare. We've got to keep you healthy until the end of our game, don't we?"

"And beyond, I hope," she said. She didn't lift her gaze to meet his. A wave of fatigue had fallen on her shoulders like a mantle of lead.

"Well, you can always hope, dear. In the meantime, I think it's better that you don't come back."

Henedy motioned at the camera, then shoved Ankou out into the hall as the door buzzed.

"That's it, then," said Bobby.

"Yes, but he gave us a lot more than he realized," said Meredeth. "Including a way to track the Highwayman down."

"Care to share with the class?" asked Kevin.

"Not here. In the car."

"Are you okay, Mere?"

"Just tired. Really, really tired."

"Then let's get you home. You can tell us your idea after you've rested."

"No, we should go out to the Branch Farm. I think Mack's first truck is there, and it will give us an idea of what he's driving now."

"But if you're tired—"

"I'll rest in the car. You work on a verbal warrant for the entire farm, looking for semi parts and vehicles, as well as records for vehicle sales. Bobby can sit up front, and I'll nap in the back. It's what, an hour's drive?"

"A little over," said Kevin. "It'll be dark by the time we get there."

"Then that will do me fine for a rest. We've got the car lights and that spotlight you like to play with."

"I suppose arguing for sanity is out of the question?"

"You know me so well, Kevin," she said with a tired smile.

CHAPTER 30

TRIPLE DIGIT RIDE

David Branch's Farm, NY

THE CAR JOUNCED its way through a particularly deep rut, and the noise, not to mention the harsh bounce, woke Meredeth from her nap. Her eyes felt hot and heavy, and her mouth tasted a little bit like a monkey's asshole, but she ignored both and sat up. "We there?"

"Well, snoring beauty awakens," said Bobby.

She smacked the back of his head for his trouble. "Answer me, Marine."

"Yes, ma'am. We are, in fact, almost at the farm. This dirt road has gone to seed since we arrested Ankou. I doubt very much any of his victims are living here or even visiting often."

"I do see some deep tire tracks that might be from a big rig," said Kevin.

"Then the Highwayman might still be around."

"I doubt it," said Bobby. "Those tire tracks look old."

Kevin applied the brakes gently. "But she's got a point, Bobby. She's in no shape for a fight—gun or otherwise. She still has the surgical bandage plastered to her tummy, and by the look of it, her wound is still oozing."

"And you let her go visit Ankou?"

"You know better than to ask me that, Bobby."

Van Zandt glanced at her over his shoulder. "Yeah," he said, then exhaled loudly. "I do. Did she say she'd get an Uber?"

"Something like that. I've given up trying to ride herd. The better she feels, the less effective I am."

"You're in good company," said Bobby. "Should we turn back?"

"No," said Meredeth, "this is too important."

"There's no way we can ascertain that none of Ankou's brainwashing victims are on the premises," said Kevin. "I could call Butch, and we could get some troopers down here to run the place for—"

"I really don't have the energy for all that," said Meredeth. "You two will protect me. And I am armed. If it comes to it, I can shoot."

"*Good Lord*," Kevin muttered.

"Relax, Chief. Mere's a badass, remember?"

"Yeah, Bobby. I remember."

"I'll stick right by you two, I promise. We'll go slow, Kevin."

"Famous last words..."

"Nah," said Bobby. "Her famous last words will be: Oh! Shiny! Then she'll leave us behind."

Meredeth slugged him in the shoulder. "I will not!"

"Ouch!" said Bobby.

"Children, don't make me turn this squad car around." Kevin lifted his foot off the brakes, and the car eased forward. "You are on Personal Security, Van Zandt, as am I. Meredeth is on 'shut up and stay behind us.'"

"My knight in shining armor," she said. She meant it as a joke, but fatigue turned it sour. "That was supposed to be funny, but evidently, my funny bone is also exhausted."

Kevin grunted and flicked on his spotlight and directed the beam at the darkness beyond the range of his headlights. The ruts were a little smoother the closer they got to the meadow in which the farmhouse sat. "Do we need the house?"

"I don't think so," said Meredeth. "Or if we do, it will come last. Let's check the barn and that rusty machine shed."

"Ten-four." Kevin let the car creep forward at idle, playing his spotlight along the side of the barn, illuminating any shadow he saw. Beside him in the front seat, Bobby sat up straight, then leaned forward a little and shielded his eyes from the low-level ambient light emitted by the dash lights and the police equipment between the two front buckets. "See something?"

"No, I...don't think so."

"What is it you don't think you saw?" asked Meredeth. She wanted to slide forward and look out between the seats, but it seemed like too much hassle.

"It was just a shadow," said Bobby. "I thought there might've... It was nothing."

"You sure?" asked Kevin.

"Yeah. You hit it with your light and there was nothing there. It was a shadow."

Kevin brought them around to the side of the barn with the big sliding doors, putting the barn between them and the house. He put the car in park but left it running. "Okay, Van Zandt. You're on point. Go open that door as wide as it will go."

Bobby opened his door and stepped out of the car. As he did so, he drew his pistol and let it hang next to his thigh as he approached the barn door. He grabbed it with his free hand and jerked hard. The door moved easily, and Bobby let go of it, wrapping his left hand around his pistol and moving into the widening opening.

The cruiser's headlights killed most of the shadows within the barn, and Kevin played the spotlight over those that had survived. The place was as Meredeth remembered it from previous searches—an eclectic mix of tools, old audio equipment, and older ECT machines.

And the boxes, of course. The wooden boxes Ankou had used to break those children he kidnapped and turn them into monsters. Meredeth's stomach churned at the thought of all those boxes. The right side of the barn was stacked floor to ceiling with them, and there were an additional two columns of boxes stacked four high, still wired to the audio and ECT machines.

"Ankou's the Henry Ford of torturing children, isn't he?"

"Yeah, though I bet the Ford family would object to that characterization."

"I just meant the assembly-line-like system he had here. The older kids breaking the younger so he can spend his time doing whatever the hell Ankou did for fun."

"I think this is it," she said in a dark voice.

Bobby finished exploring the ground floor of the barn, then jogged back to the car. "There's a basement and a loft, but there's no way a semi is in either."

"We'll come back to them if we need to."

"Right, boss." Bobby slid into the passenger seat and closed the door. "Where's this equipment shed?"

"Other side of the house. It's close to the small field on that side. Up there on the hill." Kevin drove to the big, rusting Quonset hut on the crown of the small hill that gave a little separation from the house and the fields. He repeated the same tactic of putting the car in front of the giant sliding metal doors and jerked his chin toward the building. "You're on, Van Zandt."

Bobby got out without a word and approached the shed, his hand on his holstered Glock. He turned and looked back at them, raising a hand to shade his eyes. "Padlocked," he called.

"Well, that's it, then," said Kevin. "We should've had some troopers meet us here with a set of bolt cutters and a machine gun or something."

"Get your tire iron, Kevin," said Meredeth.

"You want to break it?"

"Yes, I do. The verbal warrant will cover us here in New York, right?"

"I suppose."

"Then let's go." She opened her door and swung her legs out."

"No, FBI. You stay right where you are until I unlock the doors. Bobby and I can handle breaking a padlock without supervision."

"In a week or so, you can break my padlock."

He glanced at her in the rearview, smiling. "I'll remember that."

She smiled at him a moment, then jerked her chin toward the Quonset hut. "Let's get in there."

"Yep." Kevin left the car and used his key fob to lock the doors. He got the tire iron and a crowbar from the trunk, then walked over to Bobby. After a few minutes of talk, they got around to breaking the padlock, then each of them took one of the doors and wrestled it open.

The lights from the cruiser flooded the long, semi-cylindrical shed, touching on a four-post vehicle lift, several professional-quality toolboxes, a few workbenches, and a candy-apple red long-nosed semi-tractor with a sleeper box on the back. Kevin turned toward the car and hit the button on his key fob again, and the car's locks popped.

Meredeth wrenched herself out of the car and upright. She glanced at the darkness encircling them and had to fight off a shudder. Anyone could be out there watching them, planning to do them harm. *Maybe I should have listened to Kevin and come in the morning.* She glanced back at the Quonset hut and found Kevin's gaze on her. She smiled, then walked toward him.

"Something catch your eye?" he asked when she drew closer.

"No, nothing. I was just thinking that I might need to start listening to your arguments for sanity in the future."

Kevin's gaze flicked toward the darkness. "There's something to be said for daylight."

"Yes, it seems there is." She nodded toward the truck. "And maybe there's something to be said for jumping right on things." She smiled at him sweetly and batted her eyelashes.

"*Possibly,*" he said with an air of pretend pomposity.

"Let's go see what we can see."

They walked over to the fancy rig, and Meredeth noted the chrome, the extra lights, and the flashy paint. A lot of money had been spent making the truck just so. "Okay," she said, "let's start taking notes. Get part numbers or make and model of the aftermarket parts, especially the bling. Which one of you knows more about cars?"

"Well, I—"

"I'm pretty—"

"Good gravy," muttered Meredeth.

Both men blushed.

"One of you open the hood and see what you can figure out. I'm going inside to see if the interior has had as much attention to detail. I also want to look at the VIN tag and see if I can spot the weld." She leaned back and peered toward the other end of the shed. "No trailer?"

"Not in here," said Bobby.

"Maybe in one of the other outbuildings around the farm," suggested Kevin. "We'll look when we're done here."

"Or maybe he's still using it."

"Um, why are we getting down in the weeds on these parts?" asked Kevin.

"Profiling serial offenders is about patterns, Kev," said Meredeth as she opened the driver's door to the cab. "If he's sticking to truck manufacturers, which seems likely based on what Doe *didn't* say about the Highwayman getting something different—he'll probably use the same aftermarket part brands as well."

"If it ain't fixed..." muttered Bobby.

"Makes sense," said Kevin as he opened the hood and stared at the big diesel mill underneath. "Compound turbos, exhaust. And that's just what I can see from here. We'll need a mechanic to tear into the engine itself and figure out what's aftermarket."

Bobby thumped the massive bull bar situated in front of the grill. "This thing looks brand new. It also looks sturdy as hell."

"Check the frame for modifications," said Kevin.

Meredeth looked on the door jamb and the door itself for a VIN tag, but all she found was pristine candy-apple red paint. She climbed up into the cab and peered at the dash, looking for the VIN in the place passenger cars had them, but there was nothing there either. "Can't find a VIN plate in here," she called.

"I've got a number stamped on a brass plate mounted to the top of passenger side frame rail. Is this the plate Doe meant?" asked Bobby.

"I don't know," said Meredeth. "Take a picture."

After his phone's flash went off, he got up off the floor and dusted himself off. "There are no modifications to the frame. But that transmission looks beefy."

Meredeth gave up looking for the VIN and slid across to the passenger seat so she could get at the glove box. Inside was a sheaf of papers at least an inch think. "I might have something here." She grabbed the stack and pulled it out, and as she did, she brushed the door of the glove box with her thumb, and something felt loose.

Kevin climbed up into the driver's seat. "What did you find."

"Hold these a second." She handed over the paperwork, then turned her attention to the loose panel on the inside of the glove compartment door. She tapped it, and it rattled. She bent closer and pried the loose panel up with her fingernails. Inside was a black metal box about an inch narrower than the door itself and maybe four inches from top to bottom. Inside the hidden compartment, she found a smaller stack of papers—vehicle registrations from five different states.

Meredeth pulled the registrations out and peered down at the one on top. "New Jersey," she said. "The company name is On The Road, Limited." She flipped that one to the bottom and read the next. "Colorado. Over the Road, Inc." She moved that one to the bottom, then fanned the remaining three out on her lap. "Florida, Nebraska, South Dakota. Razor's Edge Trucking, Freight Wranglers, and last, but not least, Highway's Edge Trucking." She glanced at Kevin. "Five registrations, five companies, one single VIN."

"Truckers had to maintain separate registrations in different states at one time, but with the new unified carrier registration system, that shouldn't be necessary."

"With different company names?"

"No. I think we found out how the Highwayman—if this is *his* truck—was never arrested after one of his crimes. He just switched the license plates, and if he got pulled over, well, it's a red semi. Who would give it another glance when the plates didn't match what the witnesses reported?" Kevin shook his head. "You've got the luck of the leprechauns, Connelly."

"Ha. What do you have?"

"Service receipts, weigh station records, junk like that."

"Do they all have the same company name, or are they varied?"

Kevin shuffled through the top few documents. "Different company names, different driver names, different license plates. That must also be how he got around the drive time restrictions. Change plates, get out the logbook for that plate, and *voila*, ten more hours of driving."

"Let's find out if he had other hidden compartments in here," she said, eyes flashing.

"All right. Where should I look?"

"Sleeper," she said with a jerk of her chin. "I'll do the dash and under the seats."

"Ten-four."

"Bobby!" she called. "Look for hidden compartments out there."

"Aye-aye, boss."

"This is the motherload," she mused.

"What's that, FBI?"

"We've got a list of aliases—both for the man and his company in various states. I bet we can pull address records and find out more. And there may be a phone number associated with them."

"And what do we do with that?"

"I've got an idea," she said with a tight smile.

CHAPTER 31

MIRACLE MILE

Hanable's Valley, NY

THE NEXT DAY, the three of them sat around Kevin's kitchen table. Bobby and Meredeth had succeeded in pulling the company details for the five companies Mack had used with the original truck. Kevin had a list of customers from a couple of aftermarket parts suppliers, and they'd spent the morning cross-referencing the names from that list with the names used on the registrations and found matches for all five. Mack had been smart. He *had* ordered parts for a later model Peterbilt 379 and though he had used the same five aliases to order his new parts, he'd switched which name he used for each type of part. He used one name for exterior parts like the bull bar and various chrome enhancements, but it was a different name than he'd used for the 359. He'd done the same for interior parts, engine parts, maintenance parts, and lights.

"We know beyond a shadow of a doubt that the unsub is one careful guy," said Bobby with a sigh.

"Yes, he is," said Meredeth. "And given what we've found out, I can refine the initial profile of the Highwayman—or can we call him Mack and be done with it at this point?"

"Um, you already nailed the color of his truck," said Kevin. "How much room for refinement is there?"

"Loads," she said. "For instance, he's very intelligent but uneducated. He's self-taught on the trucks and may not have attended truck driving school after all—by his own admission, we know Ankou forged a bunch of documents for Mack already. And whether Mack or Carl or both of them is the one playing smash up derby at mile marker thirty-three, I'll bet my last dollar Ankou forged the papers for them."

"And we now know he's definitely a protégé of Ankou."

"That's right, Kevin. He's got a lot of physical strength, probably advanced training in one of the more streetwise martial arts, though he goes out of his way to avoid having to use it. He's not averse to finishing the job with tools any truck might carry—a hammer, a beater bar, a crowbar—but his primary weapon is his Peterbilt, and judging by these receipts and what we found out earlier this morning, the truck is modified to a high-degree. It's more like a show vehicle than a working freight hauler, though he still uses it as such. Along with the amount of customization he's done comes pride, perhaps hubris. He's sure his truck can handle any situation he might find himself in."

"And he's not scared of using it," said Bobby. "He's ready to rock and roll at any moment."

Meredeth nodded. "That he is, and that means he's probably hypervigilant, hyperaware, and very high strung. He's a loner who feeds his sexual needs with commercial company if you take my meaning. He spends most of his time in his truck, probably driving around the clock. Why else keep separate logbooks? And that means he's got chemical assistance, perhaps an addiction. He might have minor beefs—the prostitution, or maybe possession for personal use—but he won't have many, if any at all, traffic violations. That would put him in the same category as the people he hunts. He might have prescription meds to keep himself awake, and if he does, he probably gets the scripts online or from another of Doe's zombies."

"Zombies," said Kevin, "I like that."

"Bobby, get on the horn to Peterbilt and see if we can track down this 379 he bought parts for. Maybe he bought it new."

"Will do." Bobby moved into the other room, already searching online for the Peterbilt corporate office phone number.

"What can I do, FBI?"

"You can hold my hand while I do something risky."

"Um...what are you planning now?"

"I noticed something when looking at these corporate documents."

"Yeah?"

"Yeah. A common phone number. It's a cell phone most likely."

"And how is that risky?"

"I'm going to do something I wouldn't think twice about, except for the surgeries."

"No way." Kevin crossed his arms and shook his head. "Bobby can be the bait. Or *I* can. I'm local after all—not as intimidating as you FBI-types."

"That's not the point, Kev. The Highwayman will respond to me because Ankou taught them about me, instilled the idea that they should keep their eyes out for me, to study my cases, find out where I live, *engage* me."

"Just because he did that to Alex, doesn't—"

"*And* Michelina. She said as much, and she said he made me out as a bugbear, someone to watch, to compete against. Hell, Kevin, *I'm* the whole point of his stupid plan. Not you. Not Bobby."

"My ears are burning," said Van Zandt as he re-entered the kitchen. "What are we talking about?"

"You talk sense to her," said Kevin. "She wants to use herself as bait."

Bobby gave a little shrug. "Yeah, she does that."

"What, and that's it? She's just had two major surgeries! She's still recovering!"

"Yeah, I am," said Meredeth, "which is why I want to set this up so I don't have to be the physical bait. I'll make the call, then we'll have someone else—"

"Great. Have any idea who, or will you just have to do it yourself when no one steps up?"

"It doesn't matter who. We'll arrange things so the encounter happens at night, in a place we control."

"There's no controlling a big rig, except maybe an M1A1 Abrahams," said Kevin. "Swear to me, that no matter what, you will not be driving the bait car."

"Kevin, I—"

"Swear, or I'll have no part in it."

"Kevin, I have no intention of jumping behind the wheel at the last second and going head-to-head with a tractor-trailer. We can put manikins in the parked car or something. I will be far away. Safe. But, the goading, the challenge, that has to be me."

"We can get a female officer to—"

"No, we can't. Having me talk in her ear will add a delay to the conversation, and the Highwayman will be skittish, hypervigilant, remember? He will know something's up." She took his hand and gave it a squeeze. "Besides, the worst he can do to me over the phone is hurt my feelings."

"Yeah. And you'll be safe... *Unless* he doesn't play by your rules. Unless he decides to come after you immediately rather than at the ambush you have in mind."

"That is a risk for sure," she said. "What I need to do is give him some information about where I will be, but I need to 'slip up' and let the information come out without saying it directly to him."

"Sure," said Bobby. "One of us can barge into the room and say something about reservations at some hotel. Someplace that won't mind having the FBI run an op in their parking lot."

"That should be Kevin," said Meredeth. "I don't know how much Ankou's zombies"—she flashed a smile at Kevin—"know about my present life, but if they do, they'll know about Kevin."

"Enough to recognize his voice?" asked Bobby dubiously.

"It's possible. He's a public figure."

"And I can handle it, Van Zandt," said Kevin. "It's a one-liner."

"Okay."

"Then we're agreed?" asked Meredeth.

"Hold on, FBI. We have to figure out where we're going to do this thing."

"I know just the place."

Kevin arched an eyebrow at her.

"And I've always wanted to go there since I started coming up on the weekends."

"Yeah? Where?"

"Standing Stone."

Kevin arched his eyebrows. "The Oneida casino? I didn't know you were into gambling."

"I'm not. Oh, I might play some slots or whatever, but mostly I like casinos because they are resorts that don't gouge you on the room charge."

"And you think they'll be open to helping us?"

"It's on Oneida Indian Nation land."

"Ah. The BIA?"

"Yes, they'll manage the request for us. I've already asked them to do it, and they've already reached out to the Oneida Nation."

"Why would you do that before you'd even broached the subject with us?"

"Because Standing Stone has something else going for it."

"What's that, Mere?" asked Bobby.

"It's at mile marker thirty-three on I-90."

Bobby turned to Kevin and shrugged. "She's always got all the cards, man. Don't sweat it."

CHAPTER 32

GOT YOUR EARS ON?

Hanable's Valley, NY

THE PHONE RANG three times, and Meredeth wondered if the plan would fail due to voicemail, but just at the fourth ring started its mechanical spiel, someone picked it up. "Hello, is this the mental degenerate running people off the road and killing them?"

"What? Who is this?" said a male voice.

"My name is Meredeth Connelly, and I'm an FBI agent. I'm on your case, chickenshit, and I will put a stop to your road rage."

"Is that so?" Amusement carried across the line loud and clear.

"It is. Here's what I know already: you grew up on the Branch farm outside of Yoagoh, NY. The man that raised you is also a mental degenerate who kidnapped you after murdering the rest of your family, and you're so screwed up you're actually *loyal* to that idiot."

"*Be careful, Meredeth Connelly of the FBI!*" the man shouted.

Meredeth pumped her fist at Bobby and Kevin. "Hey, tell me something, Highwayman, did—"

"*What* did you call me?" the man hissed.

"Oh, the Highwayman? That's your serial killer nickname. Tell me this: did Ankou diddle you when you were young? Did he lose interest when you got older? Is that why you left?"

"You've got quite a mouth on you, Agent Connelly. You should work on that. It could write a check your ass can't pay."

"Yeah? Well, I make allowances by psychos who were raised by a serial killing imbecile without the brains to avoid getting caught."

"Is that so?"

"It is," said Meredeth. I just wanted you to know that Ankou is feeding us information about you. He said he raised you in his own twisted image and then gave us a description of your Peterbilt 379."

"Uh, yes, the 379."

"That's right—a real chicken-hauler by the sound of it. So many chicken-lights, Highwayman, so many chrome doodads, and that paint...candy-apple red, right? Or did you paint it since then?"

"Oh, Ankou said all that? Did he give you this number, too?" The fire that had been in his voice had gone cold, and he seemed relaxed.

"No, of course not. But he led us to a stash of corporate filings he made on your behalf. The number was in them."

"Is that so?" Again, amusement trickled over the line.

"Yes. He's so screwed up he hardly knows who he's talking to anymore. Are you as crazy as he is?"

"*HE IS NOT CRAZY!*" screamed the Highwayman. "*HE'S NOT A PEDOPHILE AND HE'S FAR SMARTER THAN YOU!*"

"Yep, sure he is. That's why it only took me a few days to nail his ass and put him in prison forever. And trust me, he's a real looney tune. I know. I've seen plenty of psychos like him. He's a nutjob, a cuckoo bird. In fact, I'm working on getting him transferred to a federal hospital for the criminally insane. I'll reserve a room there for you, too."

"Hey, sugar, you have to catch me first." The Highwayman's voice was a mixture of a bandsaw cutting metal and a teakettle about to boil over.

"That's the easy part, chum. Look me up. Once I know your mind, you are as good as caught. You might want to consider turning yourself in. Or are you too chicken? You know, the way you use your truck to do the dirty work makes you look scared."

"I'll take it under advisement, Agent Connelly. But I'm already familiar with your career. You will never track me down. No one can."

"I'm sure that's what your torturer thought, too, but look where he is now."

"Torturer?" He chuckled. "Hardly. Ankou is a great man. A visionary. He sees what's wrong with this country and—"

Meredeth pointed at Kevin.

"Hey, honey! I've got good news!" he shouted from the doorway.

"Kevin, I'm on the—"

"I got us reservations at Standing Stone! For tonight, babe, so get packed!"

"—phone..." she finished, then held her breath.

The Highwayman said nothing for a moment, then hung up.

Meredeth let the held breath race out between her parted lips. "Hook set," she said. "I think."

"Now, all we have to do is reel him in."

"Yeah," she said. Her phone rumbled that an email had come in. She opened her email app and saw a message from the AUSA for Eastern Virginia at the top. The subject line read: "Contingent on verification, let's give this woman what she wants." Meredeth scanned the email quickly, nodding to herself. "The AUSA," she said. "He's going for Michelina's proffer. He wants to set up a meeting in the next few days."

"Good deal," said Bobby.

Meredeth took a moment to send the AUSA a quick reply outlining where she was, how close they were on the

Highwayman case, and telling him she'd be available to accompany Michelina to a meeting in his office in three or four days' time. "Let me pass on the news, then we can get started on the details for tonight. She hit the compose button, selected Michelina's email, and wrote:

Dear Michelina,

I have good news! Actually, I have two pieces of good news.

The first is that I just heard from the AUSA, and though there are a few details to iron out, he's willing to extend transactional immunity to you. But as I warned you, he will require that you testify against Ankou in any cases that go to court. He also wants to depose you on the record. But don't worry, all of that is pretty standard for deals at this level. Just tell the truth during your deposition and tell *all* the truth. You're buying immunity with your knowledge of Ankou, and the only thing that can sour the deal is if he catches you in a lie—either of commission or omission, if you take my meaning.

He'd like to meet you in the next couple of days, and given where you live, I told him that was entirely possible. I'll be there, too, and I'll make sure you get what you need.

Which brings me to the second piece of news. It is my firm belief that soon, I will text you a picture of the Highwayman, so you can tell us whether it's Carl or Mack. That's right, whoever he is, I think he's made his first mistake.

And that's thanks to your help, both in giving us information about life on the farm, but also in giving us leverage over Ankou. Your information about the Cadillac and the truck he, Carl, and Mack built cowed him into cooperating.

So, yay! You'll be out from under the things he made you do. You'll be free to get on with your boring life as a software guru. :)

Congratulations!

Meredeth

She reread the email and grunted her approval, then hit send.

CHAPTER 33

TEN-THIRTY-THREE

Verona, NY

THE HOSTAGE RESCUE Team had brought a few undercover vehicles to Standing Stone, including a bobtail semi, an old van which bore an internal skeleton of chromoly and would serve as a rolling roadblock if necessary, and the motorhome Meredeth, Bobby, and Kevin lounged in. Because of the nature of the crimes and the mass of a semi-truck, they'd also brought armored personnel carriers for deployment. The bait car the Bureau had rented in her name for the operation was a three-year-old Mercedes, snow-white and brilliant under the parking lot's white LED lights. It sat all by itself on the back row of the slightly curved parking lot. Two manikins sat in the front seats—the driver dressed in one of Kevin's spare uniforms and wearing one of his HVPD ball caps, and the one in the passenger seat wearing a wig that would match Meredeth's hair in the dark and one of her BAU polo shirts and a pair of her jeans.

"We make a cute couple, sitting out there in the Mercedes, talking dirty."

"Mom!" gasped Bobby, but he could only hold the horrified expression for a few seconds before he burst into laughter.

"I sure hope this works," said Kevin, ignoring their antics. "And I'm glad you got HRT involved."

"I'm not going up against a semi with a Glock and a smile," said Meredeth. "I leave that kind of rashness to Bobby."

"Well, he's a Marine, so his smile is deadlier than yours," murmured Kevin.

"Game faces," said the HRT sergeant over the radio.

Bobby pointed toward the intersection of Patrick Road and NYSR 36. A fancied-up red semi idled in the turn lane, its blinker flashing amber. As soon as there was a break in traffic of sufficient space, the truck rumbled onto Patrick Road with the muted sound of its turbochargers. The driver made the first left—into the Standing Stone complex—and then the first right into the main parking area. The truck idled down the third lane in the center section, and when it came abreast of the rental car, it braked but didn't stop. The truck cruised slowly to the end of the lane, where it turned left and entered the last area in the lot.

"Hold steady," said the HRT leader. "Don't move until he either turns aggressive or heads to the exit."

The Peterbilt 379 began to accelerate hard, the turbos once again shrieking at the night sky, the brake lights dead. The driver turned on the roof lights, surrounding the white Mercedes in a halo of brilliant blue-white.

"Move in," Meredeth said on the radio. "He's taken the bait."

The truck roared toward the Benz from half a parking lot away, the magnificent chrome exhaust stacks belching smoke that was blacker than the night sky heavenward. The truck speared the Mercedes in the passenger door, and its momentum carried both vehicles through twenty parking spots. Gray-white steam belched from the truck, and the engine rattled to death.

The HRT van raced into the closest exit back onto Patrick Road, jerking sideways to block both lanes, but after what the truck had just done to the Mercedes, Meredeth thought it was a fool's errand. Better was the bobtailed semi-tractor driven by an HRT specialist who moved in to box the truck in place against the wreckage of the German sedan. With twin diesel roars the twin HRT APCs roared out from behind the Standing Stone Auto Care Building across Patrick Road and raced toward the truck. They ignored the pavement and jetted through Standing Stone's carefully manicured landscaping, leaving furrows through the sod and into the rich black soil that would cost the Bureau plenty.

One of the APCs slid to a stop on the passenger side of the truck, the other took the driver's side. HRT members poured out of the backs of each carrier, carrying tactical arms, and wearing tactical armor. They made a semicircular ring around the driver's door and the passenger's.

"Driver! Dismount your vehicle!" The voice of God boomed from one the APCs. "You are surrounded, and there is no escape."

The red chicken-hauler emitted a grinding shriek and puffed black smoke toward the sky, but the driver couldn't keep the beast running.

"Move in!" said the HRT leader over the APC's public address system, and a shield specialist from each team unslung his bulletproof shield and slung his rifle in favor of a Glock sidearm. Two other unit members fell in behind the shield specialist as he advanced toward his assigned truck door.

Both teams arrived at their doors at roughly the same moment, and one of the riflemen moved to the side and yanked the door open. A lanky man sat with his hands on the wheel, looking straight ahead. A thin trickle of blood ran down the left side of his face.

With the other rifleman covering the suspect, and the shield specialist virtually blocking the doorway, the remaining team member climbed the truck's steps to gain access to the cab. The one on the passenger side leveled his assault rifle on the driver, while the one on the other side crouched on the top step and took the suspect into custody from where he sat.

"That's it?" breathed Bobby. "All this preparation for...*that*?"

"Don't tempt fate," said Kevin.

"We got him, boys. We just captured the Highwayman."

"Doesn't it bother either of you that, all of a sudden, the man is stupid?"

"What do you mean?"

"He's gone eleven years, wrecking cars at will with little or no damage to his truck, then he goes for a full-on T-bone move that trashes his engine?"

Meredeth shrugged. "I did my best to enrage him."

"I think it worked," said Kevin.

"Come on, let's go talk to him," she said, and she got up, moved to the door set in the RV's side, opened it, and stepped out into the darkness. Kevin and Bobby followed a step or two behind. The three of them walked across the parking lot.

"It's eerie how much that truck looks like the one back on the farm," said Meredeth.

"It's his signature. Part of his ritual, maybe."

"Could be," said Meredeth in a distracted voice.

They approached the now relaxed HRT units lounging around the truck while one of their own searched the driver and another searched the truck. She doubted they would find anything—the Highwayman had had plenty of time to clear out any incriminating evidence, and would have if he were smart, as he'd have known the likelihood of his capture was high in such a direct approach. And he was smart. She frowned as she wondered if they'd have anything on the man besides the events of the evening, if they'd find anything linking him to the spate of road rage murders.

Meredeth approached the man and snapped his picture. "Hello, again," she said. "I'm Meredeth."

"Lady, I don't know—or care—who Meredeth is. Get away from me."

She grinned with only one side of her face. "Don't be a poor sport, Mack."

"My name isn't Mack. My name is Ralph Brenner."

"Sure thing," she said. "Whatever you want. Are you sure it isn't Carl? Do you even remember your real name?"

"*Ralph Brenner*," the man said, speaking slowly as if to a child.

Meredeth shook her head. "It's Steven Aldridge or Greg Henderson." She turned her back on him and motioned for Bobby and Kevin to follow. "He won't give us anything at the moment. We'll talk to him a few hours from now, when the reality of the situation hits him." She opened her phone. "Bobby, email the crime analyst. What's her name again?"

"Dana Jensen."

"Right, email Dana and let her know we got him. Tell her I want to meet her next week and take her to lunch."

"Roger," said Bobby.

Meredeth stopped walking and navigated to her email app. She again selected Michelina's email address and created a new message, to which she attached the photo she'd just taken. Then, she wrote, "WE GOT HIM" in the subject box and typed:

> Dear Michelina,
>
> I couldn't be happier to report that we just captured the Highwayman with no casualties. He's being processed now, but I snapped a picture, as promised.
>
> Is this Mack or Carl? He's refusing to give us his name.
>
> Your friend,
>
> Meredeth

She pressed send, and then smiled at Kevin. "I can't believe it was this easy."

"Yeah, it seems like I was worried about nothing." His eyes were far away, and his brows bunched.

"You don't—"

"Uh, did you just send an email to Michelina?" Bobby asked.

"Yes, I did."

"I just got a reply from Dana Jensen...to *your* email, not mine."

"Um, that's *interesting*. Did she hit reply on your email or is it some kind of IT snafu?"

"Look at it yourself," said Bobby, handing over his phone.

Meredeth and Kevin stepped closer together to read the email. It said:

> Meredeth, you've made a huge mistake! That's not Mack *or* Carl! You've arrested the wrong man!
>
> 10-33 10-33 10-33
>
> Michelina
>
> Today, 11:23 PM Robert Van Zandt wrote:
>
> Hi Dana,
>
> I just wanted to let you know, we found the Highwayman. He's in cuffs as I type this. Thanks so much for your help and your keen eye!
>
> Yours,
>
> BVZ

"I'll be damned," said Kevin. "Michelina is your crime analyst."

Meredeth nodded slowly. "She said at least one of Ankou's children worked in law enforcement. I thought she meant someone else. And that 10-33 is subtle."

"Right. Emergency, all units stand by."

"Hmm. And I just realized there may be a hidden meaning behind mile marker thirty-three."

"There are definitely emergencies there when the Highwayman is around," said Bobby. "But what do we do about Dana? Call McCutchins?"

"No, he'd have her arrested. I'll handle the long term, but for now..." She hit the reply button on Bobby's phone and wrote:

> Dear Dana,
>
> It's certainly nice to meet you...under this alias anyway.
>
> Don't worry, your secret is safe with me. Here's hoping it's not going to be a problem moving forward. This is one of those things you might have to tell the AUSA.
>
> In the meantime, what do you mean that isn't Mack or Carl? We pulled that guy out of a truck that has to belong to one of them—it's almost an exact match for the one the two of them rebuilt with Ankou. And he'd just rammed a car he thought I was a passenger in, and he did it with deliberation and intent.

It's been eleven years, right? Maybe he's changed?

Yours,

Meredeth and Bobby.

"There," she said. "That ought to rattle the underbrush a little." She handed the phone back to Bobby.

"What if she's right? What if that's not the Highwayman, not Mack, not Carl?" asked Bobby.

"Then we grill him until he tells us where the owner of that truck is because that beast is almost an exact match to the one back in the rusty Quonset hut." Meredeth shrugged. "Same as always, we'll use every tool in our arsenal until we get the information we need." She turned her gaze on the red truck. "But I don't understand this. Did the real Highwayman lend him the truck? And if so, why didn't the man come himself? It must have been a risk to send a patsy in his own place."

"You could call the number again," suggested Kevin.

"I suppose you're right, but what do I say? 'Sorry, we arrested your truck without you?'"

"No, you tell him we arrested his *accomplice* and he's already started talking. You tell him we'll be with him very soon," said Bobby.

Meredeth shrugged again and opened her calling app, then navigated to the recent calls tab. She scrolled through the many FBI contacts she'd spoken to that day, the CEO of Standing Stone, and the Bureau of Indian Affairs contact she had, and stared at the number for the Highwayman. "I'm not sure this is a good idea. If he's as smart as—" She jumped as her phone rang in her hand. She glanced at the caller ID, then looked at Bobby. "Dana Jensen."

"Answer it," said Bobby. "See what she has to say for herself."

"Right." Meredeth accepted the call, then clicked it on speaker. "Hello, Michelina. You're on speaker phone, but only Bobby and Chief Kevin Saunders from Hanable's Valley PD are within earshot. Kevin helped us—"

"Capture Ankou," she said in a rich mezzo soprano voice. "Yeah, I know all about him. I guess I made a big oops with that last reply."

"Sort of. I knew you had another identity and knew you lived in the area. I didn't know *you* were the crime analyst who 'found' these road rage crimes."

"Sorry for the deception. Are... Are you still willing to help me with the AUSA?"

"Of course, I am, Michelina. Nothing has changed between us, but it's nice to know *you* are the sibling in law enforcement so I can stop worrying about that."

"Oh, I'm not the one I meant, but let's save that for later. The guy you arrested is definitely *not* Mack. He's too small...too...*White*."

No one spoke for a moment. "Stephen Aldridge was White," Meredeth finally said.

"No, he wasn't. Mack is Black. He did grow up in a White household until his adoptive-mother divorced his adoptive-father and fell on hard times. His father was a drug addict, and his mother had no real work skills. Mack's younger sibling was also adopted. Chinese, I think."

"Oh, and this guy is too small," said Bobby.

"I can't believe I led with that, but I was so stunned I could hardly think."

"And I suppose Carl is Black, too?"

"No. Carl is White, but that's not Carl."

"Are you sure?"

"I am."

"He was in Mack's newest truck—a Peterbilt 379. Do you recognize the man at all? Could he be another one of Ankou's zombies?"

"No, I've never seen him before in my life."

"He might have joined the tribe after you severed contact," said Bobby.

"No, he's too old," said Kevin. "That man is forty if I'm a day older than sixteen."

"You have to be careful, Meredeth," said Michelina. "The *real* Highwayman might be in the area."

"Then why send in a patsy?"

"He's smart, Meredeth. Really smart, and really devious."

"You're starting to give me the impression that you know who is behind all this."

"I..." Michelina swallowed hard enough to be audible across the cellphone. "Look, I had a thing for Mack. I think I told you that. When we were young, I wanted to believe that Mack was playing along with Ankou and Alex, just like I was. I convinced myself he was inherently good, that he loved me. I didn't want to believe he was out there somewhere pulping drivers who pissed him off."

"But?"

"But it's got to be him, Meredeth. Never mind that for now. You've got to get out of there before he comes for you."

"Well, I'm in a parking lot with two HRT units. I think I'm safe enough. I'm going to let you go for now. I need to rest a little. I have a feeling we'll be interrogating the driver in a few hours."

"Call me before you do anything. Okay?"

"Sure, if the situation permits."

"Um, one more question. What do I do about work?"

"You go in, you keep doing what you do, and you don't say a word about this to anyone. We don't want the AUSA getting wind of it before you tell him."

"Oh. Okay."

"Goodnight, Michelina."

"Yeah, same to you three."

Meredeth hung up, then stood for a moment, shaking her head. "This is getting complicated."

"Getting complicated..."

"Shut up, Bobby," she said absently. "Hold down the fort. Let me know when you think the suspect is good to answer questions. I'm going to head back to the motorhome and take a nap until it's time." She looked at Kevin and cocked her eyebrow in a challenging manner. "You coming, or would you rather hang out with Van Zandt?"

"Mo-om! Stop talking dirty!" Bobby said, then laughed again.

CHAPTER 34

TEN-TWENTY-ONE

Verona, NY

THE PHONE WOKE her, but for the first time in months, she awoke easily and was alert and ready to go. Kevin wasn't beside her in the RV's bedroom, so she assumed he'd gone out to see if he could help with the clean-up of the parking lot. She grabbed her phone from the side table and hit accept. "Connelly," she said.

"Well, hello there," said the voice she recognized from earlier that day.

"Hello, Mr. Highwayman."

"But you caught him, right? The Highwayman, I mean?" His tone was caustic, mocking.

"No," she said calmly. "We did catch his patsy, though. Should I dispense with the nickname and start calling you Mack, or would you rather I call youCarl?"

"Poor Ralph," said the Highwayman. "Don't go too hard on him. He doesn't have a lot going on upstairs. He works for one of my trucking companies. *Worked*, I mean. I can't have employees who commit acts of road rage." He laughed.

"No, that would be bad," she said.

"He's a good man. I only convinced him to ram your rental car by offering him fifty thousand dollars in cash. He has a sick child. I thought it would help."

"Yeah, but now that sick child's father will be in prison."

The Highwayman sobered. "Don't do that. Cut him a deal to testify against me. Do that much for the man. He's never even met me. We made all our arrangements by telephone. I told him my name was Randall."

"We'll see. It depends on how cooperative he's feeling."

"He's not a criminal, Agent Connelly. He's been driving my old 379 for about two years. Since I got my new rig."

Meredeth squeezed her eyes shut. "You knew right away?"

"Of course. My father knows what kind of vehicle *I* drive." He laughed. "So much for you being smarter than my father."

"You admit you are one of Ankou's children?" In the background on the Highwayman's end, she heard the whine of a big rig's turbocharger whining.

"I've never denied it."

"Are you the one he renamed Carl? Or are you the Mack? You might as well answer—I'm evidently very far off your trail."

"But aren't you in New York?" He seemed genuinely confused, but then he shook it off. "Whatever. I'll tell you my name, but it won't help you find me. I've never used it in any official capacity."

"Then?"

"Then, yes, I'm the one he called Mack."

"The boy named Steven Aldridge."

"*Don't call me that!*" he rasped. "I left that existence in my rearview."

"And are you going to keep doing Ankou's bidding? Are you going to keep killing?"

"You will probably never know if I keep killing, but I can promise you: I'm done leaving my father's mark. I'm done with his plan."

"Would you like to understand why you have to kill, Mack?" she asked.

"I'm done with his plan, and I'm done with you, Meredeth. For now." The call went dead.

Meredeth sighed. She'd distinctly heard the turbos whining as Mack's truck battled a grade or something. He was still on the road, still driving somewhere in America, and she had no idea how to track him down.

CHAPTER 35

MOVING ON

Alexandria, VA

MEREDETH PULLED THE car to the side of the road and slowed, looking for the entrance to the parking garage attached to the United States Attorney building on Jamieson Avenue. She showed her ID to the guard in the little guard shack protected by bolsters, and he glanced at it with a bored expression dominating his slab-like face. He grunted and hit a button, causing the roll-up doors to ascend, then waved her inside. She drove around for a few minutes, looking for a spot, then lucked out and found one close to the elevators.

When she entered the outer offices of the AUSA for the Eastern District of Virginia, the reception desk was empty, but another woman was already seated on the leather couch. She looked up as Meredeth entered, and a slow smile filled her face. Meredeth approached her and held out her hand. "We meet at last."

"Hello, Meredeth," said Michelina.

"Nervous?" asked Meredeth.

"A little, I guess."

"Did you think of anything that might help us?" She didn't have to specify what she wanted help with, Michelina knew.

"No." Michelina pursed her lips. "Well, maybe. Alex was... Mack had a huge crush on Alex before it sank into his head that Alex had become male. He might have stayed in contact."

"Interesting," said Meredeth, though a lump of cold fear settled in her gut. She sank to the couch beside Michelina, then leaned close. "Did you think of anything not in the proffer letter that you need to come clean about?"

Michelina looked her in the eye and shook her head.

"That's fine. Just remember what we talked about."

"Yes," said Michelina in a clipped tone.

"Everything will be okay. I'm going to be with you the whole time."

A woman in a cream suit came walking out of an interior hallway and smiled at Michelina. "Ms. Fuchs? AUSA Brienne will see you now." She arched an eyebrow at Meredeth. "May I help you?"

"Agent Connelly," said Meredeth, flipping her ID case open. "Ms. Fuchs is my cooperating witness."

"Ah, very well." The cream-suited woman turned and held the door to an oak paneled hallway open. "Straight down the corridor to the double doors. You can go right in."

They followed the instructions, with Meredeth leading the way. She pushed open the right door of the set and stepped inside a magnificent office. "Mr. Brienne?" she asked the dapper gentleman sitting behind the wide desk scribbling notes on a legal pad.

"All day, every day, and twice on Saturdays," he said without looking up. "I've read your proffer and find it equitable. I'm willing to extend a—"

Meredeth cleared her throat. "I'm Special Agent Meredeth Connelly, sir. This"—she waved her hand at Michelina—"is Julie Fuchs." After discussing it, Michelina had agreed to use her legal name—she hadn't had much of a choice as they needed her legal name for the courts, even though it would tip Ankou off if he got wind of it.

AUSA Brienne put down his pen, lining it up precisely with the edge of his pad, which was in turn aligned with the edge of the desk. He took off a pair of glasses, folded them, and set them atop the pad. Then he lifted his gaze and looked first at Meredeth, then at Michelina. "I see. I understand using your legal name makes you uncomfortable. In deference to the special attentions you have suffered, is there another name you prefer?"

Michelina grinned nervously. "It's fine."

"We need to use your legal name for the court documents and any testifying you may do, but inside these walls, we can use any name you prefer."

The woman shrugged and said, "In that case, please call me Michelina."

"Very well, Michelina." He stood and extended his hand toward the couch and armchair arrangement setup under the window. "Please take a seat, ladies."

After they were seated in the armchairs, he sat on the couch and rested his gaze on Meredeth. "It is my firm belief that Michelina would benefit from the Marshal's Witness Protection Program after we're done with her depositions."

"I understand," said Meredeth, "and I have offered."

AUSA Brienne nodded a single time, then turned his gaze on Michelina. "Young lady, based on the information in your proffer, you are in mortal peril. I'd hate to think what these...these animals might do to you should they discover you've switched sides."

"I, uh..." She glanced at Meredeth and shrugged.

"Michelina has made other arrangements."

The AUSA's eyebrows arched comically. "Other arrangements?"

"Yes," said Meredeth, "and good ones. You can put your mind to rest on that score."

He switched his gaze back and forth between them for a moment, then nodded. He leaned forward and fixed Michelina with a stare. "It's important that you are truthful. Is there anything else I need to know before the process gets rolling?"

Michelina shook her head. "Everything I've done is in the proffer letter."

"Very well," said AUSA Brienne. "Now, there are some details we should go over before the depositions next Monday. I've blocked the rest of my afternoon to make sure you are comfortable and know what to expect."

"You're very kind," said Michelina. She glanced at Meredeth and smiled.

"Someone in your life should be," said Brienne.

CHAPTER 36

BEAR DEN

Lowell, FL

AS BOBBY PARKED their rental in front of the Lowell Correctional Institute's main building, Meredeth shivered. She'd been thinking about the amount of time they spent inside prisons or jails in stark contrast to the previous three months, most of which she'd spent hanging out at Kevin's house in Hanable's Valley. This trip was absolutely necessary as Ankou had decided not to speak to them for the time being. "Let's do this," she said at last.

"Right," said Bobby. He got out and closed the car door with a little too much exuberance.

Meredeth could feel a headache coming, and she hoped speaking with Alex Delamort might cure it before it really got going. Then again, the last time she'd spoken with Delamort she'd ended up with four inches of steel in her belly.

At least *that* had made her forget her headache.

She got out of the car, feeling a little shaky, and a nervous bubble of acid popped in the back of her throat. "Uff," she groaned.

"You okay, boss? I can talk to Alex alone."

"No," she said. "He's not going to win this one." She squared her shoulders and strode toward the main doors. "The warden knows we're coming, right?"

"Yeah. I spoke to him myself. He promised to have Delamort ready for us in an interview room."

"Good."

Bobby looked at her sidelong. "Mere, are you *sure* this is a good idea? Do we really need to speak to the serial killer that almost got you?"

"Michelina said they were close; said they might have maintained their relationship. And he's still out there, so, unless you've come up with a solid strategy for finding this ghost on wheels, yeah, we do need to speak to Alex."

"As far as we know, the Highwayman has stopped his activities."

"Right, Bobby. *As far as we know*, but a month ago, we didn't even know he existed. It's not enough for me that we *think* he's stopped. I want to know *for certain*, and the only way that works is if we put his ass behind bars for life."

"I'm with you there, boss. But listen, you don't—"

"Yes, I *do*, Bobby," she said quietly.

He treated her to a single curt nod, then led her inside and got them checked in at reception. A few minutes later, a beefy guard took them back to the interview room. Good to his word, the warden had Alex seated, chained to the table, and waiting.

He sat with his head down, but at the sound of the door, he lifted his head. His expression barely changed from the bland, spaced-out look. He looked at Bobby for a moment, then at Meredeth. "Oh..." he said. "Huh-hello."

Frowning at the long string of drool swinging from Alex's lip, Meredeth turned to the guard. "I want his medication list."

"*Her* medication list, you mean."

"Just go get the damn thing. He's not even *convicted* yet!"

The guard shrugged as though he couldn't care less what Meredeth thought. "I can't leave, but I'll radio for a runner to bring the list. The conviction is just a formality. She stabbed an FBI agent, you know. And she's been nothing but problems until we got her into the MHC program."

"MHC?"

"Mental Health Care."

"Alex isn't crazy."

The guard scoffed. "Well, the dumb bitch thinks she's a man, doesn't she?"

Meredeth narrowed her eyes a moment and treated the guard to a severe glare, after which she glanced at his name tag and jotted it in her notes. She turned her back on him and took one of the empty seats on her side of the table.

"Alex?" she asked. "Do you remember me?"

"Connelly," said Alex.

"That's right. We, uh, worked together a few months ago."

"Yeah, then I stabbed you."

Behind Meredeth, the guard grunted. "Right," she said, swallowing a sudden lump of burning coals in her throat. "Why'd you do that?" She hadn't meant to ask that question; she hadn't even meant to discuss the attack.

"You ruined my car."

"The 911?"

Alex shrugged, and the rope of spittle dropped into his lap. "Broke the...the..."

"Yes, I broke the driver's side window."

"Yes. Broke the glass with a hammer."

"And that's why you—"

"Well, I mean, you're *her*. You're *you*. And you ruined my car."

"Ankou told me you broke the rules when you attacked me."

Alex lifted his shoulders, then let them slump. "He doesn't know *everything*."

"No, he doesn't," Meredeth agreed.

Blinking hard a few times, Alex shifted his gaze to Bobby. "What..." He shook his head.

"What are we doing here?" asked Bobby, and Alex nodded.

"We need your help, Alex," said Meredeth.

Delamort closed his eyes for the time it took Meredeth's heart to make thirty beats. When he spoke, his eyes remained closed, and his voice was blurry with the effects of the sedative the prison had him on. "That's stupid of you, Meredeth. Why would I help you?"

"Because I've come to understand a little of what you went through as a child. Ankou doesn't deserve your loyalty. He betrayed you again and again as he tortured and brainwashed you."

Laughing with abandon, Alex looked around wildly as if wondering why no one laughed with him.

"We're looking for Mack," said Bobby. "We understand the two of you were close."

"Ha," grunted Alex. "He had a bro-crush on me."

"A bro-crush?"

"Yeah, but I don't swing that way if you know what I mean. I hit for the straight team." He eyed Meredeth like someone who'd had too much tequila. "*I like girls,*" he stage-whispered, "but not you."

"Um, yeah, I like girls, too," said Bobby. "Where's Mack living these days?"

Alex threw back his head and laughed. "Even if I knew, I wouldn't tell you. What's he done to warrant the attention of the great and super-awesome profiler team of...of"—the momentary competence in his voice drifted away like chaff in the wind—"you and you."

"We can't share that information with you. You know that. You were a prosecutor, after all."

"Yes," said Meredeth, "and you know how to stop all the sedatives and hypnotics and drugs they're flooding you with. You know your rights."

"Hey—" started the burly guard.

Meredeth cut him off with a sweeping chop of her hand, and Alex laughed out loud.

"What are you laughing at, *Missy*?" he snapped.

Alex lunged to his feet. "*THAT'S NOT MY NAME! ALEX DELAMORT IS MY NAME!*"

"Delamort?" snorted the guard. "Of the dead? Really? Alex of the dead? They already made that movie with a guy named Shaun."

Meredeth swiveled in her chair and pointed at the door. "Get out," she hissed at the guard.

"No, ma'am. I can't leave you alone—"

"Then *shut up*. You are interfering in a federal investigation. Don't think I won't arrest you if you continue."

The guard sneered at her but didn't venture so far as to speak.

"That's better," Delamort said.

"Alex, we're going to find Mack either way, but maybe helping us is a way out of here. We could have you taken into federal custody as a cooperating witness. You'd still do your time but in a prison the DOJ controls. Maybe the Supermax facility where you'd be alone all the time, but you wouldn't be housed with women."

"Oh, I don't mind that, so much," he said. "I like women." He narrowed his eyes at Meredeth. "Most women, anyway."

"Then something else you'd like. Use what you have to get what you want."

"You'll never allow me what I want, so stop trying to bribe me." He chuckled. "Anyway, Mack's a ghost. No one can find him. I tried four years ago, and I knew him better than Father did. You know what I found?"

"What?"

"Nothing, Meredeth. I found nothing, and I *knew* what his long-term plans were. Even with Lindsey helping me 'track down my cousin,' we found *nothing*." He waved his hand in dismissal. "You'll do no better."

"Then trade information about Ankou's crimes—"

Alex interrupted her with a slightly manic burst of guffaws. "You don't get it, Connelly. You're the *enemy*. I wouldn't give you directions out of this room."

Meredeth frowned at her note pad, then glanced at Bobby. "You know, Alex, we have some information about you that could lead to additional charges back in New York."

"We're done," scoffed Delamort. "Do your worst, Connelly, and see what it gets you. I want to go back to my cell."

"You heard her," growled the guard.

"Yes, I heard *him*," said Meredeth. She got up slowly, feeling her age, feeling the decades she'd been tracking people like Alex, feeling the missed days of recuperation she should have taken. She got her things together and turned to go.

"One more thing, Connelly," Alex rasped.

Meredeth turned to look at him.

"Don't ever come back here because the next time I see you, *I'll finish what I started in St. Petersburg Beach*." He nodded at the guard. "This neandertal won't be able to stop me, and neither will Van Zandt. Know why?"

"Why?" Meredeth asked with a sigh.

"Because I'm *committed* to your undoing. For Uncle Kenny. For Father. For *me*. I have nothing left to live for, so dying to kill you is fine by me."

Meredeth turned away and walked out the door, Bobby close on her heels.

CHAPTER 37

PLAIN WRAPPER

On the road

THE WHITE KENWORTH was plain-Jane, a fleet spec vehicle he'd picked up at an auction without a hint of personality. It had very little horsepower, relative to his Pete 389 that now stood covered with tarps in a warehouse he owned near Las Vegas. He'd given his father what he could, and now it was time for Mack to disappear.

To him, that didn't mean letting his needs go unassuaged, it meant *change*, and the Kenworth was the first step. Mack could no longer afford to stand out. He couldn't draw attention to himself, even when he killed. Connelly was onto his old gag of dropping bodies at mile marker thirty-three, and though it felt like losing an old friend to cancer or something, Mack knew it was time he gave that up.

And I have to mix up my methods. It's not just lollipop thirty-three. It's the Pete, the bull bar. It's everything. It wasn't the first time since he'd thrown Ralphie at Connelly's obvious ambush that he'd thought these thoughts. It was disturbing to contemplate the vast nature of the changes he was required to make.

But all the changes were temporary changes, and sooner or later, he'd get a message from his father, that his services were needed again. His task was to survive until then, and he planned, like always, to exceed his father's expectations.

Ahead, a bright white corvette merged from an onramp and swept across all four lanes, causing truckers to brake hard and cars to swerve. *Will you look at that drunk asshole?* he thought and smiled like a wolf as he lifted the .44 Magnum from his lap and accelerated his wheezing dragonfly of a truck toward the car.

I HOPE YOU'VE enjoyed Mile Marker 33 and want to follow Meredeth Connelly on her next adventure. The fourth book in the series is titled Sticks and Bones, and you can find it on Amazon: https://ehv4.us/4sticksandbones.

To be among the first to know what I'm up to and when the newest book I write goes live, please subscribe to my newsletter at https://ehv4.us/vvjoinehv or join my online community at https://ehv4.us/discord. You can also support me on Patreon at https://ehv4.us/patreon.

You can find my complete thriller bibliography at https://ehv4.us/booksehv. I also write supernatural fiction, and you can find my bibliography under the name Erik Henry Vick at https://ehv4.us/books.

Books these days succeed or fail based on the strength of their reviews. I hope you will consider leaving a review—as an independent author, I could use your help. It's easy (I promise). You can leave your review by clicking on this link: https://ehv4.us/2revmm33

AUTHOR'S NOTE
7/25/22

I HAD PLANNED for Meredeth's recovery to be much shorter than it turned out. There were certain things I wanted to get right, and the utter hopelessness and seemingly permanent exhaustion that went along with my own temporary ileostomy was high on that list. Also on the list was the constant fear of the ostomy leaking or exploding (it's not a fun experience, trust me), and the way the bag always made it feel like my guts were coming out as I walked. And the diet...I'm shaking my head right now because the diet is the weirdest thing—no fruit, no vegetables (well, some, but not many), and no vitamins, fiber, or supplements. Eating was a real chore and trying to eat food in a restaurant was worse still.

Everything Meredeth went through comes from my own experience—the one hundred and eighty ounces of liquids per day (think about it...that's a gallon and a half) Even her fictional surgeon is named after my own—Dr. Sam Atallah, if you missed the dedication—and in real life, he's even more impressive than I made him out here. Let's just say that his curriculum vitae is thirty pages long. On top of that, he teaches surgical techniques all over the world (and in at least three different medical schools), does clinical trials, develops new technologies for robotic surgery, and hosts interns. And, he plays the guitar. I don't know how he does it.

See? I told you. I never had any doubts entrusting him with my life. In fact, like Meredeth, I was more worried about the hospital stay than the surgeries.

Oh, yeah, my point about Meredeth's recovery... I still haven't fully recuperated—see I had this silly deadline to meet, so I pushed a little harder than I would have liked, but don't worry—I'm taking the next week off! I'm sure Dr. Atallah will be proud of me.

So, what's next for Meredeth? I have the next few novels burbling away in the back of my mind—challenging cases, some of which will be loosely based on actual cases. She will have to earn her way back into Ankou's good graces, though she will also have Michelina to provide information, and she will learn more about the woman's experiences on the Branch farm.

Kevin has a surprise for her.

Then there's Mack...who will return.

Oh, and I suppose Kenny will eventually make his appearance, but at the moment, Meredeth will have her hands full with Lucy and Carl (and new characters we will discover together).

It's now 4:08 AM, and I'm exhausted. I have a few things to take care of this week, but mostly, I'll be chilling out, reading, hanging out with Supergirl, RealSig™, and my parents.

I hope you enjoyed this little romp. I sure did. I'll see you again soon, my friend!

Until then, why not visit our Discord server? You can find it here: https://ehv4.us/discord. If you'd like to contribute monetarily to our journey, we have a Patreon page at https://ehv4.us/patreon as well.

PATRON RECOGNITION

A BIG VIKING hug to all my patrons!

Special thanks to Dawn Bogue and an anonymous patron for being the first of hopefully many patrons of the upper tiers.

ABOUT THE AUTHOR

E.H. VICK ¶is the pen name for critically acclaimed best-selling and award-winning horror author Erik Henry Vick. He specializes in pulse-pounding stories filled with nail biting tension—usually involving serial killers as villains and psychologically-flawed protagonists. As an author disabled by autoimmune diseases (also known as his Personal Monster™), Vick writes to hang on to the few remaining shreds of his sanity. He lives with his wife, Supergirl; their son; a Rottweiler named after a god of thunder; and two extremely psychotic cats. He fights his Personal Monster™ daily with humor, pain medicine, and funny T-shirts.

With a B.A. in Psychology, an M.S.C.S., and a Ph.D. in Artificial Intelligence, Vick has worked as a criminal investigator for a state agency, a college professor, a C.T.O. for an international software company, and a video game developer.

He'd love to hear from you on social media:

Website: https://ehvick.com
Facebook: https://fb.me/ehvick
Amazon author pages:
  USA: https://ehv4.us/amaehv
Goodreads Author Page: https://ehv4.us/grehv
BookBub Author Profile: http://ehv4.us/bbehv

10/28/28 - 11/1/23

Made in the USA
Monee, IL
16 October 2023